Over Sea,
Under Stone

Books by Susan Cooper available in
Aladdin Paperbacks editions

THE DARK IS RISING SEQUENCE

Over Sea, Under Stone

The Dark Is Rising

Greenwitch

The Grey King

Silver on the Tree

Seaward

Dawn of Fear

THE DARK IS RISING SEQUENCE

Over Sea, Under Stone

Susan Cooper

Aladdin Paperbacks

New York   London   Toronto   Sydney   Singapore

First Aladdin Paperbacks edition November 2000

Copyright © 1965 by Susan Cooper

Aladdin Paperbacks
An imprint of Simon & Schuster
Children's Publishing Division
1230 Avenue of the Americas
New York, NY 10020

Library of Congress Cataloging-in-Publication Data

Cooper, Susan.
  Over sea, under stone.

  (The Dark is rising sequence)
Summary: Three children on a holiday in Cornwall find an ancient manuscript which sends them on a dangerous quest for a grail that would reveal the true story of King Arthur and that entraps them in the eternal battle between the forces of the Light and the forces of the Dark.
[1. Fantasy.   2. Cornwall (England)—Fiction]
I. Title.   II. Series: Cooper, Susan. Dark is rising sequence.
PZ7.C78780v   1989   [Fic]   88-37690
ISBN: 0-689-85200-2 (Aladdin pbk.)

10 9 8 7 6 5 4 3 2 1

For my mother and father, with love

• *Chapter One* •

"Where is he?"

Barney hopped from one foot to the other as he clambered down from the train, peering in vain through the white-faced crowds flooding eagerly to the St Austell ticket barrier. "Oh, I can't see him. Is he there?"

"Of course he's there," Simon said, struggling to clutch the long canvas bundle of his father's fishing rods. "He said he'd meet us. With a car."

Behind them, the big diesel locomotive hooted like a giant owl, and the train began to move out.

"Stay where you are a minute," Father said, from a barricade of suitcases. "Merry won't vanish. Let people get clear."

Jane sniffed ecstatically. "I can smell the sea!"

"We're miles from the sea," Simon said loftily.

"I don't care. I can smell it."

"Trewissick's five miles from St Austell, Great-Uncle Merry said."

"Oh, where *is* he?" Barney still jigged impatiently on the dusty grey platform, glaring at the disappearing backs that masked his view. Then suddenly he stood still, gazing downwards. "Hey— look."

They looked. He was staring at a large black suitcase among the forest of shuffling legs.

"What's so marvellous about that?" Jane said.

Then they saw that the suitcase had two brown pricked ears and a long waving brown tail. Its owner picked it up and moved away, and the dog which had been behind it was left standing there alone, looking up and down the platform. He was a long, rangy, lean dog, and where the sunlight shafted down on his coat it gleamed dark red.

Barney whistled, and held out his hand.

"Darling, no," said his mother plaintively, clutching at the bunch of paint-brushes that sprouted from her pocket like a tuft of celery.

But even before Barney whistled, the dog had begun trotting in their direction, swift and determined, as if he were recognizing old friends. He loped round them in a circle, raising his long red muzzle to each in turn, then stopped beside Jane, and licked her hand.

"Isn't he gorgeous?" Jane crouched beside him, and ruffled the long silky fur of his neck.

"Darling, be careful," Mother said. "He'll get left behind. He must belong to someone over there."

"I wish he belonged to us."

"So does he," Barney said. "Look."

He scratched the red head, and the dog gave a throaty half-bark of pleasure.

"*No*," Father said.

The crowds were thinning now, and through the barrier they could see clear blue sky out over the station yard.

"His name's on his collar," Jane said, still down beside the dog's neck. She fumbled with the silver tab on the heavy strap. "It says Rufus. And something else . . . Trewissick. Hey, he comes from the village!"

But as she looked up, suddenly the others were not there. She jumped to her feet and ran after them into the sunshine, seeing in an instant what they had seen: the towering familiar figure of Great-Uncle Merry, out in the yard, waiting for them.

They clustered round him, chattering like squirrels round the base of a tree. "Ah, there you are," he said casually, looking down at them from beneath his bristling white eyebrows with a slight smile.

"Cornwall's wonderful," Barney said, bubbling.

"You haven't seen it yet," said Great-Uncle Merry. "How are you, Ellen, my dear?" He bent and aimed a brief peck at Mother's cheek. He treated her always as though he had forgotten that she had grown up. Although he was not her real uncle, but only a friend of her father, he had been close to the family for so many years that it never occurred to them to wonder where he had come from in the first place.

Nobody knew very much about Great-Uncle Merry, and nobody ever quite dared to ask. He did not look in the least like his name. He was tall, and straight, with a lot of very thick, wild, white hair. In his grim brown face the nose curved fiercely, like a bent bow, and the eyes were deep-set and dark.

How old he was, nobody knew. "Old as the hills," Father said, and they felt, deep down, that this was probably right. There was something about Great-Uncle Merry that was like the hills, or the sea, or the sky; something ancient, but without age or end.

Always, wherever he was, unusual things seemed to happen. He would often disappear for a long time, and then suddenly come through the Drews' front door as if he had never been away, announcing that he had found a lost valley in South America, a Roman fortress in France, or a burned Viking ship buried on the English coast. The newspapers would publish enthusiastic stories of what he had done. But by the time the reporters came knocking at the door, Great-Uncle Merry would be gone, back to the dusty peace of the university where he taught. They would wake up one morning, go to call him for breakfast, and find that he was not there. And then they would hear no more of him until the next time, perhaps months later, that he appeared at the door. It hardly seemed possible that this summer, in the house he had rented for them in Trewissick, they would be with him in one place for four whole weeks.

The sunlight glinting on his white hair, Great-Uncle Merry scooped up their two biggest suitcases, one under each arm, and strode across the yard to a car.

"What d'you think of that?" he demanded proudly.

Following, they looked. It was a vast, battered estate car, with rusting mudguards and peeling paint, and mud caked on the hubs of the wheels. A wisp of steam curled up from the radiator.

"Smashing!" said Simon.

"Hmmmmmm," Mother said.

"Well, Merry," Father said cheerfully, "I hope you're well insured."

Great-Uncle Merry snorted. "Nonsense. Splendid vehicle. I hired her from a farmer. She'll hold us all, anyway. In you get."

Jane glanced regretfully back at the station entrance as she clambered in after the rest. The red-haired dog was standing on the pavement watching them, long pink tongue dangling over white teeth.

Great-Uncle Merry called: "Come on, Rufus."

"Oh!" Barney said in delight, as a flurry of long legs and wet muzzle shot through the door and knocked him sideways. "Does he belong to you?"

"Heaven forbid," Great-Uncle Merry said. "But I suppose he'll belong to you three for the next month. The captain couldn't take him abroad, so Rufus goes with the Grey House." He folded himself into the driving seat.

"The Grey House?" Simon said. "Is that what it's called? Why?"

"Wait and see."

The engine gave a hiccup and a roar, and then they were away. Through the streets and out of the town they thundered in the lurching car, until hedges took the place of houses; thick, wild hedges growing high and green as the road wound uphill, and behind them the grass sweeping up to the sky. And against the sky they saw nothing but lonely trees, stunted and bowed by the wind that blew from the sea, and yellow-grey outcrops of rock.

"There you are," Great-Uncle Merry shouted, over the noise. He turned his head and waved one arm away from the steering-wheel, so that Father moaned softly and hid his eyes. "Now you're in Cornwall. The real Cornwall. Logres is before you."

The clatter was too loud for anyone to call back.

"What's he mean, Logres?" demanded Jane.

Simon shook his head, and the dog licked his ear.

"He means the land of the West," Barney said unexpectedly, pushing back the forelock of fair hair that always tumbled over his eyes. "It's the old name for Cornwall. King Arthur's name."

Simon groaned. "I might have known."

Ever since he had learned to read, Barney's greatest heroes had been King Arthur and his knights. In his dreams he fought imaginary battles as a member of the Round Table, rescuing fair ladies and slaying false knights. He had been longing to come to the West Country; it gave him a strange feeling that he would in some way be coming home. He said, resentfully: "You wait. Great-Uncle Merry knows."

And then, after what seemed a long time, the hills gave way to the long blue line of the sea, and the village was before them.

Trewissick seemed to be sleeping beneath its grey, slate-tiled roofs, along the narrow winding streets down the hill. Silent behind their lace-curtained windows, the little square houses let the roar

4

of the car bounce back from their whitewashed walls. Then Great-Uncle Merry swung the wheel round, and suddenly they were driving along the edge of the harbour, past water rippling and flashing golden in the afternoon sun. Sailing-dinghies bobbed at their moorings along the quay, and a whole row of the Cornish fishing boats that they had seen only in pictures painted by their mother years before: stocky workmanlike boats, each with a stubby mast and a small square engine-house in the stern.

Nets hung dark over the harbour walls, and a few fishermen, hefty, brown-faced men in long boots that reached their thighs, glanced up idly as the car passed. Two or three grinned at Great-Uncle Merry, and waved.

"Do they know you?" Simon said curiously.

But Great-Uncle Merry, who could become very deaf when he chose not to answer a question, only roared on along the road that curved up the hill, high over the other side of the harbour, and suddenly stopped. "Here we are," he said.

In the abrupt silence, their ears still numb from the thundering engine, they all turned from the sea to look at the other side of the road.

They saw a terrace of houses sloping sideways up the steep hill; and in the middle of them, rising up like a tower, one tall narrow house with three rows of windows and a gabled roof. A sombre house, painted dark-grey, with the door and windowframes shining white. The roof was slate-tiled, a high blue-grey arch facing out across the harbour to the sea.

"The Grey House," Great-Uncle Merry said.

They could smell a strangeness in the breeze that blew faintly on their faces down the hill; a beckoning smell of salt and seaweed and excitement.

As they unloaded suitcases from the car, with Rufus darting in excited frenzy through everyone's legs, Simon suddenly clutched Jane by the arm. "Gosh—*look*!"

He was looking out to sea, beyond the harbour mouth. Along his pointed finger, Jane saw the tall graceful triangle of a yacht under full sail, moving lazily in towards Trewissick.

"Pretty," she said, with only mild enthusiasm. She did not share Simon's passion for boats.

"She's a beauty. I wonder whose she is?" Simon stood watching, entranced. The yacht crept nearer, her sails beginning to flap; and then the tall white mainsail crumpled and dropped. They heard the rattle of rigging, very faint across the water, and the throaty cough of an engine.

"Mother says we can go down and look at the harbour before supper," Barney said, behind them. "Coming?"

"Course. Will Great-Uncle Merry come?"

"He's going to put the car away."

They set off down the road leading to the quay, beside a low grey wall with tufts of grass and pink valerian growing between its stones. In a few paces Jane found she had forgotten her handkerchief, and she ran back to retrieve it from the car. Scrabbling on the floor by the back seat, she glanced up and stared for a moment through the windscreen, surprised.

Great-Uncle Merry, coming back towards the car from the Grey House, had suddenly stopped in his tracks in the middle of the road. He was gazing down at the sea; and she realised that he had caught sight of the yacht. What startled her was the expression on his face. Standing there like a craggy towering statue, he was frowning, fierce and intense, almost as if he were looking and listening with senses other than his eyes and ears. He could never look frightened, she thought, but this was the nearest thing to it that she had ever seen. Cautious, startled, alarmed . . . what was the matter with him? Was there something strange about the yacht?

Then he turned and went quickly back into the house, and Jane emerged thoughtfully from the car to follow the boys down the hill.

* * *

The harbour was almost deserted. The sun was hot on their faces, and they felt the warmth of the stone quayside strike at their feet through their sandal soles. In the center, in front of tall wooden warehouse doors, the quay jutted out square into the water, and a great heap of empty boxes towered above their heads. Three sea-gulls walked tolerantly to the edge, out of their way. Before them, a small forest of spars and ropes swayed; the tide was only half high, and the decks of the moored boats were down below the quayside, out of sight.

"Hey," Simon said, pointing through the harbour entrance. "That yacht's come in, look. Isn't she marvellous?"

The slim white boat sat at anchor beyond the harbour wall, protected from the open sea by the headland on which the Grey House stood.

6

Jane said: "Do you think there is anything odd about her?"

"Odd? Why should there be?"

"Oh—I don't know."

"Perhaps she belongs to the harbour-master," Barney said.

"Places this size don't have harbour-masters, you little fathead, only ports like Father went to in the navy."

"Oh yes they do, cleversticks, there's a little black door on the corner over there, marked Harbour-Master's Office." Barney hopped triumphantly up and down, and frightened a sea-gull away. It ran a few steps and then flew off, flapping low over the water and bleating into the distance.

"Oh well," Simon said amiably, shoving his hands in his pockets and standing with his legs apart, rocking on his heels, in his captain-on-the bridge stance. "One up. Still, that boat must belong to someone pretty rich. You could cross the Channel in her, or even the Atlantic."

"Ugh," said Jane. She swam as well as anybody, but she was the only member of the Drew family who disliked the open sea. "Fancy crossing the Atlantic in a thing that size."

Simon grinned wickedly. "Smashing. Great big waves picking you up and bringing you down swoosh, everything falling about, pots and pans upsetting in the galley, and the deck going up and down, up and down—"

"You'll make her sick," Barney said calmly.

"Rubbish. On dry land, out here in the sun?"

"Yes, you will, she looks a bit green already. Look."

"I don't."

"Oh yes you do. I can't think why you weren't ill in the train like you usually are. Just think of those waves in the Atlantic, and the mast swaying about, and nobody with an appetite for their breakfast except me. . . ."

"Oh shut up, I'm not going to listen"—and poor Jane turned and ran round the side of the mountain of fishy-smelling boxes, which had probably been having more effect on her imagination than the thought of the sea.

"Girls!" said Simon cheerfully.

There was suddenly an ear-splitting crash from the other side of the boxes, a scream, and a noise of metal jingling on concrete. Simon and Barney gazed horrified at one another for a moment, and rushed round to the other side.

Jane was lying on the ground with a bicycle on top of her, its front wheel still spinning round. A tall dark-haired boy lay sprawled across the quay not far away. A box of tins and packets of food had spilled from the bicycle carrier, and milk was trickling in a white puddle from a broken bottle splintered glittering in the sun.

The boy scrambled to his feet, glaring at Jane. He was all in navy-blue, his trousers tucked into Wellington boots; he had a short, thick neck and a strangely flat face, twisted now with ill temper.

"Look where 'ee's goin', can't 'ee?" he snarled, the Cornish accent made ugly by anger. "Git outa me way."

He jerked the bicycle upright, taking no heed of Jane; the pedal caught her ankle and she winced with pain.

"It wasn't my fault," she said, with some spirit, "You came rushing up without looking where you were going."

Barney crossed to her in silence and helped her to her feet. The boy sullenly began picking up his spilled tins and slamming them back into the box. Jane picked one up to help. But as she reached it towards the box the boy knocked her hand away, sending the tin spinning across the quay.

"Leave 'n alone," he growled.

"Look here," Simon said indignantly, "there's no need for that."

"Shut y' mouth," said the boy shortly, without even looking up.

"Shut your own," Simon said belligerently.

"Oh Simon, don't," Jane said unhappily. "If he wants to be beastly let him." Her leg was stinging viciously, and blood trickled down from a graze on her knee. Simon looked at her flushed face, hearing the strain in her voice. He bit his lip.

The boy pushed his bicycle to lean against the pile of boxes, scowling at Barney as he jumped nervously out of the way; then rage suddenly snarled out of him again. "—off, the lot of 'ee," he snapped; they had never heard the word he used, but the tone was unmistakable, and Simon went hot with resentment and clenched his fists to lunge forward. But Jane clutched him back, and the boy moved quickly to the edge of the quay and climbed down over the edge, facing them, the box of groceries in his arms. They heard a thumping, clattering noise, and looking over the edge they saw him lurching about in a rowing-dinghy. He untied its mooring-rope from a ring in the wall and began edging out through the other boats into the open harbour, standing up with one oar thrust down over

8

the stern. Moving hastily and angrily, he clouted the dinghy hard against the side of one of the big fishing-boats, but took no notice. Soon he was out in open water, sculling rapidly, one-handed, and glaring back at them in sneering contempt.

As he did so they heard a clatter of feet moving rapidly over hollow wood from inside the injured fishing-boat. A small, wizened figure popped up suddenly from a hatch in the deck and waved its arms about in fury, shouting over the water towards the boy in a surprisingly deep voice.

The boy deliberately turned his back, still sculling, and the dinghy disappeared outside the harbour entrance, round the jutting wall.

The little man shook his fist, then turned towards the quay, leaping neatly from the deck of one boat to another, until he reached the ladder in the wall and climbed up by the children's feet. He wore the inevitable navy-blue jersey and trousers, with long boots reaching up his legs.

"Clumsy young limb, that Bill 'Oover," he said crossly. "Wait'll I catch 'n, that's all, just wait,"

Then he seemed to realize that the children were more than just part of the quay. He grunted, flashing a quick glance at their tense faces, and the blood on Jane's knee. "Thought I heard voices from below," he said, more gently. "You been 'avin' trouble with 'n?" He jerked his head out to sea.

"He knocked my sister over with his bike," Simon said indignantly. "It was my fault really, I made her run into him, but he was beastly rude and he bashed Jane's hand away and—and then he went off before I could hit him," he ended lamely.

The old fisherman smiled at them. "Ah well, don't 'ee take no count of 'n. He'm a bad lot, that lad, evil-tempered as they come and evil-minded with ut. You keep away from 'n."

"We shall," Jane said with feeling, rubbing her leg gingerly.

The fisherman clicked his tongue. "That's a nasty old cut you got there, midear, you want to go and get 'n washed up. You'm on holiday here, I dessay."

"We're staying in the Grey House," Simon said. "Up there on the hill,"

The fisherman glanced at him quickly, a flicker of interest passing over the impassive brown wrinkled face. "Are 'ee, then? I wonder maybe"—then he stopped short, strangely, as if he were quickly

9

changing his mind about what he had been going to say. Simon, puzzled, waited for him to go on. But Barney, who had not been listening, turned round from where he had been peering over the edge of the quay.

"Is that your boat out there?"

The fisherman looked at him, half taken aback and half amused, as he would have looked at some small unexpected animal that barked. "That's right, me 'andsome. The one I just come off."

"Don't the other fishermen mind you jumping over their boats?"

The old man laughed, a cheerful rusty noise. "I'd'n no other way to get ashore from there. Nobody minds you comin' across their boat, so long's you don't mark 'er."

"Are you going out fishing?"

"Not for a while, midear," said the fisherman amiably, pulling a piece of dirty rag from his pocket and scrubbing at the oil-marks on his hands. "Go out with sundown, we do, and come back with the dawn."

Barney beamed. "I shall get up early and watch you come in."

"Believe that when I see 'n," said the fisherman with a twinkle. "Now look, you run and take your little sister home and wash that leg, don't know what scales and muck have got into it off here." He scuffed at the quay with his glistening boot.

"Yes, come on, Jane," Simon said. He took one more look out at the quiet line of boats; then put up his hand to peer into the sun. "I say, that oaf with the bicycle, he's going on board the yacht!"

Jane and Barney looked.

Out beyond the far harbour wall, a dark shape was bobbing against the long white hull of the silent yacht. They could just see the boy climbing up the side, and two figures meeting him on the deck. Then all three disappeared, and the boat lay deserted again.

"Ah," said the fisherman. "So that's it. Young Bill were buying stores and petrol and all, yesterday, enough for a navy, but nobody couldn't get it out of him who they was for. Tidy old boat, that'n—cruisin', I suppose. Can't see what he made all the mystery about."

He began to walk along the quay: a rolling small figure with the folded tops of his boots slapping his legs at every step. Barney trotted beside him, talking earnestly, and rejoined the others at the corner as the old man, waving to them, turned off towards the village.

"His name's Mr. Penhallow, and his boat's called the *White*

10

Heather. He says they got a hundred stone of pilchard last night, and they'll get more tomorrow because it's going to rain."

"One day you'll ask too many questions," said Jane.

"Rain?" said Simon incredulously, looking up at the blue sky.

"That's what he said."

"Rubbish. He must be nuts."

"I bet he's right. Fishermen always know things, specially Cornish fishermen. You ask Great-Uncle Merry."

* * *

But Great-Uncle Merry, when they sat down to their first supper in the Grey House, was not there; only their parents, and the beaming red-cheeked village woman, Mrs Palk, who was to come in every day to help with the cooking and cleaning. Great-Uncle Merry had gone away.

"He must have said *something,*" Jane said.

Father shrugged. "Not really. He just muttered about having to go and look for something and roared off in the car like a thunderbolt."

"But we've only just got here," Simon said, hurt.

"Never mind," Mother said comfortably. "You know what he is. He'll be back in his own good time."

Barney gazed dreamily at the Cornish pasties Mrs Palk had made for their supper. "He's gone on a quest. He might take years and years. You can search and search, on a quest, and in the end you may never get there at all."

"Quest my foot," Simon said irritably. "He's just gone chasing after some stupid old tomb in a church, or something. Why couldn't he have told us?"

"I expect he'll be back in the morning," Jane said. She looked out of the window, across the low grey wall edging the road. The light was beginning to die, and as the sun sank behind their headland the sea was turning to a dark grey-green, and slow mist creeping into the harbour. Through the growing haze she saw a dim shape move, down on the water, and above it a brief flash of light; first a red pinprick in the gloom, and then a green, and white points of light above both. And she sat up suddenly as she realized that what she could see was the mysterious white yacht, moving out of Trewissick harbour as silently and strangely as it had come.

• *Chapter Two* •

Next day, as they sat eating breakfast, Great-Uncle Merry came back. He loomed in the doorway, tall and hollow-eyed under the thatch of white hair, and beamed at their surprised faces.

"Good morning," he said cheerfully. "Any coffee left?" The ornaments seemed to rattle on the mantelpiece as he spoke; Great-Uncle Merry always gave the impression of being far too big for any room he was in.

Father reached out imperturbably to pull up another chair. "What's it like out this morning, Merry? Doesn't look so good to me."

Great-Uncle Merry sat down and helped himself to toast, holding the slice in one large palm while he spread butter on it with Father's knife. "Cloud. Thick, coming in from the sea. We're going to have rain."

Barney was fidgeting with unbearable curiosity. Suddenly, forgetting the family rule that they should never ask their mysterious great-uncle questions about himself, he burst out: "Gumerry, where have you *been?*" In the heat of the moment he used the pet name which he had invented when he was very small. They all used it sometimes still, but not for everyday.

Jane hissed quietly between her teeth, and Simon glared at him across the table. But Great-Uncle Merry seemed not to have heard. "It may not last," he went on conversationally to Father, through a mouthful of toast. "But I think we shall have it for most of the day."

"Will there be thunder?" Jane said.

Simon added hopefully, "Shall we have a storm at sea?"

Barney sat silent while their voices eddied round the table. The weather, he said to himself in exasperation, all of them talking

12

about the weather, when Great-Uncle Merry's just come back from his quest.

Then over their voices there came a low rumble of thunder, and the first spattering sounds of rain. As everyone rushed to the window to look out at the heavy grey sky, Barney crossed unnoticed to his great-uncle and slipped his hand into his for a moment.

"Gumerry," he said softly, "did you find it, what you were looking for?"

He expected Great-Uncle Merry to look past him with the familiar amiable-obstinate expression that greeted any question. But the big man looked down at him almost absently. The eyebrows were drawn forbiddingly together on the craggy, secret face, and there was the old fierceness in the dark hollows and lines. He said gently, "No, Barnabas, I didn't find it this time." Then it was as if a blanket came down again over his face. "I must go and put the car away," he called to Father, and went out.

The thunder rolled quietly, far out over the sea, but the rain fell with grey insistence, blurring the windows as it washed down outside. The children wandered aimlessly about the house. Before lunch they tried going for a walk in the rain, but came back damp and depressed.

Half-way through the afternoon Mother put her head round the door. "I'm going upstairs to work until supper. Now look, you three—you can go where you like in the house but you must promise not to touch anything that's obviously been put away. Everything valuable is all locked up, but I don't want you poking at anyone's private papers or belongings. All right?"

"We promise," Jane said, and Simon nodded.

In a little while Father muffled himself in a big black oilskin and went off through the rain to see the harbour-master. Jane wandered round the bookshelves, but all the books within reach seemed to have titles like *Round the Horn,* or *Log-Book of the* Virtue, *1886,* and she thought them very dull.

Simon, who had been sitting making darts out of the morning paper, suddenly crumpled them all up irritably. "I'm fed up with this. What shall we do?"

Barney stared gloomily out of the window. "It's raining like anything. The water in the harbour's all flat. And on our first proper day. Oh I hate the rain, I hate it, I hate it, I hate the rain. . . ." He began to chant morosely.

13

Simon prowled restlessly around the room, looking at the pictures on the dark wallpaper. "It's a very dreary house when you're shut up inside. He doesn't seem to think about anything but the sea, does he, the captain?"

"This time last year you were going to be a sailor too."

"Well, I changed my mind. Oh well, I don't know. Anyway, I should go on a destroyer, not a potty little sailing-ship like that one. What is it?" He peered up at the inscription under an engraving. *"The Golden Hind."*

"That was Drake's ship. When he sailed to America and discovered potatoes."

"That was Raleigh."

"Oh well," said Barney, who didn't really care.

"What useless things they discovered," Simon said critically. "I shouldn't have bothered about vegetables, I should have come back loaded with doubloons and diamonds and pearls."

"And apes and peacocks," said Jane, harking vaguely back to a poetry lesson at school.

"And I should have gone exploring into the interior and the rude natives would have turned me into a god and tried to offer me their wives."

"Why would the natives be rude?" said Barney.

"Not that sort of rude, you idiot, it means—it means—well, it's the sort of thing natives *are*. It's what all the explorers call them."

"Let's be explorers," Jane said. "We can explore the house. We haven't yet, not properly. It's like a strange land. We can work from the bottom all the way up to the top."

"And we should have to take provisions with us, so we can have a picnic when we get there," said Barney, brightening.

"We haven't got any."

"We can ask Mrs Palk," said Jane. "She's making cakes for Mother in the kitchen. Come on."

Mrs Palk, in the kitchen, laughed all over her red face and said, "What will 'ee think of next, I wonder?" But she gave them, neatly wrapped, a stack of freshly-baked scones cut in half, thickly buttered and put together again; a packet of squashed-fly biscuits, three apples and a great slab of dark yellowy-orange cake, thick and crumbling with fruit.

"And something to drink," said Simon commandingly, already captain of the expedition. So Mrs Palk good-humouredly added a big bottle of home-made lemonade "to finish 'n off."

"There," she said, "that'll take 'ee to St Ives and back, I reckon."

"My rucksack's upstairs," said Simon, "I'll get it."

"Oh really," said Jane, who was beginning to feel a little foolish. "We aren't even going outdoors."

"All explorers have rucksacks," Simon said severely, making for the door. "I won't be a minute."

Barney nibbled at some yellow cake-crumbs from the table. "This is smashing."

"Saffron cake," Mrs Palk said proudly. "You won't get that in London."

"Mrs Palk, where's Rufus?"

"Gone out, and a good job too, though I dare say we shall have his great wet feet all over the floor afore long. Professor took'n for a walk. Now stop pickin' at that cake, midear, or you'll spoil that picnic o' yours."

Simon came back with his rucksack. They filled it, and went out into the little dark passage away from the kitchen, Mrs Palk waving them farewell as solemnly as if they were off to the North Pole.

"Who did she say had taken Rufus for a walk?" said Jane.

"Great-Uncle Merry," Barney said. "They all call him the Professor, didn't you know? Mr. Penhallow did as well. They talk as if they've known him for years."

They were on the first-floor landing, long and dark, lit only from one small window. Jane waved her hand at a big wooden chest half hidden in one corner. "What's that?"

"It's locked," said Simon, trying the lid. "One of the things we mustn't touch, I suppose. Actually it's full of native gold and ornaments, we'll collect it on the way back and stow it in the hold."

"Who's going to carry it?" demanded Barney practically.

"Easy, we've got a string of native porters. All walking behind in a row and calling me Boss."

"Catch me calling you Boss."

"Actually you ought to be the cabin-boy, and call me Sir. Aye, aye, Sir!" Simon bellowed suddenly.

"Shut up," said Jane. "Mother's working at the other end of the landing, you'll make her do a smudge."

"What's in here?" said Barney. There was a dark door in the shadows at the far end of the landing. "I haven't noticed it before."

He turned the handle, and the door opened outward with a slow creak. "I say, there's another little corridor down some steps, and a door at the end of it. Come on."

They went down over the worn carpet, beneath rows of old maps hanging on the walls.

The little corridor, like all the house, had a smell of furniture polish and age and the sea; and yet nothing like these things really but just the smell of strangeness.

"Hey," said Simon as Barney reached for the door. "I'm the captain, I go first. There might be cannibals."

"Cannibals!" said Barney with scorn, but he let Simon open the door.

It was an odd little room, very small and bare, with one round leaded window looking out inland across the grey slate roofs and fields. There was a bed, with a red-and-white gingham coverlet, and a wooden chair, a wardrobe, and a wash-stand with an outsize willow-pattern bowl and ewer. And that was all.

"Well, that's not very interesting," said Jane, disappointed. She looked about, feeling something was missing. "Look, there isn't even a carpet, just a bare floor."

Barney pattered across to the window. "What's this?" He picked something up from the window-sill, long and dark with the glint of brass. "It's a sort of tube."

Simon took it from him and turned it about curiously. "It's a telescope in a case." He unscrewed the case so that it came apart in two halves. "No it's not, what a swizz, it's just the case with nothing inside."

"Now I know what this room reminds me of," Jane said suddenly. "It's like a cabin in a ship. That window looks just like a porthole. I think it must be the captain's bedroom."

"We ought to take the telescope with us in case we lose our way," said Simon. Holding it made him feel pleasantly important.

"Don't be silly, it's just an empty case," Jane said. "Anyway, it's not ours, put it back."

Simon scowled at her.

"I mean," Jane said hastily, "we're in the jungle, not at sea, so there are landmarks."

"Oh all right." Simon put the case down reluctantly.

They emerged from the little dark corridor, its door, as they closed it behind them, vanishing once more into the shadows so that they could hardly see where it had been.

"Not much else here. That one's Great-Uncle Merry's bedroom, there's the bathroom this side of it and Mother's studio room the other."

"What an odd way this house is built," Simon said, as they turned into another narrow corridor towards the stairs leading up to the next floor. "All little bits joined together by funny little passages. As if each bit were meant to be kept secret from the next."

Barney looked round him in the dim light, tapping at the half-panelled walls. "It's all very solid. There ought to be secret panels and things, secret entrances into native treasure-caves."

"Well, we haven't finished yet." Simon led the way up the stairs to the familiar top landing, where their bedrooms were. "Isn't it getting dark? I suppose it's the low clouds."

Barney squatted on the top stair. "We ought to have torches, burning brands to light the path and keep the wild animals off. Only we couldn't because there are hostile natives all round, and they'd see."

Simon took over. Somehow imagination worked easily in the friendly silence of the Grey House. "Actually they're already after us, creeping along our tracks up the hill. We'll be able to hear their feet rustling soon."

"We ought to hide."

"Make camp somewhere that they can't get at."

"In one of the bedrooms, they're all caves."

"I can hear them *breathing,*" Barney said, gazing down the dark stairs into the shadow. He was half beginning to believe it.

"The obvious caves wouldn't do," Simon said, remembering he was in command. "They'd look there first of all." He crossed the landing and began thoughtfully opening and shutting doors. "Mother's and Father's room—no good, very ordinary cave. Jane's—just the same. Bathroom, our room, no escape route anywhere. We shall all be turned into sacrifices and eaten."

"Boiled," said Barney sepulchrally. "In a great big pot."

"Perhaps there's another door, I mean cave, that we haven't noticed. Like the one downstairs." Jane peered round the darkest end of the landing, beside her brothers' door. But the passage came to a dead end, the wall running unbroken round all three sides. "There ought to be one. After all the house goes straight up, doesn't it, and there's a door directly underneath there"—she pointed at the

17

blank wall—"and a room behind it. So there ought to be a room the same size behind this wall."

Simon became interested. "You're quite right. But there isn't any door."

"Perhaps there's a secret panel," Barney said hopefully.

"You read too many books. Have you ever seen a real secret panel in a real house? Anyway there isn't any panelling on this wall, just wallpaper."

"Your room's on the other side," Jane said. "Is there a door in there?"

Simon shook his head.

Barney opened the door into their bedroom and went in, kicking his slippers under the bed as he went past. Then he stopped suddenly.

"Hey, come in here."

"What's the matter?"

"That bit between our beds, where the wall makes a sort of alcove for the wardrobe. What's on the other side?"

"Well, the landing, of course."

"It can't be. There's too much wall in here. You stand in the doorway and look on both sides—the landing stops before it gets that far."

"I'll bang on the wall where it does stop, and you listen in here," said Jane. She went outside, pulling the door shut, and they heard a faint tapping on the wall just over the head of Barney's bed.

"There you are!" Barney said, hopping with excitement. "The landing only reaches to there, but the wall in here goes on for yards, right over your bed to the window. So there *must* be a room on the other side."

Jane came back into the bedroom. "The wall doesn't look nearly as long out there as it does in here."

"It isn't. And I think that means," Simon said slowly, "that there must be a door behind the wardrobe."

"Well that finishes it, then," Jane said, disappointed. "That wardrobe's enormous, we shall never be able to move it."

"I don't see why not." Simon looked thoughtfully at the wardrobe. "We shall have to pull it from down low, so the top doesn't overbalance. If we all pull at one end perhaps it'll swing round."

"Come on then," Jane said. "You and I pull, and Barney hold

18

the top and shout if he feels it overbalancing."

They both bent and heaved at the nearest leg of the wardrobe. Nothing happened.

"I think the stupid thing's nailed to the floor," said Jane in disgust.

"No it's not. Come on, once more. One, two, three—*heave!*"

The great wooden tower squeaked unwillingly a few inches across the floor.

"Go on, go on, it's coming!" Barney could hardly stand still.

Simon and Jane tugged and puffed and blew, their sneakers slithering on the linoleum; and gradually the wardrobe moved out at an angle from the wall. Barney, peering into the gloom behind, suddenly shrieked.

"There it is! There *is* a door! Ouf—" He staggered backwards, gasped, and sneezed. "It's all covered in dust and cobwebs, it can't have been opened for years."

"Well go on, try it," panted Simon, pink with breathlessness and success.

"I hope it doesn't open towards us," Jane said, sitting weakly on the floor. "I can't pull this thing another inch."

"It doesn't," Barney said, muffled from behind the wardrobe. They heard the door creak protestingly open. Then he reappeared, with a large dark smudge down one cheek. "There isn't a room. It's a staircase. More like a ladder really. It goes up to a sort of hatchway and there's light up there." He looked at Simon with a crooked grin. "You can go first, Boss."

One by one they slipped behind the wardrobe and through the little hidden door. Inside, it was at first very dark, and Simon, blinking, saw before him a wide-stepped ladder, steeply slanting, rising towards a dimly-lit square beyond which he could see nothing. The steps were thick with dust, and for a moment he felt nervous about disturbing the stillness.

Then very faintly, he heard above his head the low familiar murmur of the sea outside. At once the comfortable noise made him more cheerful, and he even remembered what they were supposed to be. "Last one up shut the door," he called down over his shoulder. "Keep the natives at bay." And he began to climb the ladder.

• *Chapter Three* •

As Simon's head emerged through the hatch at the top he caught his breath just as Barney had: "Aah—aah—" and sneezed enormously. Clouds of dust rose, and the ladder shook.

"Hey," said Barney protestingly from below, drawing his face back from his brother's twitching heels.

Simon opened his watering eyes and blinked. Before him and all round was one vast attic, the length and breadth of the whole house, with two grubby windows in its sloping roof. It was piled higgledy-piggledy with the most fantastic collection of objects he had ever seen.

Boxes, chests and trunks lay everywhere, with mounds of dirty grey canvas and rough-coiled ropes between them; stacks of newspapers and magazines, yellow-brown with age; a brass bedstead and a grandfather clock without a face. As he stared, he saw smaller things: a broken fishing-rod, a straw hat perched on the corner of an oil-painting darkened by age into one great black blur; an empty mousetrap, a ship in a bottle, a glass-fronted case full of chunks of rock, a pair of old thigh-boots flopped over sideways as if they were tired, a cluster of battered pewter mugs.

"Gosh!" said Simon.

Muffled noises of protest came from below, and he hauled himself out through the opening and rolled sideways out of their way on the floor. Barney and Jane came through after him.

"Simon!" said Jane, gazing at him in horror. "You're filthy!"

"Well, isn't that just like a girl. All this round you, and you only see a bit of dust. It'll brush off." He patted ineffectually at his piebald shirt. "But isn't it marvellous? Look!"

Barney, cooing with delight, was picking his way across the

littered floor. "There's an old ship's wheel . . . and a rocking-chair . . . and a saddle. I wonder if the captain ever had a horse?"

Jane had been trying to look insulted, but failed. "This is something *like* exploring. We might find anything up here."

"It's a treasure-cave. This is what the natives were after. Hear them howling with frustrated rage down there."

"Dancing round in a circle, with the witch-doctor cursing us all."

"Well, he can curse away," Barney said cheerfully. "We've got enough provisions for ages. I'm hungry."

"Oh not yet, you can't be. It's only four o'clock."

"Well, that's tea-time. Anyway, when you're on the run you eat little and often, because you daren't ever stop for long. If we were Eskimos we'd be chewing an old shoelace. My book says—"

"Never mind your book," Simon said. He fished inside the rucksack. "Here, have an apple and keep quiet. I want to look at everything properly, before we have our picnic, and if I can wait so can you."

"I don't see why," Barney said, but he bit into his apple cheerfully and wandered across the floor, disappearing between the high brass skeleton of the old bed and an empty cupboard.

For half an hour they poked about in a happy dusty dream, through the junk and broken furniture and ornaments. It was like reading the story of somebody's life, Jane thought, as she gazed at the tiny matchstick masts of the ship sailing motionless for ever in the green glass bottle. All these things had been used once, had been part of every day in the house below. Someone had slept on the bed, anxiously watched the minutes on the clock, pounced joyfully on each magazine as it arrived. But all those people were long dead, or gone away, and now the oddments of their lives were piled up here, forgotten. She found herself feeling rather sad.

"I'm ravenous," Barney said plaintively.

"I'm thirsty. It's all that dust. Come on, let's unload Mrs Palk's tea."

"This attic's rather a swizz," Simon said, squatting on a crackling edge of canvas and undoing the rucksack. "All the really interesting boxes are locked. Look at that one, for instance." He nodded towards a black metal chest with two rusting padlocks on its lid. "I bet it's full of the family jewels."

"Well," Jane said regretfully, "we aren't supposed to touch anything locked, are we?"

"There's a lot not locked," Simon said, handing her the bottle of lemonade. "Here. You'll have to swig from the bottle, we forgot to bring any cups. Don't worry, we won't pinch anything. Though I shouldn't think anyone's been up here for years."

"*Food*," Barney said.

"The scones are in that bag there. Help yourself. Four each, I've counted."

Barney reached out an extremely dirty hand.

"Barney!" Jane squeaked. "Wipe your hand. You'll eat all sorts of germs and get typhoid or—or rabies or something. Here, have my handkerchief."

"Rabies is mad dogs," Barney said, looking with interest at the black finger-prints on his scone. "Anyway, Father says people make too much fuss about germs. Oh all *right*, Jane, stop waving that silly thing at me, I've got a proper handkerchief of my own. I don't know how girls ever blow their noses."

Scowling, he thrust his free hand into his pocket, and then his expression changed to disgust. "Ugh," he said, and brought out a brown, squashed apple core. "I'd forgotten that. All cold and horrible." He flung the core away from him into the far corner of the attic. It bounced, slithered, and rolled into the shadows.

Simon grinned. "Now you'll bring the rats out. All attics have rats. We shall hear greedy little squeakings and see twin green points of fire and there'll be rats all over the floor. First they'll eat the apple core, and then they'll come after us."

Jane turned pale. "Oh no. There wouldn't be rats up here, would there?"

"If there were they'd have eaten all the newspaper," Barney said hopefully. "Wouldn't they?"

"I expect they don't like ink. All old houses have rats. We've got them at school, you can hear them scuttling about in the roof sometimes. Come to think of it their eyes are red, not green." Simon's voice began to lose its brightness. He was beginning to feel slightly unhappy about the rats himself now. "I think maybe you'd better pick that apple core up, you know, just in case."

Barney gave an exaggerated sigh and got to his feet, swallowing his scone in two gigantic bites. "Where did it go, then? Over there somewhere. I wonder why they didn't put anything in this corner."

He crawled about on his hands and knees, aimlessly. "Come and help, I can't find it." Then he noticed a triangular gap in the sloping wall of the attic where its planks joined the floor. He peered through, and saw daylight gleaming dimly through the tiles. Just inside the gap the floorboards ended and he could feel wide-spaced beams.

"I think it must have gone through this hole," he called. "I'm going to look."

Jane dived across the floor towards him. "Oh do be careful, there might be a rat."

"Couldn't be," Barney said, half-way through the gap. "There's light coming through the tiles and I can see, more or less. Can't see any core, though. I wonder if it fell between the floorboards and the underneath part. Ow!"

His rear half jerked suddenly.

"What is it? Oh do come out!" Jane tugged at his shorts.

"I touched something. But it can't be a rat, it didn't move. Where's it gone . . . here it is. Feels like cardboard. Blah—here's that disgusting core next to it as well."

His voice grew suddenly louder as he backed out of the hole, flushed and blinking. "Well, there it is," he said, triumphantly, flourishing the apple core. "Now the rats'll have to come and get it. I still don't believe there are any."

"What's that other thing you've got?" Simon looked curiously at a tattered, scroll-like object in Barney's other hand.

"Piece of wallpaper, I think. I bet you've eaten all the scones, you pigs." Barney bounded back across the floor, making the floorboards rattle. He sat down, pulled out his handkerchief, waved it ostentatiously at Jane, wiped his hands, and began to munch another scone. As they ate, he reached over and idly unrolled the scroll he had found, holding one end down on the floor with his toe and pushing the other back with a piece of wood until it lay stretched open before them.

And then, as they saw what it was, they all suddenly forgot their eating and stared.

The paper Barney had unrolled was not paper at all, but a kind of thick brownish parchment, springy as steel, with long raised cracks crossing it where it had been rolled. Inside it, another sheet was stuck down: darker, looking much older, ragged at the edges, and covered with small writing in strange squashed-looking dark brown letters.

Below the writing it dwindled, as if it had been singed by some

23

great heat long ago, into half-detached pieces carefully laid back together and stuck to the outer sheet. But there was enough of it left for them to see at the bottom a rough drawing that looked like the uncertain outline of a map.

For a moment they were all very quiet. Barney said nothing, but he could feel a strange excitement bubbling up inside him. He leant forward in silence and carefully stretched the manuscript flat, pushing the piece of wood aside.

"Here," Simon said, "I'll get something to weight the edges down."

They put an old paper-weight, a pewter mug and two carefully dusted chunks of wood on the corners, and sat back on their heels to look.

"It's terribly old," Jane said. "Centuries, thousands of years."

"Like those papers in glass cases in museums, with little curtains to keep the light out."

"Where did it come from? How did it get up here?"

"Somebody must have hidden it."

"But it's older than the house. I mean look at it, it must be, some of the writing's nearly faded away."

"It wasn't hidden," Barney said, with absolute conviction, though he had no clear idea why. "Someone just threw it down where I found it."

Simon whooped suddenly, making them jump. "This is terrific! Do you realize, we've got a real live treasure map? It could lead us to anything, anywhere, secret passages, real hidden caves—the treasure of Trewissick"—he rolled the words lovingly round his tongue.

"There isn't much map, it's all writing."

"Well then, that's instructions. Look in ye little room on ye second floor, I expect it says, ye second floorboard on the, I mean ye, left—"

"When this was written there weren't such things as floorboards."

"Oh come off it, it's not that old."

"I bet it is," Barney said, quietly. "Anyway, you look at this writing. You can't read it, it's all in some funny language."

"Course you can read it if you look properly," Simon said impatiently. In his mind he was already half-way through a sliding panel, throwing back the lid of a chest to reveal hoards of untold wealth. He could almost hear the chink of doubloons.

"Let's have a look." He leant forward, the floorboards hard and rough under his knees, and peered at the manuscript. There was a long pause. "Oh," he said at last, reluctantly.

Barney said nothing, but looked at him very expressively indeed.

"Well all right," said Simon. "There's no need to look so cocky. It isn't in English. But that doesn't mean we shan't be able to find out what it says."

"Why isn't it in English?"

"How on earth should I know?"

"I mean," Barney said patiently, "that we're in England, so what other language could it possibly be in?"

"Latin," Jane said unexpectedly. She had been looking quietly at the manuscript over Simon's shoulder.

"Latin?"

"Yes. All old manuscripts are written in Latin. The monks used to write them down with a goose-feather for a pen, and put flowers and birds and things all squiggling round the capital letters."

"There isn't anything squiggling here. It looks as if it's been written in rather a hurry. I can't even see any capital letters at all."

"But why *Latin?*" demanded Barney.

"I don't know, the monks just always used it, that's all, it was one of their things. I suppose it's a religious-sounding kind of language."

"Well, Simon does Latin."

"Yes, come on, Simon, translate it," Jane said maliciously. At school she had not yet begun Latin, but he had been learning it for two years, and was rather superior about the fact.

"I don't think it's Latin at all," Simon said rebelliously. He peered at the manuscript again. "This writing's so odd, the letters all look the same. Like a lot of little straight lines all in a row. The light in here isn't very good either."

"You're just making excuses."

"No, I'm not. It's jolly difficult."

"Well, if you can't even recognize Latin when you see it you can't be nearly as good as you make out."

"Have another look," said Barney hopefully.

"I think it's in two parts," Simon said slowly. "One little paragraph on top, and then a lot more all together after a gap. The second bit I can't make out at all, but the first paragraph does look as if it might be Latin. The first word looks like *cum*, that means with, but I can't see what comes after it. Then later on there's *post mul-. tos annos*, that's after many years. But the writing's all so small and squashy I can't—wait a minute, there's some names in the last line. It says *Mar*— no, *Marco Arturoque*."

"Like Marco Polo," Jane said doubtfully. "What a funny name."

"Not one name, it's two. *Que* means and, only they put it on the end instead of in the middle. And *o* on the end is the ablative of *us*, so this means by with or from Marcus and Arturus."

"By with or from? What a—Barney! Whatever's the matter?"

Barney, red in the face and spluttering, had suddenly thumped his fist on the floor, caught his breath trying to say something, and collapsed into a thunderous fit of coughing. They patted him on the back and gave him a drink of lemonade.

"Marcus and Arturus," he said hoarsely, gulping his breath back. "Don't you see, it's Mark and Arthur! It's about King Arthur and his knights. Mark was one of them, and he was King of Cornwall. It must be about them

"Gosh," Simon said. "I think he's right."

"It *must* be that. I bet old King Mark left some treasure behind somewhere and that's why there's a map."

"Suppose we find it."

"We'd be rich."

"We'd be famous."

"We shall have to tell Mother and Father," Jane said.

The two boys stopped thumping each other ecstatically and looked at her.

"Whatever for?"

"Well—" Jane said lamely, taken aback. "I suppose we ought to, that's all."

Barney sat back on his heels again, frowning, and riffled his fingers through his hair, which by now looked several shades darker than it had when they came up to the attic.

"I wonder what they'd say?"

"I know what they'd say," Simon said promptly. "They'd say it was all our imagination, and anyway they'd tell us to put the manuscript back where we found it because it isn't ours."

"Well," said Jane, "it isn't, is it?"

"It's a treasure trove. Finding's keepings."

"But we found it in someone else's house. It belongs to the

captain. You know what Mother said about not touching anything."

"She said anything that was put away. This wasn't put away, it was just chucked down in a comer."

"I found it," Barney said. "It was all forgotten and dusty. I bet you anything the captain hadn't a clue it was there."

"Oh honestly, Jane," Simon said. "You can't find a treasure map and just say, 'Oh, how nice,' and put it back again. And that's what they'd make us do."

"Oh well," Jane said doubtfully, "I suppose you're right. We can always put it back afterwards."

Barney had turned to the manuscript again. "Hey," he said, "look at this top part, the old manuscript that's stuck down on the parchment. What's it made of? I thought it was parchment like the outside bit, but when you look properly it isn't, and it's not paper either. It's some funny thick stuff, and it's hard, like wood."

He touched an edge of the strange brown surface gingerly with one finger.

"Be careful," Jane said nervously. "It might crumble away into dust before our eyes or something."

"I suppose you'd still want to go showing everyone even then," Simon said acidly. " 'Look what we've found, does it matter if we touch it?' and show them a little heap of dust in a match-box."

Jane said nothing.

"Oh well, never mind," Simon said, relenting. She meant well, after all. "Hey, it's getting awfully dark up here, d'you think we ought to go down? They'll be looking for us soon, Mother will have stopped painting."

"It *is* getting late." Jane looked round the attic and shivered suddenly. The big echoing room was growing dark, and there was a dismal sound now to the rain faintly tapping on the glass.

Back in their bedrooms, the boys' wardrobe pushed in again to hide the small secret door, they washed and changed hurriedly as the curt clang of the ship's bell calling them to supper echoed up the stairs. Simon changed his dusty shirt, rolling the clean one into a crumpled ball before he put it on, and hoping no one would notice it was fresh. There was not very much they could do about Barney's hair, now khaki. "It's like what Mother says about that rug in the living-room at home," Jane said in despair, trying to brush out the dust while her brother wriggled in protest. "It shows every mark."

27

"Perhaps we ought to wash it." Simon peered at Barney critically.

"*No,*" Barney said.

"Oh well, there isn't time really. Anyway, I'm hungry. You'll just have to sit away from the light."

* * *

But when they were all sitting round the supper-table, it soon became clear that no one was going to ask questions about where they had been. The evening began as one of those times when everything seemed determined to go wrong. Mother looked tired and depressed, and did not say very much; signs, they knew, that her day's painting had not been a success. Father, gloomy after the grey day, erupted into wrath when Rufus bounced in dripping from his walk, and banished him to the kitchen with Mrs Palk. And Great-Uncle Merry had come in silent and thoughtful, mysteriously brooding. He sat at one end of the table, alone, staring into the middle distance like a great carved totem-pole.

The children eyed him warily, and took care to pass him the salt before he had to ask. But Great-Uncle Merry scarcely seemed to see them. He ate automatically, picking up his food and guiding it to his mouth without taking the slightest notice of it. Barney wondered for a wistful moment what would happen if he were to slip a cork table-mat on to his great-uncle's plate.

Mrs Palk came in with an enormous apple tart and a dish of mounded yellow cream and clattered the dirty plates into a pile. She went out down the hall, and they heard the rich rolling contralto of "O God, our help in ages past" echoing into the distance.

Father sighed. "There are times," he said irritably, "when I could dispense with devotions at every meal."

"The Cornish," boomed Great-Uncle Merry from the shadows, "are a devout and evangelical people."

"I dare say," said Father. He passed Simon the cream. Simon helped himself to a large spoonful, and a yellow blob dropped from the spoon to the table-cloth.

"Oh *Simon,*" Mother said. "Do look what you're doing."

"I couldn't help it. It just fell."

"That comes of trying to take too much at once," Father said.

"Well, you like it too."

"Possibly. But I don't try to transport a quart in a pint pot."

"What d'you mean?"

"Never mind," Father said. "Oh for heaven's sake, Simon, that's

28

just making it worse." Simon, in an attempt to retrieve the blob of cream with his spoon, had left a large yellow smear on the cloth.

"Sorry."

"I should think so."

"Did you go fishing today, Father?" Jane said hopefully from across the table, feeling that it was time to change the subject.

"No," said Father.

"Don't be stupid," Simon said ungratefully, still smarting. "It was raining."

"Well, Father does go fishing in the rain sometimes."

"No, he doesn't."

"Yes, he does."

"If I may be allowed to explain my own actions," Father said with heavy sarcasm. "Occasionally I have been known to go fishing in the rain. Today I did not. Is that comprehensible?"

"Have some apple tart, dear," said Mother, handing him a plate.

"Hrmm," Father said, glancing at her sideways, and he lapsed into silence. After a moment he said, hopefully: "Might be an idea if we all went for a walk after supper. It seems to be clearing up."

Everyone looked out of the window, and the temperature of the room rose several degrees. Over the sea the clouds had broken, leaving a deepening blue sky, and the opposite headland glowed suddenly a brighter green as the sinking sun shone for the first time that day.

Then they heard the doorbell ring.

"Bother," Mother said wearily. "Whoever can that be?"

Mrs Palk's footsteps rang briskly past the door, and then back again. She put her head in. " 'Tis some people for you, Dr. Drew."

"Stand by to repel boarders," Father said, and he went out into the hall. In a few moments he was back, talking to someone over his shoulder as he came through the door. ". . . very kind of you indeed, we hadn't really thought what we were going to do tomorrow. They're an independent lot, you know. Well, here we are." He beamed heartily round with what the family called his public face. "My wife, Simon, Jane, Barney . . . this is Mr. and Miss—er—Withers. From that yacht you admire so much, Simon. We met in the harbour this morning."

A man and a girl stood behind him in the doorway. Both were dark-haired, with beaming smiles bright in sun-tanned faces. They looked like beings suddenly materialised from another very tidy

29

planet. The man stepped forward, holding out his hand: "How do you do, Mrs Drew?"

They sat staring blankly at him as he advanced towards Mother; he wore dazzling white flannel trousers, and a blazer, with a dark-blue scarf tucked in the neck of his white shirt, and they had not expected to see anything like him in Trewissick at all. Then they jumped up hastily as Mother stood to shake hands, and Simon knocked over his chair. Into the confusion Mrs Palk appeared with a large teapot and a tray of cups and saucers.

"Two extra cups," she said, smiling blandly, and departed again.

"Do sit down," the girl said. "We only popped in for a moment, we didn't want to interrupt." She bent to help Simon pick up his chair. Her black curls bobbed forward over her forehead. She was a very pretty girl, Jane thought, watching her. Much older than any of them, of course. She wore a bright green shirt and black trousers, and her eyes seemed to twinkle with a kind of hidden private laughter. Jane suddenly felt extremely young.

Mr. Withers, showing a lot of very white teeth, was talking to Mother. "Mrs Drew, do please forgive this intrusion, we had no intention of breaking into your supper."

"Not at all," said Mother, looking faintly bemused. "Won't you have a cup of tea?"

"Thank you, no, no, most kind, but we have a meal waiting on the boat. We simply came to issue an invitation. My sister and I are in Trewissick for some days, with the yacht to ourselves—on our way round the coast, you know—and we wondered whether you and the children would care to spend a day out at sea. We have—"

"Gosh!" Simon nearly upset his chair again. "How marvellous! You mean go out in that fabulous boat?"

"I do indeed," said the smiling Mr. Withers.

Simon spluttered without words, his face glowing with delight. Mother said hesitantly: "Well . . ."

"Of course I realise we're descending on you out of the blue," Mr. Withers said soothingly. "But it would be pleasant to have company for a change. And when we met your husband in the harbour-master's office this morning, and discovered we are neighbours in London—"

"Are you?" said Barney curiously from the table. "Where?"

"Marylebone High Street, just round the corner from you," said

30

the girl, dimpling at him. "Norman sells antiques." She looked across at Mother. "I expect you and I use the same shops, Mrs Drew—you know that little *pâtisserie* where you can get those gorgeous rum babas?"

"I try not to," Mother said, beginning to smile. "Well really, this is very kind, considering we're strangers. But I'm not sure whether . . . well, the three of them can be rather a handful, you know."

"Mother!" Simon looked aghast.

Mr. Withers puckered his nose boyishly at her. "But my invitation extends to the whole family, Mrs Drew. We sincerely hope you and your husband will join our little crew as well. Just a trip out and back, you understand—round the bay, as the commercial gentlemen have it. With perhaps a little fishing. I shall enjoy showing off the boat. Tomorrow perhaps? They say it should be a fine day."

What an old-fashioned way of talking he has, Jane thought idly; perhaps it comes of selling antiques. She looked at Simon and Barney, both all eagerness at the idea of a day on the strange yacht, gazing anxiously at their parents; and then back at Mr. Withers' immaculate white flannels and folded scarf. I don't like him, she thought. I wonder why?

"Well, thank you very much indeed," Mother said finally. "I don't think I shall come, if you'll forgive me—if the sun comes out I shall go and work up above the harbour. But I know Dick and the children would love to go."

"Ah yes, Dr. Drew was telling us about your painting," Mr. Withers said warmly. "Well, the loss will be ours—but if the muse calls, dear lady. . . . The rest of the family will come, though, I hope?"

"Not half," said Simon swiftly.

"It sounds smashing," Barney said. He added, as an afterthought: "Thank you very much."

"Well," said Father cheerfully, "this is a noble gesture, I must say. We're all very grateful to you. As a matter of fact"—he looked vaguely round the room—"there should have been one other member of the family here, but he seems to have disappeared. My wife's uncle. He rented the house for us."

The children automatically followed his gaze round the room. They had forgotten Great-Uncle Merry. Now they realized that there had been no sign of him since the two sudden visitors appeared. The door that led into the breakfast room at the back of the house stood slightly open—but when Barney ran across to look in, there was no one there.

"Professor Lyon, you mean?" the girl said.

"That's right." Father stared at her for a moment. "I didn't think I'd mentioned him this morning. D'you know him, then?"

Mr. Withers answered for her, quickly and smoothly. "I believe we have met, once or twice. In another sphere than this. In the course of our work, you know. A charming old gentleman, as I remember, but a little unpredictable."

"That he certainly is," Mother said ruefully. "Always dashing off somewhere. He hasn't even finished his supper this time. But do let me give you some tea, or coffee."

"Thank you, but I think we should be getting back," the girl said. "Vayne will have supper waiting."

Mr. Withers pulled down the edges of his immaculate blazer with a precise, feminine gesture. "You're quite right, Polly, we mustn't be late." He swung his white smile round the room like a lighthouse. "Vayne is our skipper—the professional on board. And an excellent chef too. You must sample his cooking tomorrow. Well now, shall we see you all down in the harbour, if the weather is fine? Nine thirty, perhaps? We will have the dinghy waiting at the quay."

"Splendid." Father moved with him out into the hall, and everyone straggled after them. On the way Polly Withers paused, and looked up over Simon's head at the old Cornish maps hanging among the oil-paintings on the dark wall. "Do look, Norman. Aren't they marvellous?" She turned to Mother. "This really is a wonderful house. Did your uncle rent it from a friend?"

"A Captain Toms. We've never met him—he's abroad. Quite an old man—a retired sailor of some kind. I believe his family have owned the Grey House for years."

" A fascinating place." Mr. Withers was looking about him with a professional eye. "He has some beautiful old books, I see." He reached one hand idly down to the door of a long low bookcase in the hall; but it would not open.

"I keep everything locked," Father said. "You know what it is with a furnished house—one's always nervous of damaging things."

"An admirable principle," Mr. Withers said formally. But his sister was smiling down at Simon. "I bet it's a wonderful place to explore, though, isn't it?" she said. "Have you children been looking for secret tunnels and things yet? I know I should have done, in an old house. Do let us know if you find one."

Simon said politely, feeling Barney's anxious eyes on his back: "Oh, I don't think there's anything like that here."

"Well, till tomorrow, then," Mr. Withers said from the doorstep; and they were gone.

"Isn't that terrific?" Barney said eagerly, when the door closed. "A whole day out on that yacht! D'you think they'll let us help sail her?"

"Mind you keep out of their way until you're asked," said Father. "We don't want any casualties."

"Well, you could be ship's doctor."

"I'm on holiday, remember?"

"Why didn't you tell us you'd met them?" demanded Simon.

"I was going to," Father said meekly. "I expect I was too busy being irritable." He grinned. "You can let Rufus out now if you want to, Barney—but he's *not* going on the boat tomorrow, so don't ask."

Jane said suddenly: "I don't think I will either."

"Well, for goodness' sake!" Simon stared at her. "Why ever not?"

"I should get seasick."

"Of course you wouldn't—not under sail. There won't be any smelly old engine running. Oh come on, Jane."

"No," said Jane, more firmly. "I'm not batty about boats like you are. I really don't want to go. They won't mind, will they, Father?"

Simon said in disgust: "You must be nuts."

"Leave her alone," said his father. "She knows her own mind. No, they'll understand, Jane. No-one would want you to be worried about getting ill. See how you feel about going in the morning, though."

"I do think it would be safer not," Jane said. But she said nothing about her real reason for not wanting to go. It would have sounded too silly to explain that she felt a strange uneasiness about the tall white yacht, and about the smiling Mr. Withers and his pretty sister. The more she thought about it, the sillier it seemed; so that in the end she convinced herself, as well as everybody else, that her reason for avoiding the trip was nothing but fear of seasickness.

But again nobody knew where Great-Uncle Merry had gone.

• *Chapter Four* •

A white morning haze lay over the sea, and down in the harbour the boats shifted idly on still water, bright under the sun. Jane peered down from her window. The fishing-boats were deserted, but she could see two small figures clambering from a dinghy beside the quay.

Simon said, behind her: "I brought this for you to look after, if you really aren't coming." She turned and saw him holding out a grey woollen sock. It looked peculiarly stiff and cylindrical.

"What on earth's so special about your socks?"

Simon grinned, but lowered his voice. "It's the manuscript. I couldn't think of anything else to put it in."

Jane laughed, took the sock and pulled the manuscript out half-way. But even though she handled it gently, the edges cracked and crumbled ominously as they caught in the wool. "Hey," she said, alarmed. "If that's going to happen every time, the whole thing'll fall to bits in a week. It was all right up in the attic, lying there for years without anyone touching it, but if we're going to carry it around—"

Simon looked anxiously at the curled parchment, its battered edges dark with age, and saw cracks that had not been there before. He said, troubled: "But we'll have to handle it so much if we're going to find out what it means . . . wait a minute, though. That room—"

Leaving Jane baffled, he seized the manuscript and ran downstairs to the small dark door on the first-floor landing which led to the passage they had discovered on the way to the attic. It was still unlocked. He stepped down into the tiny passage, and across to the bare, austere room that they had decided was the captain's

34

bedroom. It was just as it had been the day before, and the telescope case was still lying on the window-sill.

Simon picked up the case, and unscrewed it. The thread of each half was bright and untarnished, shining with a faint film of oil; and the copper lining inside, when he held it up to the light, glinted dry and clean. He dropped the rolled manuscript inside. It fitted perfectly, resting snugly between the two halves when he screwed them together again. Simon looked thoughtfully round the room, as if it might tell him something. But there was nothing but the silence and the mysterious lived-in emptiness, and he closed the door again, gently, and ran back upstairs.

"Look," he said to Jane. "Might have been made for it."

"Perhaps it was," said Jane, taking the case.

"You'd better hide it somewhere," said Simon. "What about the top of our wardrobe?"

"I'll think of a good place," said Jane thoughtfully.

But Simon, half-way back to his own room already, hardly heard her; already his mind was racing ahead to the day on the Witherses' yacht. And by the time he, Barney and Father were gone, in a great scuffle of argument over oilskins and pullovers and bathing-trunks, Jane was almost beginning to wish she had changed her mind and gone too.

But she said firmly, to Simon's final jeers: "No. I'd only spoil it all if I got sick." And instead she stood watching from the window as they ran down to the quay, and the little dinghy bobbed out to the tall, slim white yacht.

Her mother, easel under one arm and a bag of sandwiches and paints in the other hand, looked at her doubtfully. "Darling, are you sure you aren't going to be lonely?"

"Goodness no," said Jane stoutly. "I shall just wander about, it'll be fun. Honestly. I mean, you don't get lonely when you're painting, do you?"

Mother laughed. "All right, independence, you wander. Don't get lost. I shall be up above the harbour on the other side if you want me. Mrs Palk's going to be here all day, she'll get your lunch. Why don't you take Rufus for a walk?"

She went out into the sunshine, her eyes already vague with the shape and colour of her painting. Jane felt a wet nose push at her hand, looked down at Rufus' large hopeful brown eyes, laughed, and ran off with him down into the village, through the small strange streets and the Cornish voices lilting from the doorways of the shops.

But all the morning she felt curiously restless, as if something were jostling to push itself to the front of her mind. As if, she thought, her mind were trying to say something to her that she couldn't quite hear. When she brought Rufus home, to collapse in a panting red heap in the kitchen beside Mrs Palk, she was still thoughtful and subdued.

"Nice walk, lovey?" said Mrs Palk, sitting back on her heels. She had a bucket of soapy water beside her, and her face was red and shiny; she had been scrubbing the grey slate floor.

"Mmm," Jane said vaguely. She fiddled with the bow on her pony-tail.

"Have 'ee's lunch ready in just a minute," Mrs Palk said, scrambling to her feet. "My, just look at that dog, proper wore out. Needs a drink of water, I'll be bound—" She reached for Rufus's dish.

"I'll go up and wash." Jane wandered out through the hall, the cool dark passage with the sunlight shafting in on one of the old maps that Polly Withers had exclaimed over with delight. Miss Withers . . . why should she and her brother have seemed sinister? They were perfectly ordinary people, there was no real reason to think otherwise. It was kind of them to have asked everyone out for the day on the yacht. . . . Odd, though, that remark she had made about exploring, and finding things. . . .

Finding things. Half-way up the stairs, Jane remembered with a sudden shock of guilt that she had left the manuscript alone all the morning, shut in its new case in the drawer of her bed-side table. Should she have taken it with her? No, don't be silly, she thought; but she scuttled up the stairs and into her room anxiously, and felt a surge of relief as she saw the case lying quietly glinting in the drawer.

She drew out the brown roll of parchment and took it to the window, gingerly straightening it out. The lines of cramped black lettering gave her the same shiver of uneasy excitement that she had felt in the attic, at that moment when suddenly they had all three realised what they were looking at. She peered at it, but the squat chunks of words were no more legible now than they had been then. She could just make out the initials of the words that Simon had said were Mark and Arthur.

How were they ever to find out what it all meant?

36

She looked down at the bottom of the curling sheet, at the few thin wavering lines that they had thought might be a map. In the dim light of the attic there had been little there to see; but now Jane had the full white glare of midday. She bent closer, suddenly realising that there were more lines in the map than she had noticed at first; lines so faint that before she had mistaken them for cracks. And among them, fainter still, some words were written.

It was a very rough map, as if it had been hurriedly drawn. It seemed to be coastline, looking rather like a letter W lying on its side, with two inlets and a headland. Or was it two headlands and an inlet? There was no way of telling which side was supposed to be the sea. And although she could just see that there was a word written across one of the projecting arms of land—or sea—it was made totally unreadable by one of the breaks in the ancient crumbling parchment: a crack crossing the word out as neatly as if it had been a thick ink line.

"Bother," said Jane crossly, aloud. She realised as she said it that she had become determined in the last half-minute to have some discovery of her own about the manuscript to announce to Simon and Barney when they came back from their day on the boat. That was what had been niggling at the back of her mind all the morning.

One other name was written across the map. If it was a name. The letters were small and brown, but more distinct than those on the rest of the manuscript. Jane worked them out one by one and found they made three words. "Ring Mark Hede." She stared, disappointed. It meant nothing. Ring, mark, heed," she said experimentally. It wasn't even a place. How could a place have a name like that?

The clang of the ship's bell in the hall came echoing up the stairs, breaking into the stillness of the sea's murmur and the distant gulls, and she heard Mrs Palk calling faintly below. "Jane! Ja—ne!" Hastily she rolled up the manuscript and dropped it back into the telescope case, screwing the two halves tight together. She opened the drawer of her bed-side table, hesitated for a moment, then shut it again. Better not to let it out of her sight. She snatched a cardigan from the bed, wrapped it round the case, and ran out and down the stairs two at a time.

But she ran too fast. Swinging round a comer of the first-floor landing, she bumped heavily against a long low wooden chest lying in the shadows, and yelped with pain. It *would* have to be the same leg she had hurt down on the quay . . . but as she bent to rub her knee, something drew her attention away. The chest she had knocked against was the one they had noticed the day before, with the lid locked. "Native gold and ornaments," Simon had said, and then found he couldn't open it. But now the lid had sprung open a few inches, and was rocking gently up and down. It must have been stuck, not locked, her collision had jerked it loose.

Curiously Jane lifted it fully open. There was not much inside: some old newspapers, a big pair of leather gloves, two or three heavy woollen sweaters and, half hidden, a small black-covered book. A very dull treasure, she thought. But the book might be interesting. She reached down inside and picked it up.

"Ja—ne!" Mrs. Palk's voice was nearer, coming up the stairs. Guiltily Jane dropped the lid and bundled the little book inside the folds of her cardigan with the telescope case. Mrs. Palk's face puffed into view through the banisters.

"Coming," Jane said meekly.

"Ah, there, thought 'ee'd gone to bed. Gettin' too fat for they stairs, I am." Mrs. Palk beamed at her. "Lunch is on the table. I were takin' me pastry out of the oven or I'd not have kept 'ee so long." She waddled back to the kitchen. A mounded plateful of ham and salad waited for Jane in the dining-room, like a small bright island in the glossy sea of the polished mahogany table. Beside it was a dish of gooseberry tart and a small jug of cream.

Jane sat down and ate everything absently, leafing with one hand through the little book she had found in the chest. It was a guide-book to the village, written by the local vicar. "*A Short Guide to Trewissick*" said the title-page, in flowing, curly type. "Compiled by the Reverend E.J. Hawes-Mellor, M.A. (Oxon.) LL.D. (Lond.), Vicar of the Parish Church of St John, Trewissick."

Not exciting, thought Jane, her interest dying. She flipped through the narrow pages, full of details of "rambles" through the country-side around. The words from the manuscript were still swimming before her mind. If only she could have something to tell Simon and Barney about the map. . . .

It was then that the guide-book fell open at its center page under her fingers. Jane glanced down idly, and then paused. The page showed a detailed map of Trewissick village, with every street, straight and winding, patterned behind the harbour that lay snug

38

between its two headlands. The churches, the village hall, were all separately marked; she saw with a quick thrill of pride that the Grey House was marked by name, on the road that led up to the tip of Kemare Head and then faded into nothing. But what caught her attention was the name written neatly across the headland. It read: "King Mark's Head."

"King Mark's Head," said Jane slowly, aloud. She reached down to the bundled cardigan lying beside her chair, drew out the telescope case, and unrolled the manuscript on the table. The words stared up at her, cramped and enigmatic: "Ring Mark Hede". And as she looked she saw that the first letter of the first word, blurred with age and dirt, might very well be not an "R" but a "K." She gulped with excitement and took a deep breath.

King Mark's Head: the same name on both maps. So that the map on the manuscript from the attic must be a map of Trewissick—of that very part of Trewissick on which the Grey House stood. The strange words must be an old name for Kemare Head.

But when the first delighted shock had washed over her she looked again from one map to the other, and her spirits sank a little. There was something very odd about the wavering outline of the coast drawn on the old manuscript; something more than the inaccuracies you always found in a rough free-hand drawing. The lines of the coast were not the same as those on the guide-book map; the headlands bulged strangely, and the harbour was the wrong shape. Why?

Puzzled, Jane fetched a stub of pencil from the sideboard and did her best to draw a faint copy of the manuscript coastline over the one on the guide-book. There was no doubt about it; the shapes were not the same.

Perhaps the manuscript didn't show Trewissick after all. Perhaps there were two headlands in Cornwall called King Mark's Head. Or perhaps the coast had changed its shape in the hundreds of years since the manuscript had been drawn. How on earth were they to find out?

She put the manuscript reluctantly away, and stared at the two outlines, one in print, one in pencil, that she now had on the page of the book. But still she could find no answer. In exasperation she flipped back the pages of the book, and suddenly caught sight of the title-page again.

". . . the Reverend E.J. Hawes-Mellor, M.A. . . ."

Jane jumped to her feet. That was it! Why not? The vicar of Trewissick must know all about the district. He was the expert, he had written the guide-book. He would know whether the coast had changed its shape, and what it had been like before. That was the way to find out—the only way. He was the only person who wouldn't ask why she wanted to know; he would think she was just interested in his book. She must go and find him, and ask.

And then think how much she would have to tell Simon and Barney when they came home. . . .

That was the final thought which decided Jane, normally the shy member of the family, on the way she would spend her afternoon. She turned quickly as the door opened, and Mrs. Palk came rolling in. "Finished, 'ave 'ee? Enjoy it?"

"Lovely. Thank you very much." Jane gathered up the guide-book and the precious woolly bundle of her cardigan. "Mrs. Palk," she said tentatively, "do you know the vicar of Trewissick?" Surely, she thought, with all those hymns . . .

"Well, not meself personally, no." Mrs. Palk became very grave and solemn. "Bein' chapel, I don't have no contact with'n, though I see 'n about, of course. Tur'ble clever man, they do say the vicar is. Was 'ee thinkin' of takin' a look at the church, midear?"

"Yes," Jane said. After all I probably shall, she added defensively to herself.

" 'Tis a beautiful old place. Long way though—up the hill at the top of the village. You can just see the tower through the trees going up Fish Street, from the quay."

"I think I know."

"Don't get sunstroke, now." Mrs. Palk sailed benevolently out with the dishes, and in a moment Jane heard "Abide with më" echoing with rich gloomy relish down the hall from the kitchen. She ran upstairs, looked hastily round for a place where she might hide the manuscript case, and finally tucked it among the covers at the foot of her bed, so that it could lie along the edge of the mattress and leave no bump. Then before her nervousness could get the better of her new idea, she went out, clutching her guide-book, into the sleepy afternoon sun.

* * *

The church at the top of the hill seemed cut off from the sea. Jane could see nothing from there but trees and the hills, and even the little village houses ended some twenty yards down the road. The

square grey church with its low tower, and the big gate-posts opposite it, might have been in any wooded valley a hundred miles from
the sea.

In the churchyard a wizened old man in shirt-sleeves and braces
was cutting the grass with a pair of shears. Jane stopped near him
on the other side of the wall. "Excuse me," she said loudly, "but is
that the vicarage over there?"

The old man, wheezing, straightened himself by holding one arm
round to push himself in the small of the back. "A's right," he said
laconically, and then just stood there, staring without expression,
watching her all the way across the road and up the drive. Jane
heard her feet crunching on the gravel, enormously loud in the
silent afternoon. The big square grey house, its windows empty and
lifeless, seemed to dare her to disturb it.

It was a very scruffy house, she thought, for a vicarage. The
gravel of the drive was clotted with weeds, and in the rambling garden hydrangea bushes grew spindly and neglected, with the grass of
the lawns as high as hay. She pressed the bell-push by the side of
the peeling door, and heard a bell ring faintly inside the house,
echoing a long way off.

After a long time, when she had just begun to decide with relief
that no one was there to answer the bell, she heard footsteps inside
the house. The door opened, creaking resentfully as if it did not
often open at all.

The man standing there was tall and dark, untidy in an old sports
jacket, but at the same time forbidding, with the thickest black eyebrows that Jane had ever seen growing almost straight across his
brow without a break in the middle. He stared down at her.

"Yes?" His voice was very deep, without a trace of accent.

"Is Mr. Hawes-Mellor in, please?"

The tall man frowned. "Mr. who?"

"Mr. Hawes-Mellor. The vicar."

His face cleared a little, though still the intent blackbrowed stare
did not relax. "Ah, I see. Mr. Hawes-Mellor, I'm afraid, is no longer
vicar here. He died a number of years ago."

"Oh," said Jane, and stepped back off the doorstep, not at all
sorry at the chance to go away. "Oh well, in that case—"

"Perhaps I can be of some help," he said in the deep mournful
voice. "My name is Hastings, I have replaced Mr. Hawes-Mellor
here."

41

"Oh," Jane said again; she was beginning to find the lone Mr. Hastings and his strange neglected house and garden rather unnerving. "Oh no, I don't want to be a nuisance, it was only something about a book he wrote, a guide-book to the village."

A flicker of interest seemed to wake in the vicar's dark face. "A guide-book to Trewissick? There was some talk that he had written one, but I have never been able to trace a copy. What was it that you wanted to ask? I am afraid that if you are looking for the book I can be of no help—"

"Oh no," Jane said, not without pride. "I've got one." She held her little guide-book up to show him. "It was just something inside it, about the village, that I wondered if he'd got wrong."

The vicar stared down at the book, opened his mouth to say something and then seemed to change his mind. He held the door wider open and moved his mouth into an uneasy smile. "Well, do come in for a few moments, young lady, and we'll see what we can do. I know a little about Trewissick myself after my years here."

"Thank you very much," Jane said nervously. She stepped inside the door, hitching up the ribbon on her pony-tail as she followed him down the passage, and hoping she looked reasonably tidy. Not that she would have been out of place if she had been in rags: she thought, looking around her, that the vicarage was one of the most unloved-looking and shabbiest houses she had ever seen. It was big, and rambling, with more sense of space than the Grey House; but the paint was peeling, the walls grubby and the floors all bare with one or two faded rugs. She began to feel rather sorry for the vicar as he strode stiffly along ahead of her.

He led her into a room which was obviously his study, with a big desk strewn with papers, two battered cane chairs with faded cushions, and shelves of books all round the walls. Tall French windows stood wide open to show the stretch of long grass that Jane had glimpsed from the front drive.

"Now," he said, sitting down behind his desk and clearing a space impatiently in the litter of papers on its top. "Sit yourself down and tell me what you were going to ask Mr. Hawes-Mellor. You've found a copy of his book, have you?"

He stared again at the book in Jane's hand. It seemed to fascinate him.

"Yes," Jane said. "Would you like to have a look at it?" She held the book out to him.

The vicar took it, slowly, closing his long fingers round the narrow cover as if it were something infinitely precious. He did not open it, but put it down on the desk before him and looked at it so hard that he seemed not to be seeing it but thinking about something else. Then he turned his grave, heavy-browed face towards Jane again.

"You are on holiday here?"

"Yes. My name's Jane Drew. I'm staying with my family in the Grey House."

"Are you indeed? That is not a house I am very familiar with." Mr. Hastings smiled rather grimly. "Captain Toms has no time for me, I am afraid. A strange, solitary man."

"We've never met him," Jane said. "He's gone abroad."

"And this book of yours." His fingers caressed its cover almost unconsciously. "Is it interesting?"

"Oh, tremendously. I love all the stories about Trewissick when there were smugglers and things." For a moment Jane wondered doubtfully whether to mention the map after all. But her curiosity overcame any doubts. She stood up and crossed to stand beside him, leafing through the book to the page with the map of south Cornwall. "This was the bit that puzzled me, the shape of the coastline. I wanted to ask if it had ever been different, once."

Standing behind the vicar, she could not see his face, but his shoulders seemed to stiffen as he looked at the map, and the fingers of his hand lying on the desk curled gently underneath into the palm.

"A curious question," he said.

"I just wondered."

"I see there is another line pencilled over the coastline of the map here. Is that yours?"

"Yes."

"From your imagination?" The deep voice was very quiet.

"More or less. Well, that is . . . I saw something like it somewhere, in a book or something." Jane floundered, trying to avoid mentioning their manuscript from the attic without actually telling untruths. "If you know about Trewissick, Mr. Hastings, do you know if the coast has always been the same shape?"

"I should have thought so. A granite coast takes a very long time to change." He was staring at the pencilled line. "You say you saw this outline in a book?"

43

"Oh, a book, or another map, or something," Jane said vaguely.

"In the Grey House?"

"We don't touch the captain's books," Jane said automatically, forgetting that the guide-book must be one of them.

"But you have looked around them, no doubt?" The vicar rose to his feet, towering above her, and reached out a long arm to take a book from one of the shelves. He handed it to Jane; it was very old and covered with shiny scuffed leather, and the pages crackled and gave off a smell of musty age when she opened it. It was called *Tales of Lyonesse,* and a lot of the "s"s were printed like "f"s.

"Have you seen any book there like that?" His voice was persistent. He stood between Jane and the light, and looking up at him, she could see nothing but a faint glint of light reflected from his eyes in the shadowed face. The effect was for a moment exceedingly sinister, and Jane felt creeping over her the small cold uneasiness that was becoming familiar about the holiday: a sense of something mysterious, that everyone else knew about but that was hidden from her brothers and her.

"No, I don't think so."

"Are you sure? A title like that, perhaps? You might have seen a map in such a book?"

"No, really. We just haven't looked."

"Might you not have seen a volume on a shelf similar to this?"

"I honestly don't know," Jane said, shrinking back in her chair at the urgency that had come into his voice. "Why don't you ask the captain?"

Mr. Hastings took the book back from her and tucked it back in its place on the shelf. The grave near-frown was back on his face. "He is not a communicative man," he said shortly.

Uneasiness was nudging more insistently at Jane's mind, and she began to fidget from one foot to another.

"Well, I must be off home," she said, using one of Mother's phrases brightly and hoping it sounded polite. "I'm sorry to have interrupted you." She glanced rather wildly from the window to the door.

The vicar, standing silent and intent, pulled himself together and moved towards the French windows. "You can come out this way, it's quicker. The front door is seldom used."

He held out his hand to Jane. "I am pleased to have met you, Miss Drew. I am sorry not to have been more helpful, but I must say

I think it unlikely that our coast here has ever had any characteristics that are not shown on Mr. Hawes-Mellor's map. He was, I understand, a cartographer of some repute. I am glad you came to see me."

He inclined his head gravely as he shook Jane's hand, with a strange, archaic gesture that reminded her suddenly of Mr. Withers when he left the Grey House. But this, she thought, seemed more genuine, as if it were something which Mr. Withers had been trying to imitate.

"Good-by," she said quickly, and ran off through the long feathery grass towards the drive of the silent shabby house, and the road that led back home.

• *Chapter Five* •

When Jane reached the Grey House, Simon and Barney were chattering like monkeys in the living-room to Great-Uncle Merry, who sat quietly listening from the depths of a big arm-chair. Both boys were glowing with excitement, and even Barney's fair skin had been flushed by the wind and sun to a faint pinkish-brown.

"There you are, darling," Mother said. "I was just beginning to worry about you."

Simon hailed her with a yell from across the room, "Oh you should have *come!* It was fabulous, like being right out at sea, and when the wind was behind us we went tremendously fast, far better than a motor boat . . . only we came back in on the engine, because the wind dropped, and that was fun too. Mr. Withers came back with us for a drink, but he's gone now. Father went with him, to fetch up some of the mackerel we caught."

"And what's Jane been doing?" said Great-Uncle Merry quietly from his corner.

"Oh, nothing much," Jane said. "Wandering about."

But when all three children were upstairs (sent early up to bed because, Father said ominously when Simon imitated a lightship siren right behind his chair, they were all "overtired"), Jane knocked at the door of the boys' room and went in to tell them about her discovery and her visit to the vicar. She did not meet quite the enthusiastic response that she had expected.

"You copied out part of the manuscript?" Simon demanded, his voice rising to a squeak of horror. "And showed it to him?"

"Yes, I did," Jane said defensively. "Well, for goodness' sake, what harm can that possibly do? A little pencilled line in a guide-book can't mean anything to anybody."

"You jolly well shouldn't have done anything connected with the manuscript unless we all agreed it together."

"It wasn't connected with the manuscript, not as far as he knew. I just told him I wanted to find something out about the coast." Jane forgot any uneasiness she had felt about the vicar in building a defense against Simon's indignation. "I thought you'd be grateful, my finding out the manuscript map shows Kemare Head."

"She's quite right, you know," Barney said from his pillow. "It's terrifically important finding that out. For all we knew up to now it might have been a map of Timbuctoo. And if it turns out from what the vicar says that Trewissick hasn't changed since when our map was drawn, that's going to help us when we find if there are any clues in the manuscript."

"I dare say," Simon said grudgingly, clambering into bed and kicking off all the blankets. "Oh well, yes, it does help. We'll talk about it tomorrow."

"Then we can start our quest," Barney said sleepily. " 'Night, Jane. See you in the morning."

"Goodnight."

* * *

But the morning brought more than any of them had bargained for.

Simon woke first, very early. The air was still as warm as it had been the day before. He lay in his pyjamas staring up at the ceiling for a little while, listening to Barney's peaceful breathing from the other bed. Then he grew restless, so he went out and padded downstairs barefoot, feeling hungry. If he found Mrs. Palk already in the kitchen he might manage to have two breakfasts.

But Mrs. Palk seemed not to have arrived yet. and the house was quite silent. It was not until he reached the flight of stairs leading down into the hall that Simon first noticed something wrong.

Always on his way down to breakfast he stopped to look at the old map of Cornwall that hung on the wall at the turn of the stairs. But when he looked for it this morning, it was not there. Only a rectangular mark on the wallpaper showed where it had hung; and as Simon glanced along the wall of pictures down the stairs he saw there were several more gaps as well.

Puzzled, he went slowly down into the hall. He found several strange naked-looking patches where pictures had been taken down, and the barometer, next to one empty space, was leaning sideways.

Simon went across and straightened it, feeling the bare wooden blocks of the floor cool under his bare feet. Looking down the long hall, he could see nothing else unusual at first. Then he noticed that at the far end, where the sun was streaming in from the kitchen through the open doorway, several of the blocks had been wrenched out and were strewn all over the floor. Simon stared, puzzled.

He started down the hall towards the kitchen, and then on an impulse turned to his right and reached for the handle of the door into the living-room. It squeaked under his touch as it always did, and nervously Simon opened the door and peered round. Then he gasped.

The room looked as though a tornado had blown through it in the night. The pictures hung crooked on the walls, or lay torn from their frames on the floor, and the furniture seemed to Simon's first startled glance to be completely buried in books.

Everywhere there were books, scattered over the floor, open, closed, upside-down; heaped on the tables and chairs, mounded on the sideboard; and a lonely few still lying on the empty shelves. All the locked bookcases around the walls, that they had been forbidden to touch, were empty. The glass doors hung loose from their hinges with splintered wood showing round their locks; and one or two, completely wrenched away, were propped against the wall. The shelves had been swept clear of everything they held, and the drawers below were open, with papers spilling from them loose on to the chaos of books on the floor. There was a faint musty smell, and a thin pall of dust seemed to hang in the air.

For one frozen moment Simon stood staring, aghast. Then he turned on his heel and raced upstairs, shouting for his father.

Everyone was woken out of their early half-sleep by his shouts. Led by Father, they all stumbled out into the passage in pyjamas and night-dresses and followed Simon downstairs, trying dazedly to understand the words tumbling over each other out of his mouth.

"What is it?"

"What's the matter, is the house on fire?"

"Burglars!" Father said incredulously, following down the stairs. "But you don't get burgled in a village like—good heavens!" He caught sight of the devastation in the living- room through the open door. As Mother, Jane and Barney followed his gaze they fell silent too, but not for long.

48

Wherever they went on the ground floor of the house they found the same thing. The doors of bookcases had been ripped off, and the books tumbled off the shelves into a chaotic jumble on the floor. Every locked drawer or cupboard had been forced, and the papers from inside scattered wildly about. Even in the breakfast room half a dozen elderly cookery books had been scattered from a shelf.

"I don't understand this," Father said slowly. "The place is practically wrecked, but one or two obvious things that are clearly valuable haven't been touched. That statuette on the mantelpiece there, for instance, and that big silver cup on the sideboard in the front room. There doesn't seem any point to it all."

"Someone was rejoicing in destruction," Barney said solemnly.

Simon said slowly, "They must have made an awful noise. Why didn't it wake us up?"

"We're two floors away," Barney said. "You can't hear anything up there. I like this, it's mysterious."

"I don't," Jane shivered. "Imagine someone wandering about down here all night while we were asleep upstairs. It gives me the creeps."

"Perhaps there wasn't anyone," Bamey said.

"Don't be an idiot, of course there was. Or do you think all the books jumped off the shelves?"

"It needn't have been human. It might have been one of those special sort of ghosts that throws things about just for fun. A polter—polt—"

"Poltergeist," said Father absently. He was opening all the silver cupboards to see if anything had gone.

"There you are. One of those."

"Well, Mrs. Palk says the house is supposed to be haunted," Jane said. "Oh dear."

They all looked at one another round-eyed, and suddenly shivered.

Mother said, appearing suddenly in the doorway and making them all jump: "Well, it's the first ghost I've ever heard of who wore crêpe-soled shoes. Dick, come and have a look out here."

Father straightened up and followed her out into the kitchen, with the children close at his heels. Mother pointed, without a word.

Two kitchen windows were open, the big one over the sink and a small one above it; and so was the door. And on the flat white tiles

49

of the table-top beside the sink there was the faint but unmistakable outline of a footprint. A large footprint, with bar markings across the sole; and traces of the same markings on the window-sill above.

"Gosh!"

"There's your ghost," Father said cheerfully, though he did not look cheerful at all.

Then he turned on them briskly. "Now come on, all of you, off upstairs and get dressed. You've seen all there is to see. No"—he waved his hands as all three children began to protest vigorously. "This isn't a game, it's extremely serious. We shall have to call the police, and I don't want anything touched before they arrive. *Off!*"

Father had one voice which stopped all argument, and this was it. Simon, Jane and Barney trailed reluctantly out of the kitchen door and along the hall, and then stopped still at the foot of the stairs, looking up. Great-Uncle Merry was heavily descending the stairs towards them, clad in a pair of brilliant red pyjamas and with his white hair all standing up on end.

He was yawning prodigiously and rubbing his eyes in a puzzled kind of way. "Won't do," he was muttering to himself. "Can't make it out . . . heavy sleep . . . most unusual . . ." Then he caught sight of the children. "Good morning," he said with dignity, as if he were fully and impeccably dressed. "Befuddled though I am this morning, a great clamour has been penetrating up the stairs from down here. Is anything wrong?"

"We've had *burglars* . . . !" Simon began, but Father came striding out after them from the kitchen and clapped his hands. "Come on, come on, I told you to go and get dressed. . . . Oh good, there you are, Merry. The most extraordinary thing has happened—" He glared at the children, and they hastily ran upstairs.

After breakfast the police arrived from St Austell: a solid, red-faced sergeant and a very young constable following him like a mute shadow. Simon was looking forward to eager questions about his discovery of the crime. At the very least, he thought vaguely, he would have to make a statement. He was not quite sure what this meant, but it sounded familiar and important.

But the sergeant only said to him, his warm Cornish accent stroking the words: "Came down first, did 'ee?"

"Yes, that's right."

"Touch anythin'?"

"No, not a thing. Well, I did straighten the barometer. It was crooked." Looking round at the chaos, Simon thought how silly this sounded.

"Ah. Hear anythin'?"

"No."

"All quite as usual, eh, apart from the mess?"

"Yes, it was really."

"Ah," said the sergeant. He grinned at Simon sitting eagerly on the edge of his chair. "All right, I'll let 'ee off this time."

"Oh," said Simon, deflated. "Is that all?"

"I reckon so," the sergeant said placidly, tugging his jacket down over his stout middle. "Now, sir," he said to Father, "if we might take a look at this footprint you say you found . . ."

"Yes, of course." Father led them out to the kitchen. The children, drifting behind, peeped through the door. The sergeant gazed impassively at the footprint for some moments, said to his speechless constable, "Now take good note o' that, young George," and moved ponderously out to the disorder of the living-room.

"You say there seems to be nothin' gone, sir?"

"Well, it's difficult to tell, of course, since it's a rented house," Father said. "But certainly nothing valuable seems to be missing. The silver's all intact, not that there's much of it anyway. That cup, as you see, wasn't touched. But they seemed to go for the books, and I can't vouch for those. There may well be some missing that we don't know about."

" 'Tis a proper mess, surely." The sergeant bent down, with some effort, and picked up a book. A small deflated black cobweb lay along the top of its pages. "Very old, these—valuable, maybe. Quite well off, the captain is, I believe."

"If I might suggest, sergeant—" Great-Uncle Merry said diffidently, from the edge of the group.

"What is it, Professor?" The sergeant beamed at him all over his rosy countryman's face; even he seemed to know Great-Uncle Merry inexplicably well.

"I had no chance to look very thoroughly, since most of the bookcases were locked. But I should have said that very few of the books in this house were valuable, to a dealer at any rate. None of them was worth more than a few pounds, at the outside."

"Funny. They seem to have been looking for something . . . hey, look here." The sergeant shifted aside some of the papers whitening the floor, and they saw a pile of empty picture-frames.

"Those are from the hall," Simon said at once. "That bumpy gold frame had a map in it at the top of the stairs."

"Hmm. No map in it now. All of 'em been ripped out. Still, I dare say we'll find them somewhere in all this clutter." The sergeant rocked to and fro on his heels, gazing with an expression of mild regret at the battered bookcases and piles of books. He rubbed one of his shiny silver buttons thoughtfully, and finally turned to Father with an air of decision. "Sheer hooliganism, I reckon, sir. Can't be no other explanation. Seldom is round these parts, anyway."

"Ah," said the young constable regretfully, and immediately turned crimson and looked down at his feet.

The sergeant beamed at him. "Someone with a grudge against the captain, I dare say, havin' a go at his belongings. Might well be one or two people hereabouts don't like him, he's a funny old bird. Wouldn't 'ee say so, Professor?"

"You might call him that," Great-Uncle Merry said abstractly. He was standing looking about him with a puzzled frown.

"Breakin' in idn' difficult in a place the size of Trewissick," the sergeant said. "People don't expect it, they leave their windows open . . . did 'ee lock up last night, Dr. Drew?"

"Yes, I always do, back and front." Father scratched his head. "I could swear there weren't any windows open downstairs, but I must admit I didn't go round trying them all."

"Well no, you wouldn't expect this sort of thing . . . beats me why anyone should want to take the risk, just to rough the place up and not pinch anything. Now if I could have one more look at that print—" He led the way out of the room.

Simon beckoned Jane and Barney to stay behind. "Hooligans," he said thoughtfully. He picked up a book that lay sprawled open face downwards on the carpet, and shut its covers gently.

"It doesn't sound right somehow," Jane said. "It's all so thorough. Every drawer opened, and almost every book taken down."

"And every map taken out of its frame," said Barney. "It's just the maps, have you noticed? None of the pictures."

"The burglars must have been looking for something."

"And they went on all through the house because they couldn't find it."

"Perhaps it wasn't down here," Simon said slowly.

"Well, it couldn't have been upstairs."

"How d'you know?"

"Don't be silly, there just isn't anything upstairs. Except us."

"Isn't there?"

"Well—" Jane said, and then suddenly they were all three looking at one another in horror. They turned and dashed out of the room and up the stairs, to the second-floor bedroom where the great square wardrobe stood between Simon's and Barney's beds.

Simon hastily dragged a chair forward and jumped up on it to feel round on top of the wardrobe. His face went blank with alarm. "It's gone!"

There was a fearful moment of silence. Then Jane sat down with a bump on Barney's bed and began to giggle hysterically.

"Stop it!" Simon said sharply, sounding for a moment as authoritative as his father.

"Sorry . . . it's all right, it hasn't gone," Jane said weakly. "It's in my bed."

"In your *bed*?"

"Yes, I've got it. It's still there. I clean forgot," Jane babbled, then pulled herself together. "When I went to see the vicar I didn't want to take it with me, and 1 had to hide it somewhere in my room. So I shoved it right down under the bed-clothes. It was the nearest place. Then last night I forgot it was there, and I must have gone to sleep without feeling it. Come on."

The front bedroom was full of sunlight, and through the window the sea sparkled as merrily as if nothing could ever disturb the world. Jane hauled back the sheet of her rumpled bed and there, tucked in a corner at the bottom, was the telescope case.

They perched in a row on the edge of the bed, and Jane opened the case on her lap. They stared in silent relief at the familiar hollow cylinder of the old manuscript inside.

"Do you realize," Simon said gravely, "this was the safest place it could possibly have been? They could have looked anywhere else, but not in your bed without waking you up."

"You don't think they came up and looked in our rooms?" Barney turned pale.

"They might have looked anywhere."

"Oh, but this is silly." Jane swung her pony-tail as if she were trying to clear her head. "How on earth could they have known anything about the manuscript at all? We found it in the attic, all hidden away, and it had obviously been there for years and years. And no one can even have been up in the attic for ages—think of all that dust on the stairs."

"I don't know," Simon said. "There's a lot of things I don't understand. I only know I've been feeling funny about the manuscript ever since you said that vicar of yours got all excited about the copy of the map."

Jane shrugged. "I don't see how a vicar could be bad. Anyway he didn't know about the manuscript. He asked a few questions, but I think he was just being nosy."

"Wait a minute," Barney said slowly. "I've remembered something. There was someone else asking questions. It was Mr. Withers, on the boat yesterday, when I was down in the cabin with him getting lunch. He started saying a lot of peculiar things about the Grey House, and to tell him if we saw anything that looked very old . . . any"—he swallowed—"any old books or maps or papers. . . ."

"Oh no," Simon said. "It couldn't have been him."

"But whoever it was," said Barney in a small clear voice, "they were looking for the manuscript—weren't they?"

Sitting there in the silence of the Grey House they all three knew that it was the truth.

"They must want it awfully badly." Simon looked down at the manuscript. "It's that map part, that's what it is. Somehow someone knows it's in the house. Oh, I wish we knew what it said."

"Look here," Jane said, making up her mind, "we've got to tell Mother and Father about finding it."

Simon stuck his chin out. "It wouldn't do any good. Mother would be worried stiff. Anyway, don't you see, we shouldn't have a chance to work it out ourselves then. And suppose it *does* lead to buried treasure?"

"I don't want to find any beastly treasure. Something horrible's bound to happen if we do."

Barney forgot his fright in outraged ownership. "We can't tell anyone about it now. We found it. I found it, it's my quest."

"You're too young to understand," Jane said pompously. "We shall have to tell someone about it—Father, or the policeman. Oh do see," she added plaintively. "We've got to do something, after last night."

"Children!" Mother's voice came from the stairs outside, very close. They jumped guiltily to their feet at once, and Simon held the manuscript case behind his back.

"Hallo?"

"Oh there you are." Mother appeared in the doorway; she looked preoccupied. "Look, the house is going to be chaotic all this morning—would you like to go off swimming and come home for a late lunch—about one thirty? Then this afternoon Great-Uncle Merry wants to take you all out."

"Fine," Simon said, and she vanished again.

"That's it!" Barney thumped the pillow in excitement and relief. "That's it, of course, why didn't we think of it before? We can tell someone and still have things all right. We can tell Great-Uncle Merry!"

• *Chapter Six* •

"Now then," said Great-Uncle Merry as they strode down the hill to the harbour. "It's a splendid afternoon for a walk. Which way d'you want to go?"

"Somewhere lonely."

"Somewhere miles from anywhere."

"Somewhere where we can talk."

Great-Uncle Merry looked down at them, from one strained face to the next. His bleak, impassive expression did not change and he simply said, "Very well," and lengthened his stride so that they had to trot to keep up. He asked no questions, but walked in silence. They climbed the winding little street on the side of the harbour opposite Kemare Head and the Grey House, and followed the cliff path past the last straggling houses of the village, until the great purple-green sweep of the opposite headland rose before them.

Up the slope they toiled, through heather and prickling gorse, past rough outcroppings of grey rock patched yellow with lichen and weathered by the wind. There had been no breath of a breeze down in the harbour, but here the wind was loud in their ears.

"Gosh," Barney said, pausing and turning outwards to look down. "Look!" They turned with him, and saw the harbour far below and the Grey House tiny on the threading road. Already they were higher than their own headland. and still the rock-scarred slope stretched above them to meet the sky.

They turned again and scrambled up the slope, and at last they were at the top of the headland, with the line of the surf laid out like a slow-moving map below them on either side, and beyond it the great blue sweep of the sea. One big slanting boulder of granite stood higher than any they had passed on the way up, and

Great-Uncle Merry sat down with his back against it, his legs arched up before him long and knobbly, in their flapping brown corduroys. The children stood together, looking down. The land before them was unfamiliar, a silent, secret world of mounded peaks and invisible valleys, all its colours merging in a haze of summer heat.

"Hic incipit regnum Logri . . ." Great-Uncle Merry said, looking out with them across it all, as if he were reading out an inscription.

"What does that mean?"

"Here begins the realm of Logres. . . . Now come on, the three of you, and sit down."

They squatted down beside him, in a semi-circle before the big rock. Great-Uncle Merry surveyed them as if he were enthroned. "Well," he said gently, "who tells me what's wrong?"

In the quiet with only the sound of the wind stirring the air Jane and Barney looked at Simon. "Well, it was the burglar," he said haltingly. "We were worried . . ." and then the three of them were all tumbling out the words.

"When Miss Withers came the other night she was asking questions about the Grey House, and whether we'd found anything."

"And so did Mr. Withers on their yacht, he asked me about old books."

"And whoever it was last night, they only touched the books and all the old maps . . ."

". . . they were looking for it, they must have been . . ."

". . . only they didn't know where to look, and they didn't know we already had it."

"Suppose they know we've got it, they might come after us . . ."

Great-Uncle Merry raised one hand, though he did not move. His chin was up. He looked as if he were waiting for something. "Gently now," he said, "If you have found something in the Grey House, what is it you have found?"

Simon felt inside the rucksack. He drew out the case and handed the parchment to Great-Uncle Merry. "We found this."

Great-Uncle Merry took the parchment without a word, and gently unrolled it on his knees. He gazed at it in silence for a long while, and they could see his eyes moving over the words.

The wind on the headland whined softly round them, and although, as they watched, Great-Uncle Merry's expression did not change, they suddenly knew that some enormous emotion was flooding through him. Like an electric current it tingled in the air, exciting and frightening at the same time; though they could not understand what it was. And then he raised his head at last and looked out across the hills of Cornwall rolling far into the distance; and he breathed a great sigh of relief that was like a release from all the worry of the whole world.

"Where did you find it?" he said, and the three children jumped at the quiet, ordinary tone of his voice as if it brought them out of a spell.

"In the attic."

"There's a great big attic, all full of dust and junk, we found a door behind our wardrobe, and a staircase leading up."

"I found it," Barney said. "I threw my apple core away, and I went to get it back because of the rats, and I found the manuscript by accident in a comer under the floor."

"What is it, Gumerry?"

"What does it say?"

"It's terribly old, isn't it?"

"Is it important? Is it about buried treasure?"

"In a way," Great-Uncle Merry said. His eyes seemed dazed, unable to focus anywhere, but there was a twitching at the corners of his mouth. Somehow, without smiling, he looked happier than they had ever seen him look before. Jane thought, watching: it is a sad face usually, and that's why there is such a difference.

He laid the manuscript down on his lap and looked from Jane to Simon to Barney and back again. He seemed to be searching for words.

"You have found something that may be more important than you can possibly realise," he said at last.

They stared at him. He looked away again over the hills.

"You remember the fairy stories you were told when you were very small—'once upon a time . . .' Why do you think they always began like that?"

"Because they weren't true," Simon said promptly.

Jane said, caught up in the unreality of the high remote place, "Because perhaps they were true once, but nobody could remember when."

Great-Uncle Merry turned his head and smiled at her. "That's right. Once upon a time . . . a long time ago . . . things that happened once, perhaps, but have been talked about for so long that nobody really knows. And underneath all the bits that people have added, the magic swords and lamps, they're all about one thing— the good hero fighting the giant, or the witch, or the wicked uncle. Good against bad. Good against evil."

"Cinderella."

"Aladdin."

"Jack the Giant-killer."

"And all the rest." He looked down again, his fingers caressing the curving edge of the parchment. "Do you know what this manuscript is about?"

"King Arthur," Barney said promptly. "And King Mark. Simon found the names, in Latin."

"And what do you know about King Arthur?"

Barney looked round triumphantly at his captive audience and drew breath for a long recital, but somehow found himself stammering instead.

"Well . . . he was King of England, and he had his knights of the Round Table, Lancelot and Galahad and Kay and all of them. And they fought jousts and rescued people from wicked knights. And Arthur beat everyone with his sword Excalibur. It was good against bad, I suppose, like you said about in the fairy stories. Only he was real."

Great-Uncle Merry's quiet pleased smile was flickering again. "And when was Arthur King of England?"

"Well—" Barney waved his hand vaguely. "A long time ago . . ."

". . . like in the fairy stories," Jane finished for him. "I see. But Gumerry, what are you trying to tell us? Was King Arthur a fairy story too?"

"No!" Barney said indignantly.

"No," said Great-Uncle Merry. "He was real. But the same thing has happened, d'you see—he lived such a long time ago that there's no record of him left. And so he's become a story, a legend, as well."

Simon fidgeted with the strap of his rucksack. "But I don't see where the manuscript comes in."

The wind over the headland stirred Great-Uncle Merry's white hair outlined against the sky, and as he glanced down he looked magisterial and severe.

"Patience a little. And listen carefully now, because you may find this difficult to understand.

"First of all, you have heard me talk of Logres. It was the old name for this country, thousands of years ago; in the old days when the struggle between good and evil was more bitter and open than it is now. That struggle goes on all round us all the time, like two armies fighting. And sometimes one of them seems to be winning and sometimes the other, but neither has ever triumphed altogether. Nor ever will," he added softly to himself, "for there is something of each in every man.

"Sometimes, over the centuries, this ancient battle comes to a peak. The evil grows very strong and nearly wins. But always at the same time there is some leader in the world, a great man who sometimes seems to be more than a man, who leads the forces of good to win back the ground and the men they seemed to have lost."

"King Arthur," Barney said.

"King Arthur was one of these," Great-Uncle Merry said. "He fought against the men who wanted Logres, who robbed and murdered and broke all the rules of battle. He was a strong and good man, and the people of those days trusted him absolutely. With that faith behind him, Arthur's power was very great—so great that in the stories that have grown up since, people have talked about his having magical help. But magic is just a word."

"I suppose he didn't win," Jane said with sudden conviction, "or there wouldn't have been any wars since."

"No, he didn't win," Great-Uncle Merry said, and even in the clear afternoon sunshine he seemed with every word to become more remote, as ancient as the rock behind him and the old world of which he spoke.

"He wasn't altogether beaten, but he didn't altogether win. So the same struggle between good and evil sides has gone on ever since. But the good has grown very confused, and since the ancient days of Logres it has been trying to regain the strength it was given by Arthur. But it never has. Too much has been forgotten.

"But those men who remembered the old world have been searching for its secret ever since. And there have been others searching as well—the enemies, the wicked men, who have the same greed in their cold hearts as the men whom Arthur fought."

Great-Uncle Merry looked out into the distance, his head outlined against the sky like the proud carved head of a statue, centuries old and yet always the same. "I have been searching," he said. "For many, many years."

The children stared at him, awed and a little afraid. For a moment he was a stranger, someone they did not know. Jane had a sudden fantastic feeling that Great-Uncle Merry did not really exist at all, and would vanish away if they breathed or spoke.

He looked down at them again. "I was beginning to know that this part of Cornwall held what we sought," he said. "I did not know that you children would be the ones to find it. Or what danger you would be putting yourselves in."

"Danger?" Simon said incredulously.

"Very great danger," said Great-Uncle Merry, looking him full in the face. Simon swallowed. "This manuscript, Simon, puts you all right in the middle of the battle. Oh, nobody will stick a knife in your back—their methods are more subtle than that. And perhaps more successful." He looked down at the manuscript again. "This," he said more normally, "is a copy."

"A copy?" said Barney. "But it's so old."

"Oh yes, it's old. About six hundred years old. But it's a copy of something even older than that—written more than nine hundred years ago. The part at the beginning is in Latin."

"There, I said so," Jane said in triumph.

Simon stuck out his lower lip. "Well, I translated bits of it, didn't I? Not much, though," he confessed to Great-Uncle Merry. "I couldn't recognise any of the words."

"I don't suppose you could. This is medieval Latin, not like the Latin you learn at school . . . it's written by a monk who must have lived near here, and I think about six hundred years ago, though there's no date. He says, roughly, that near his monastery an old English manuscript has been found. He says it tells of an old legend from the days of Mark and Arthur, and that he has copied out the story to save its being lost, because the manuscript was falling to bits. He says he copied out a map that was with the manuscript too. Then all the rest, underneath, is the story that he copied out—and you can see the map right at the bottom."

"If the original manuscript was so old that it was falling to bits six hundred years ago . . ." Barney said, bemused.

Simon broke in impatiently. "Gumerry, can you understand the copied-out part? That's not Latin, is it?"

"No, it's not," Great-Uncle Merry said. "It's one of the Early English dialects, the old language that used to be spoken centuries ago. But it's a very old form of it, full of words from the old

Cornish and even some from Brittany. I don't know—I'll read it out as best I can. But I may turn it into rather curious English, and I may have to stop. . . ."

He peered at the manuscript again. Then, stumblingly and with many pauses while he held it to the sunlight or fumbled in his mind for a word, he began to read, in his deep, far-away voice. The children sat and listened, with the sun hot on their faces and the wind still whispering in their ears.

"This I write, that when the time comes it shall be found by the proper man. And I leave it in the care of the old land that soon shall be no more.

"Into the land of Cornwall, the kingdom of Mark, there came in the days of my fathers a strange knight fleeing towards the west. Many fled hither in those days, when the old kingdom was broken by the invader and the last battle of Arthur was lost. For only in the western land did men still love God and the old ways.

"And the strange knight who came to the place of my fathers was called Bedwin, and he bore with him the last trust of Logres, the grail made in the fashion of the Holy Grail, that told upon its sides all the true story of Arthur soon to be misted in men's minds. Each panel told of an evil overcome by Arthur and the company of God, until the end when evil overcame all. And the last panel showed the promise and the proof of Arthur's coming again.

"For behold, said the knight Bedwin to my fathers, evil is upon us now, and so shall it be for time beyond our dreaming. Yet if the grail, that is the last trust of the old world, be not lost, then when the day is ripe the Pendragon shall come again. And at the last all shall be safe, and evil be thrust out never to return.

"And so that the trust be kept, he said, I give it into your charge, and your sons', and your sons' sons', until the day come. For I am wounded near death from the last of the old battles, and I can do no more.

"And very soon he died, and they buried him over the sea and under the stone, and there he lies until the day of our Lord.

"And so the grail passed to my fathers' charge, and they guarded it in the land of Cornwall where men still strove to keep alive the old ways, while in the east the men of evil grew more numerous and the land of Logres grew dark. For Arthur was gone, and Mark was dead, and the new kings were not as the old had been. And with each turn of years the grail came to the charge of the eldest son, and at the last it came to me.

"And since the death of my father I have kept it safe as best I might, in secret and in true faith; but now I grow old, and am childless, and the greatest darkness of all comes upon our land. For the heathen men of evil, who came to the east in years past and slew the Englishmen and took their land, are turning westward now, and we shall not long be safe from them.

"The darkness draws toward Cornwall, and the long ships creep to our shore, and the battle is near which must lead to final defeat and the end of all that we have known. No guardian for the grail is left, since my brother's son whom I loved as my own is turned already to the heathen men, and guides them to the west. And to save my life, and the secret of the grail that only its guardian knows, I must flee even as Bedwin the strange knight fled. But in all the land of Logres no haven remains, so that I must cross the sea to the land where, they say, Cornishmen have fled whenever terror comes.

"But the grail may not leave this land, but must wait the Pendragon, till the day comes.

"So therefore, I trust it to this land, over sea and under stone, and I mark here the signs by which the proper man in the proper place, may know where it lies: the signs that wax and wane but do not die. The secret of its charge I may not write, but carry unspoken to my grave. Yet the man who finds the grail and has other words from me will know, by both, the secret for himself. And for him is the charge, the promise and the proof, and in his day the Pendragon shall come again. And that day shall see a new Logres, with evil cast out; when the old world shall appear no more than a dream."

Great-Uncle Merry stopped reading; but the children sat as still and speechless as if his voice still rang on. The story seemed to fit so perfectly into the green land rolling below them that it was as if they sat in the middle of the past. They could almost see the strange knight Bedwin riding towards them, over the brow of a slope, and the long ships of the invaders lurking beyond the grey granite headland and its white fringe of surf.

Simon said at last, "Who is the Pendragon?"

"King Arthur," Barney said.

Jane said nothing, but sat thinking of the sad Cornishman sailing away over the sea from his threatened land. She looked at Great-Uncle Merry. He was gazing unseeing down at the sea and the headland beyond Trewissick, the taut lines of his face relaxed and wistful. ". . . when the old world," he repeated softly to himself, "shall appear no more than a dream . . ."

Simon scrambled to his feet and went to crouch close to him, peering at the manuscript on his knee. "Then the map must show where the grail is. I say, suppose we find it! What will it mean?"

"It will mean all kinds of things," Great-Uncle Merry said grimly. "And not all of them pleasant, perhaps."

"What will it look like? What is a grail, anyway?"

"A kind of drinking-vessel. A chalice. A cup. But not like an ordinary cup." Great-Uncle Merry looked at them gravely. "Now listen to me. This map you have found shows the way to a sign which men have been seeking for centuries. I said that I had been looking for it. But you remember I said that there were others too—the enemy side, if you like. These people are evil, and they can be very, very dangerous indeed." Great-Uncle Merry spoke with great seriousness, leaning forward, and the children gazed rather nervously back.

"They have been very close to me for a long time now," he said. "And here in Trewissick they have been close to you too. One of them is the man Norman Withers. Another is the woman who calls herself his sister. There may be others, but I do not know."

"Then the burglary." They stared at him and Jane said, "Was it them?"

"Undoubtedly," Great-Uncle Merry said. "Not in person, perhaps. But they must have been behind it all—the ransacked books, the stolen maps, the attempt to look for a secret hiding-place under the floor. They were very near, you know, nearer than I. When I rented the Grey House it was no more than a shot in the dark. I had narrowed the search down to the Trewissick area, but that was all. And I had no idea what I was looking for. It might have been anything. But they knew. Somehow, in some dark way, they had found out about the manuscript and they came after it last night. Only, they hadn't bargained for your finding it by chance first." He smiled slightly. "I should like to see Withers' face today."

"Everything fits now," Simon said slowly. "The way he made friends so quickly with Father, the way he took us out in the boat—" For an unpleasant moment he heard GreatUncle Merry's voice saying again emphatically, "They can be very dangerous indeed. . . ."

Barney said: "But Gumerry, did you know that *we* should find whatever it was? Us, I mean, me and Simon and Jane?"

His great-uncle looked at him sharply. "What makes you say that?"

"Well—I don't know—" Barney fumbled for words. "You must have looked yourself, before we came, and not found anything. But when we did come, you were never there. You kept on disappearing, almost as if you were leaving the house to us."

Great-Uncle Merry smiled. "Yes, Barney," he said, "I did have an idea you might find it, because I know you three very well. That was one idea I had before our friends did, so that for all their interest in the Grey House they were still worried about what I was up to. And I led them a high old dance all over south Cornwall while you were at home. I was, you might say, a red herring."

"But what—" Barney said.

"Oh never mind," Simon broke in. He had been hovering restlessly at Great-Uncle Merry's elbow. "It's all obvious now. The thing is, what about the map?"

"You're quite right." Great-Uncle Merry sat down by the rock again. "We haven't any time to lose."

"It's a map of Trewissick," Simon said eagerly. "Jane found that out. Only the coast seems to have changed—"

"I was comparing it with the map in a guide-book at the Grey House," Jane said. It hardly seemed worth mentioning her visit to the vicar. "The funny thing is that though the outlines of the coast don't look alike, the names are the same. If you look very closely on the manuscript one of the headlands is called King Mark's Head, only it's spelt all wrong. And that's the name the guide-book uses for Kemare Head. So the manuscript must show Trewissick."

"That's right," Great-Uncle Merry said, bent over the parchment. "Simple corruption, dropping consonants—" His head shot up. "*What* did you say?"

Jane looked puzzled. "Mmm?"

"Did you say it was called King Mark's Head in the guide-book?"

"Yes, that's right. Does it matter?"

"Oh no." The usual remote expression came back over Great-Uncle Merry's face like a veil. "Only that particular name hasn't been used for a very long time, and most people have forgotten about it. I should like to have a look at that guide-book of yours."

"I don't understand this." Simon was peering over the old map. "Even if it is Trewissick, where does that get you? It's the most useless treasure map I ever saw, there are all sorts of peculiar marks on it but none of them means anything. Nothing leads to anything else, so how can it show you where the grail is?"

Great-Uncle Merry pointed at the manuscript. "Remember what the text says—for the proper man in the proper place, to find . . ."

"Perhaps it's like one of those mazes you see in books sometimes," Jane said, thinking hard. "The ones that are simple once you get going but it's awfully hard to find where to start. That could be what he meant by 'in the proper place.' If you took the map to the right starting-point, then it would tell you where to go from there."

Simon almost wailed, "But how do we find out where to start from?"

Barney, standing at Great-Uncle Merry's elbow, had not been listening. He had lapsed into one of his dreaming silences, gazing wide-eyed out over the harbour and occasionally glancing back at the map. "I know what it reminds me of," he said musingly.

No one took any notice. Barney went on dreamily to himself, "It's like one of Mother's drawings, the ones she calls perspective sketches. It looks like a picture, not a map at all really. You've got the bump of this hill coming over the edge of the harbour when you look down, and the headland curving like that"—he traced his finger through the air over the view before him—"and those stones on top of it make the funny little knobs on the side of the map . . ."

"Golly, he's got it!" Simon shouted, jerking Barney out of his reverie. "That's what it is, look! It is a picture, and not a map, and that's why the shape looked all wrong compared with the guide-book. Look, you can see—" He took the manuscript carefully from Great-Uncle Merry's hands and held it up in front of them, against the long rocky arm of Kemare Head. And as they looked from the headland back to the manuscript, the scrawled

66

brown lines suddenly seemed so obviously a picture of the scene before them that they wondered how they could possibly have thought it was a map.

"Well then," Jane said, incredulity spreading over her face as she looked from one to the other, "*this* must be the proper place. The beginning of the maze. All this time without knowing it we've been standing on the very same spot as the man who drew the picture. Just think!" She looked at the manuscript in awe.

"Well, come on," Barney said, glowing with excitement at what he had discovered. "We know where he started from. How do we find out where he went from here?"

"Look at the picture. There's a sort of blodge marked on this headland."

"There are blodges all over the place. Half of them are blots and the rest are dirt marks."

"The marks of age," Great-Uncle Merry said sepulchrally.

"No, but this one's intentional," Simon persisted. "Right here, where—gosh! It must be that rock you're leaning on, Gumerry!"

His great-uncle looked round critically. "Well, it's possible, I suppose. Yes indeed, it's possible. A natural outcropping, I think, not erected by the hands of men."

Barney got up and trotted all round the rock, gazing closely at its yellow lichened scars and every small crevice and cleft, but noticing nothing unusual. "It looks very ordinary," he said in disappointment, reappearing at the other side.

Jane burst out laughing. "You look just like Rufus, sniffing along after a rabbit and then finding there's nothing there after all."

Barney slapped his knee. "I knew we should have brought Rufus. He'd have been terrifically useful on a hunt, sniffing things out."

"You can't sniff things out when they've been hidden for centuries, idiot."

"I don't see why not. You wait, I bet you he'll help."

"Not a hope."

"Where is he, anyway?"

"With Mrs. Palk. Shut up somewhere, I suppose, poor thing. You know Father said he wouldn't have him in the house any more when he got in a rage the other night."

"Mrs. Palk takes him home every evening."

"If she hadn't taken him home yesterday evening he might have caught the burglars."

"Gosh, so he would." There was a moment's silence as they all digested the thought.

"I don't trust Mrs. Palk," Jane said darkly.

"Well, don't worry about it," Great-Uncle Merry said easily. "From what I know of that dog he'd just have licked their hands and told them to go ahead."

"He doesn't like Mr. Withers," Barney said. "He came to meet us wagging his tail when we came in off the boat yesterday, but when he saw Mr. Withers his tail went right down and he barked. We all laughed about it at the time," he added thoughtfully.

"Well, we'll bring him out tomorrow. But we shall have to go home soon and we still aren't any nearer the beginning. Gumerry, could this rock really mean anything?" Simon rubbed its grey surface doubtfully.

"Perhaps it's in line with something," Jane said hopefully. "Like a compass bearing. Look on the map, I mean the picture."

"Doesn't help. It could be in line with any one of those blodges."

"Well then, we ought to find out where all the blodges are and go and see if there's anything near one of them."

"But that would take months."

"Oh!" Barney stamped his foot with impatience. "This is awful. What are we going to do?"

"Leave it," Great-Uncle Merry said unexpectedly.

"*Leave* it?" They stared at him.

"Leave it until tomorrow. Come to it with fresh minds. We haven't much time, and it's going to be a race in the end, but we're all right at the moment. The other side doesn't know that we've found anything. They watch me like hawks, but they don't suspect you, and with any luck they won't. You can afford to go away and think about it for tonight."

"Won't they come back and burgle us again?" Jane said nervously.

"They wouldn't dare. No, that was a long shot—they staked everything on being able to find a clue the first time, and they failed. They'll try something different now."

"I wish we knew what."

"Great-Uncle Merry," Simon said, "why can't we tell the police it was them? Then they wouldn't be able to come after us at all."

"Yes," said Jane, eagerly. "Why not?"

"We can't possibly," Barney said with conviction.

"Why not?"

"I don't know."

They looked at Great-Uncle Merry.

He said non-committally, "Why didn't you tell the police that you thought you knew what the burglars had been after?"

"Well—they'd have laughed. They'd have thought it was just an old bit of paper."

"And if we'd gone to them it wouldn't have been a secret any more and we shouldn't have been able to follow up the map."

"And anyway," Jane said, with a return of the old guiltiness, "we hadn't told Mother and Father about finding it in the first place."

"Well," Great-Uncle Merry said, "you would have said to them, 'We found an old parchment in the attic and we think that's what the burglars were looking for when they turned the house upside-down.' And our worthy sergeant, who is satisfied that the culprits were just hooligans, would have smiled indulgently and told you to go away and play."

"That's right, that's just it. That's why we didn't."

Great-Uncle Merry smiled. "Now, I could go to him and say this manuscript is a clue to a kind of ancient cup, called a grail, that is hidden in Trewissick. It tells the real story of King Arthur. The man from the yacht called the *Lady Mary* wants it, and he burgled the house, and he has me followed night and day to discover if I have found it before him. And what would happen?"

"They'd go and arrest Mr. Withers," Simon said hopefully, but he sounded less convinced than before.

"The sergeant would go to Mr. Withers, who would of course have a perfect alibi for the night of the burglary, and he would question him rather apologetically about my odd-sounding story. Mr. Withers would impress him as a courteous and gentlemanly antique-dealer on a harmless holiday with his pretty sister."

"That's what we thought he was." Barney pointed out.

"The sergeant knows of me," Great-Uncle Merry went on, "and knows I do things that sometimes seem" —he chuckled—"eccentric. He would think things over, and he'd say to himself: Poor old Professor, 'tis all been too much for 'n at last. All that book-learnin', tidn' natural, it do 'ave turned the poor old chap's head."

"You do it even better than Simon," Jane said admiringly.

"I see now," Simon said. "It would just sound fantastic. And if we told the sergeant about Mr. Withers and his sister asking questions about old books, it would just seem perfectly normal to him and not suspicious at all."

He looked up and grinned. "Of course, we couldn't possibly tell them. Sorry. I didn't think."

"Well, you must think now, and seriously." Great-Uncle Merry said, turning his grave dark eyes on each face in turn. "I'm going to say something I shan't say again. You may think the same as the sergeant would, that this is all a business of a private rivalry. An old professor and a book-collector, both intent on beating the other to something that doesn't matter much to anyone else anyway."

"No!"

"Of course not."

"It's much more than that," Jane said impulsively. "I've got a feeling . . ."

"Well—if you all have a feeling, if you understand just a little of the things I was trying to say earlier on, then that's more than enough. But I am not happy about having the three of you mixed up in this at all, and I should be even less happy if I thought you didn't have any idea of what you were doing."

"You make it sound fearfully serious," Simon said curiously.

"So it is. . . . I worry because I can only be on the edge all the time, acting as decoy, making them think they have nobody to bother about except me. So that you are left all on your own, with the responsibility of unravelling this." He touched the manuscript in Simon's hand. "Step by difficult step."

"Smashing," Barney said happily.

Simon glanced at his brother and sister and drew himself up, trying to look as dignified as it is possible to look in shorts and sandals.

"Well, I'm the eldest—"

"Only by eleven months," said Jane.

"Well I am, anyway, and I'm responsible for you two and I ought to be spokesman, and—and"—he floundered, and then gave up all attempt at dignity in a rush—"and honestly, Gumerry, we do know what we're doing. In a way it is a kind of quest, like Barney said. And it isn't as if we were altogether on our own."

"All right," Great-Uncle Merry said. "It's a bargain." And he shook hands solemnly with each of them in turn. Everyone looked at everyone else, wide-eyed and a little breathless, and then they all suddenly felt rather foolish, and burst out laughing. But behind the laughter they were dimly aware of a new kind of comforting closeness, in the face of possible danger.

When they packed up, and were starting down the hill, Great-Uncle Merry said, stopping them in their tracks, "Take a good look at it first." He swept his arm out over the harbour, the cliffs and the sea. "Take the real picture back with you too. Learn what it looks like."

They looked across from the slope once more. The sun was setting down in the westward sky, over Kemare Head and the Grey House, lighting the top of the headland and the strange grey rocks that prickled its skyline. But the harbour was already darkening into shadow. As they looked, the sun seemed gradually to fall, until the unbearable brightness of it was over the outlined fingers of the group of standing stones, and the stones themselves became invisible in the blaze.

• *Chapter Seven* •

"Well, *I* think it's underneath the Grey House."

"Yes—look how the burglars tried to take up the floor."

"But they were looking for the map, not the grail."

"No they weren't. Remember what Great-Uncle Merry said. They didn't know what they were looking for, nor did he. It might have been a clue to it, like the map, or it might have been the thing itself."

"Well, the clue was there, why shouldn't the thing itself be there as well?"

"But look, idiot," Simon said, unrolling the map, "the Grey House isn't marked. There isn't even a blodge. It just wasn't there then. Remember our Cornishman lived nine hundred years ago."

"Oh."

They were sitting on the grass half-way up Kemare Head, at the side of one of the rough-trodden tracks which ran zigzagging up its slope. Great-Uncle Merry had left them on their own. "A day's grace to find the first clue," he had said, "while I draw off the hounds. Just one piece of advice—don't start till the afternoon. Spend the morning on the beach or something. Then you'll be sure the hounds are gone."

Then he had gone out fishing for the day with Father, who was intent on trying a part of the sea off a headland a mile down the coast. And sure enough, as their small boat puttered out of the harbour with Father at the tiller and Great-Uncle Merry towering stiff-backed in the bows, the yacht *Lady Mary,* gleaming white in the sun, had within minutes moved silently out after them, her engine purring faintly over the quiet morning sea. Watching from the house, they had seen her sails gradually unfurl and billow as she came into the bay. She took a wide course out to sea, but one from which Great-Uncle Merry and Father would always be just in sight.

Up on the headland now the afternoon sun prickled their bare legs, and there was a small breeze. "Oh dear," Jane said despondently, edging a blade of grass from its sheath and nibbling it. "This is hopeless. We just don't know where to start. Perhaps we should go back to where we were yesterday."

"But we know what things look like from there."

"Well, so what? Which things?"

"Well—the headland, and the sea, and the sun—and those stones up on the top there." Barney gestured vaguely above their heads, up the slope. "I think they've got something to do with it. The Cornishman must have been able to see them. Gumerry says they're three thousand years old, so they'd have been almost as ancient-looking nine hundred years ago as they are now."

"You can certainly see them clear enough from the other side." Simon sat up, interested.

"But they're such a long way across," Jane pointed out. "I mean, the first clue might be that you have to take ten paces to your left, or something. It always is in stories about buried treasure. But to get to the standing stones, up here, from over there, you'd have to take thousands of paces right across the harbour. It doesn't make sense."

"It doesn't have to be like that," Simon said. "It could be the thing like compass bearings again. You know—perhaps we have to get something in line with something else to lead us on to a third thing."

Barney closed his eyes and screwed up his face, trying to bring back a picture of the scene they had gazed at so hard the evening before. "D'you remember when the sun set yesterday?" he said slowly. "The biggest standing stone was right bang in line with the sun, from where we were. I remember because you could only see it if you didn't look straight at it, if you see what I mean."

Simon looked closely at the manuscript again, excitement beginning to dawn on his face.

"D'you know, I think you've got something there. This round thing drawn here over the standing stones, that we thought was just decoration—perhaps it's supposed to be the sun. I mean, if he knew the map wouldn't be found for years and years and years he'd have to use signs like the sun that wouldn't be likely to change."

"Come on then, let's go further up and look." Jane jumped eagerly to her feet; and then suddenly she froze, stock-still. "Simon, quick," she said quietly, in a strained, tight voice. "Put the map away. Hide it."

Simon frowned. "What on earth—"

"Quickly! It's Miss Withers. She's coming up the path, and someone else with her. They'll be right on top of us in a minute."

Simon hastily rolled up the manuscript and stuffed it into his rucksack. "Who is it with her?" he hissed.

"I can't see—yes, I can." Jane turned away quickly as if it hurt her to look, and sat down again. She was very flushed. "It's that boy. The one who knocked me over. I *knew* he was mixed up in all this somehow."

They heard voices then, coming nearer up the slope. Miss Withers' clear tones floated up to them. "I don't care, Bill, we have to check on everything. He may already have—" Then she was on them, silhouetted against the skyline, and she stopped short as she saw the three children all sitting looking expressionlessly up at her. The boy stopped too, glowering.

For a moment Miss Withers stood with her mouth slightly open, taken aback. Then she pulled herself together and flashed a smile at them. "Well!" she said pleasantly, coming forward. "What a nice surprise! All the Drew family at once. I hope you boys didn't feel too tired after all that sea air we gave you the other day."

"Not a bit, thank you," Barney said in his clearest, most public voice.

"It's a marvellous boat," said Simon, equally distant and polite.

"And what are you all doing up here?" Miss Withers inquired innocently. She was wearing slacks, with a sleeveless white blouse that made her arms look very brown; and her dark hair was tumbled by the breeze. She looked very attractive and healthy.

She glanced at Jane expectantly. Jane gulped. "We were just looking at the sea. We saw your boat go out this morning."

"We thought you'd be on board her," Simon added, without thinking.

A flicker of wariness crossed Polly Withers' face. She said easily, "Ah, I'm not the best of sailors, as I probably told you."

Simon looked deliberately down at the sea. It lay as flat and unrippled as a pond. Miss Withers said, following his gaze, "Ah, it'll blow up later, you mark my words."

74

"Oh?" Simon said. His face was expressionless still, but there was the faintest note of insolent disbelief in his tone. For the first time Miss Withers' smile faded slightly.

Before she could say anything, the boy with her spoke. "Miss Polly be allus right about the sea," he said gruffly, glaring at Simon. "She do know more about 'n than all they old men down there put together." He jerked his head contemptuously down at the harbour.

"Oh—I haven't introduced you," Miss Withers said brightly. "Do forgive me. Jane, Simon, Barnabas, this is Bill, our right-hand man. Without him the *Lady Mary* couldn't do a thing."

The boy flushed darkly and looked down at his grubby sneakers after a quick glance up at her. Jane thought pityingly: he thinks she's wonderful.

"We've met before," Simon said shortly.

Barney said: "How is your bicycle?"

"No better for your askin'," the boy snapped.

"Watch your manners, Bill." Through the sweet smile Miss Withers' voice was cold and tight as a steel wire. "That's not the way we speak to our friends."

Bill looked at her in sullen reproach, jerked forward and went on up the path without a word.

"Oh dear," Miss Withers sighed. "Now I've hurt his feelings. These village people are so touchy." She made a charming, conspiratorial little grimace at them. "I suppose I'd better go after him." She turned to follow the boy, and then swung round again. The words shot out like a flick of lightning: "Have you found a map?"

For a moment of roaring silence that seemed like an hour they stared at her. And then Barney, driven by pure naked alarm, took refuge in gabbling nonsense. "Did you say a map, Miss Withers? Or was it a gap? We did find a gap in the hedge, down there, that was how we got through up on to the headland. But we haven't got a map, at least I haven't, I don't know about Simon and Jane . . . don't you know your way up the hill?"

Miss Withers, staring fixedly at them, relaxed into friendliness again. "Yes, that's right, Barnabas, a map . . . I don't know my way about at all well, as a matter of fact. And I couldn't find a map anywhere in the shops this morning. There's one little foot-path I'm looking for, just over the other side, and Bill isn't very much help."

"I believe Great-Uncle Merry has a map," Jane said, vaguely. She was watching closely from the corner of her eye; but not a muscle moved in Miss Withers' face. "You haven't met our great-uncle, have you, Miss Withers? He's gone out fishing with Father today. What a pity. I'm awfully sorry we can't help."

"I do hope you find your way," Simon said kindly.

"Well, well, I expect I shall," Miss Withers said. She flashed her brightest smile at them, and turned away up the path, raising her hand. "Good-by, all of you."

They watched in silence until she disappeared over the line where the slope met the sky. Then Barney flung himself face down on the ground and rolled over and over, letting out a long relieved breath. "Wheeee-ee-ee-ee! How awful! When she suddenly said . . . !" He buried his face in the grass.

"D'you think she realises?" Jane said anxiously to Simon. "Did we give it away?"

"I don't know." Simon gazed thoughtfully up the quiet green slope. There was no sign there now of Miss Withers, or of anything except one far-away grazing sheep. "I don't think so. I mean, we must have all looked pretty silly when she asked about a map, I know you did."

"So did you. Like a fish."

"All right . . . well, we could perfectly well have looked surprised anyway, her saying it out of the blue like that. I don't think she'd be able to tell if we were looking guilty or just startled. I expect," he added, gaining confidence as he went on, "she believes we really did think she just wanted an ordinary map to find her way."

"Perhaps that's all she did want."

"No fear," Barney said, emerging from the grass. "She was testing us out, all right. Otherwise why did she say 'found'? Have you *found* a map? Any normal person would have said, I say, have you *got* a map?"

"He's quite right." Simon stood up, rubbing the dust from his legs. "Great-Uncle Merry was right too. They aren't taking chances. Miss Withers was surprised to see us, you could tell, but it wasn't five seconds before she was having a go about the map."

"It was nasty altogether," Jane said, wriggling her shoulders as if she could shake off the memory. She looked up the slope. "How can we go on up there now? We shan't be able to tell if she and that horrible boy are hidden away somewhere, watching everything we do."

76

"Well, it's no good letting that stop us," Simon stuck out his chin. "If we think about being watched we shall never do anything. So long as we behave normally, as if we were just wandering about, it ought to be all right." He picked up his rucksack. "Come on."

The side of Kemare Head was steeper than the opposite headland had been, and for a long time as they toiled up the zigzag path they saw nothing above them but the line of the slope against the sky, with the sun blazing down into their eyes. The end of the headland, rocky and grey, stretched out far beyond them into the sea, and sweeping towards it the land looked immensely solid, as if it were all rock and the soil above it no more than a skin.

And then they were at the top of the slope, where the grass grew short in a great dry-green sweep, and they could see the standing stones. As they drew nearer, the stones seemed to grow, pointing silently to the sky, like vast tombstones set on end.

"Stones," Simon said, "is the biggest understatement I've ever heard. Like calling Nelson's Column a stick."

He stood considering the giant granite pillars rising above him. There were four of them; one much higher than the rest, with the other three grouped irregularly round it.

"Perhaps the grail's buried under one of those," Barney said tentatively.

"It can't be, they're too old . . . anyway, I think you're wrong about it being buried."

"Oh come on, it must be," Jane said. "How else could anything stay hidden all that time?"

"And remember that bit in the manuscript," said Barney. "Over sea and under stone."

Simon rubbed his ear, still dissatisfied. "We aren't over the sea here. The sea's miles away. Well all right, not miles, but I bet it's four hundred yards to the end of the headland."

"Well, we're still above the sea, aren't we?"

"I'm sure that's not what he meant. Over sea, over sea—I wonder—anyway, we're trying to go too fast. Step by step, Gumerry said. We ought to stick to the step we're on."

Simon looked at the sun, gradually sinking over the coast where cliff after cliff curved into the mist beyond Kemare Head. "Have a look at the stones. The sun'll be as low as it was yesterday soon."

"They look so different when you're close." Jane wandered round the weather-beaten grey pillars of rock. "We want to know

77

which one it was that looked in line with the sun from the other side, isn't that it? But how do we find that out from here?"

"It was the biggest one," Barney said. "It stood up higher than the rest."

The sun glowed deep towards the horizon, casting an orange-gold warmth over their faces. "Look at the shadows," Simon said suddenly. His shadow on the ground before him moved a long arm, dapple-edged by the grass, as he pointed. "That's the way we can do it from this side. *Backwards*. If one stone was directly between us and the sun yesterday, that means that from here its shadow would be pointing directly to where we were standing then. Towards the rock Gumerry was sitting against. Look, you can just see it from here."

Following his arm, they saw the one chunky rock on the opposite headland; a small far-away bump on its skyline, lit bright by the gold of the setting sun. It was higher than the standing stones on Kemare Head, and further out towards the sea. But it was undoubtedly the spot where they had stood the day before.

Jane gazed at Simon in open and unusual admiration. He flushed slightly, and became very brisk. "Come on, Barney, quick before the sun goes. Which stone d'you think it was?"

"Well, it was the biggest, so it must have been this one."

Barney moved a yard or two downhill to the tallest stone. He crossed to its other side, facing the harbour, and crouched down in the shadow, peering at the lone stone across the bay. He frowned, doubtfully. Simon and Jane moved to one side of him, waiting impatiently.

Barney, his frown deepening, suddenly lay down on his stomach in the grass, so that he was lying along the line of the pointing shadow and looking straight ahead. "Am I lying straight?" he said, rather muffled.

"Yes, yes, dead straight. Is it the right one?"

Barney scrambled to his feet, looking doleful. "No. That shadow doesn't point exactly at the rock. You can see the rock clearly enough, but you have to shift your eyes slightly to be looking straight at it. And that's cheating."

"But you *said* it was the tallest stone you saw."

"I still say it was."

"I don't see how it could have been," Jane said, petulant with disappointment.

Simon was thinking hard, holding the rucksack swinging by its strap and banging it absently against his leg. He turned and looked back at the other three stones, standing black now and gold-rimmed against the blaze of the sun. Then he yelped, dropped the rucksack and rushed towards the furthest stone, scrambling down as Barney had done to lie in its shadow. Holding his breath, he dropped his chin to the grass and shut his eyes.

"Move your top half a bit to the left, you're not straight," Jane said, close beside him, beginning to understand.

Simon shifted a few inches, raising himself on his elbows. "That right?"

"Okay."

Simon crossed his fingers and opened his eyes. Straight in front of him over the blades of grass, right in the middle of his line of vision, the bright sunlit rock on the opposite headland was staring him in the face. "This is the one," he said in a curiously subdued voice.

Barney rushed across and dropped down beside him. "Let me, let me—" He elbowed Simon out of the way and squinted across the harbour at the rock. "You're right," he said rather reluctantly. "But it was the biggest stone that I saw, I know it was."

"That's right," said Jane.

"What d'you mean, that's right?"

"Look at the way the stones are put up. Look at the way the ground slopes. This is the top of the headland, but it isn't flat, and the big stone is lower down than the others. The one you're next to now is higher up the hill, even though it's not the tallest. So where you saw its outline against the sky yesterday, it *looked* as if it were the tallest."

"Gosh," Barney said. "I never thought of that."

Simon said loftily, "I thought you might get there in the end."

"It was jolly clever of you," Jane said. "If you hadn't been so quick we might never have realised. The shadows'll be gone soon." She pointed down at the grass. The blaze of the sun was sinking over the far horizon behind them, and the shadow creeping up over the ground, swallowing up the long shadows of the stones. But across the harbour the rock on the other headland, higher up and longer exposed to the sun, still shone bright like a beacon.

Barney whooped with delight. "We've got it! We've got it!" He thwacked one hand against the hard warm rock of the standing stone, and whirled round in a circle. "We're on the first step, isn't it fabulous?"

"Only the first step, though," Simon said. But pleasure was bubbling within him as well. They all three felt suddenly enormously energetic.

"But we've started . . ."

"We know where to look for the next clue now."

"We go from here." Barney ran his hand over the surface of the standing stone again. "From this one."

"But where?" Simon said, determined to be realistic. "And how?"

"We shall just have to look at the map again. It's bound to tell us. I mean, really the first clue was marked plain as plain, how to get from the other headland over to the stone here, if only we'd known how to understand it." Barney ran across to where Simon had dropped his rucksack, flipped the straps open and fumbled inside, bringing out the grubby brown roll of the manuscript from its case. "Look," he said, sitting down with a bump and spreading it out on the grass before him. "Here's where the stone's marked . . ."

"Bring it farther up," Simon said, looking over his shoulder. "The sun's still on the grass a bit higher up, and you need the brightest light you can get to look at it. Anyway it'll be warmer."

Barney clambered obligingly up the slope, past the massive grey foot of the last and tallest standing stone, to where the grass was still a brighter green in the last golden light of the sun. Simon and Jane followed him, standing on either side so that their own shadows should not darken the faint indistinct scrawl on the curling parchment. They bent down, intent, staring at the crude quick outline that was the Cornishman's picture, made nine hundred years before, of the standing stones.

Miss Withers' voice said, behind them: "So you have found a map after all."

A great wave of horror enveloped Barney, and he froze hunched over the manuscript. Simon and Jane wheeled round in alarm.

Miss Withers stood close behind them, higher up the slope. Her outline was dark and menacing against the sunset sky, and they could not see her face. The boy Bill appeared silently behind her, and stood at her elbow. The sight of them both poised there filled Jane with panic, and she suddenly felt frightened at the silence and emptiness of the headland.

Barney's finger unconsciously curled into his palm, and the edge of the manuscript, released, sprang back into a closed roll. The faint crackle of its movement sounded like a gunshot in the silence. "Oh, don't put it away," Miss Withers said clearly. "I want to have a look."

She took a step forward, stretching out her hand, and in terror of the flat expressionless voice Jane cried out suddenly.

"Simon!"

As the dark figure loomed swiftly towards him from the hill, Simon felt himself wake up. Quicker than his own thought he swung round, dipped swiftly and snatched up the manuscript from Barney's knee. And then he was gone, half slithering, half running down the slanting side of Kemare Head, towards the village.

"Bill! Quickly!" Miss Withers snapped. The big silent figure beside her shot into sudden life, tearing down the hill at Simon's heels. But he was too clumsy for his speed, and in mid-flight on the edge of the slope he stumbled and half fell. He recovered himself almost at once, but not before Simon, running and slipping straight down over the grass and the zigzagging paths, had gained thirty yards' lead.

"He won't catch him," Jane said, her voice wavering with excitement, feeling a broad smile of relief spreading over her stiff cheeks.

"Run it, Simon!" Barney shrilled down the hill, scrambling to his feet.

Miss Withers came down towards them, and they drew back from the sight of her face, twisted by rage into something frightening and unfamiliar, no longer attractive, no longer even young. She snarled at them: "You stupid children, tampering with things you don't understand—"

She swung away from them and made off down the slope in the same direction that Simon had taken, in a long quick stride. They watched her angry erect back cross and recross the slope on the zigzag path, until she disappeared over the edge of the headland.

"Come on," Barney said. "We've got to find Gumerry. Simon's going to need help."

* * *

The dry grass was like polished wood under Simon's feet, giving no grip as he slipped and slithered down the hillside; now on his feet, now flat on his back and elbows, holding one arm up always to keep the manuscript from damage. Behind him he heard the noise of the boy from the village slipping and stumbling more heavily, his breath rasping in his throat, and an occasional gasping curse as he lost his footing and fell.

Facing outwards across the harbour as he ran down, Simon felt that he could almost jump straight out into the sea. The slope seemed much steeper than when they had climbed up by the path, dropping below him in an endless green curve. His heart was thumping wildly, and he was too intent on getting away to imagine what might happen if the boy caught up with him. But gradually, minute by minute, the panic at the pit of his stomach was disappearing.

Everything depended on him now—to keep the manuscript safe, and get away. He was almost enjoying himself. This was something that he could understand; it was like a race or a fight at school, himself against the boy Bill. And he wanted to win. Panting, he glanced over his shoulder. The boy seemed to be gaining on him a little. Simon flung himself down the rest of the slope, sliding and bumping on his back, alarmingly fast, now and again coming to his feet for a couple of staggering steps.

And then suddenly he was at the bottom of the slope, stumbling and gulping for breath. With a brief glance up at the pursuing Bill, who yelled and glared at him as he saw him looking round, Simon was off and away over the field, running like a hare and feeling confidence surge stronger as he ran. But he could not lose the boy behind him. Stronger, bigger and longer-legged, the village boy pounded after him with grim determination, striding more heavily but never losing ground.

Simon made for a stile in the hedge at the far side of the field and leapt over, gripping the shaky wooden bar at its top with one hand. He came out at the other side into a quiet lane, pitted with deep dry ruts hard as rock, lined with trees, arching overhead in a thick-leaved roof. With the sunlight quite gone now, it was half dark under the branches, and both ends of the lane vanished within a few yards into impenetrable shadow.

Simon looked wildly up and down, clutching the manuscript and feeling the sweat damp in the palms of his hands. Which way would lead him to the Grey House? He could no longer hear the sea.

Making a blind choice, he turned right and ran up the lane. Behind him he heard the clatter of the boy's boots climbing over the stile. The lane seemed never-ending as he ran, dodging light-footed from side to side to avoid the ruts. Round every bend there stretched another, curving on in a gloomy tunnel of branches and banks, with no break anywhere into a gateway or another field.

He could hear the beat of the boy's feet behind him on the hard dry mud of the lane.

The boy shouted nothing now, but pounded along in grim silence. Simon felt a thread of panic creep back into his mind, and he ran more wildly, longing to get out of the cavernous lane and into the open air.

Then facing him round the next bend he saw the sky, bright after the gloom, and within moments he was out again, running on a paved road past quiet walls and trees. Again he turned automatically without time to think where he was going, and the rubber soles of his sneakers pattered softly along the deserted road.

The long high grey wall along one side, and the hedge of a field on the other, gave no sign to tell him where he was running—more slowly now, he knew, for try as he might he was beginning to tire. He began to long for someone, anyone, to appear walking along the road.

The boy's footsteps rang more loudly behind him now, over the quiet evening twitter of birds hidden in the trees. The sound of the feet so much noisier than his own gave Simon the beginnings of an idea, and when at last the road branched off he put on a desperate burst of speed and ran down the side turning.

The wall ended at two battered gate-posts through which he glimpsed an overgrown drive. Further down the road he caught sight of the rising tower of Trewissick church, and his heart sank as he realised how far he was from home.

The boy Bill had not turned the corner yet; Simon could hear his steps gradually growing louder from the main road. Quickly he slipped inside the deserted gateway of the long drive and wriggled into the bushes which grew in an unruly tangle beside the gate-post. He jumped with pain as thorns and sharp twigs stuck into him from all sides. But he crouched quite still behind the leaves, trying to quiet his gasping breaths, certain that the pounding of his heart must be audible all up and down the road.

The idea worked. He saw Bill, dishevelled and scarlet, pause at the end of the road, peering up and down. He looked puzzled and angry, listening with his head cocked for the sound of feet. Then he turned and walked slowly towards Simon's hiding-place down the side road, glancing back uncertainly over his shoulder.

Simon held his breath, and crouched further back into the bushes.

Unexpectedly he heard a noise from behind him. Turning his head sharply, wincing as a fat purple fuchsia blossom bobbed into his eye, he listened. In a moment he recognised the sound of feet crunching on gravel, coming towards the road down the drive. The gaps of light through the branches darkened for an instant as the figure of a man passed very close to him, walking down the drive and out through the gateway. Simon saw that he was very tall, and had dark hair. but he could not see his face.

The figure wandered idly out into the road. Simon saw now that he was dressed all in black; long thin black legs like a heron, and a black silk jacket with the light glinting silvery over the shoulders. The boy Bill's sullen face brightened as he caught sight of the man, and he ran forward to meet him in the middle of the road. They stood talking. but out of earshot, so that Simon could hear their voices only as an indistinct low blur. Bill was waving his hands and pointing back behind him to the road and then down the drive. Simon saw the tall dark man shake his head, but still he could not see his face.

Then they both turned back towards the drive and began to walk in his direction, Bill still talking eagerly. Simon shrank nervously back into his hiding-place, feeling suddenly more frightened than he had been since the chase began. This was no stranger to Bill. The boy was smiling. This man was someone he had recognised with relief. Someone else on the enemy side. . . .

He could see nothing now but the leaves before his face, and did not dare move forward to peer through a gap. But the footsteps ringing on the metalled road outside did not change to the crunch of gravel; they went past, outside the wall, and on up the road. Simon heard the murmur of voices, but could distinguish nothing except one phrase when the village boy raised his voice. ". . . got to get 'n, she said, 'tis surely the right one, and now I've lost . . ."

Lost me, thought Simon with a grin. His terror faded as their footsteps died away, and he began to feel triumphant at having out-witted the bigger boy. He glanced down at the manuscript in his hand and gave it a conspiratorial squeeze. There was silence again now, and he could hear nothing but the song of the birds in the approaching dusk. He wondered how late it was. The chase seemed to have lasted for a week. The muscles of his legs began to nag protestingly at their long cramped stillness. But still he waited, straining his ears for any sound showing that the man and the boy were still near.

At last he decided that they must have gone out of sight down the road. Clutching the manuscript firmly, he parted the bushes before his face with one hand and stepped out into the drive. No one was there. Nothing moved.

Simon tiptoed gingerly across the gravel and peered up and down round the gate-post. He could see no one, and with growing cheerfulness he crossed from the gateway to make his way back to the road from which he had come.

It was not until he was several paces out in the open that he saw the boy Bill and the dark man standing together beside the wall fifty yards away, in clear view.

Simon gasped, and felt his stomach twist with panic. For a moment he stood there, uncertain whether to bolt back to the shelter of the drive before they could see him. But as he hesitated, mesmerized, Bill turned his head, shouted and began to run, and the man with him, realising, turned to follow. Simon swung round and dashed for the main road. The silence all round seemed suddenly as menacing as the leaf-roofed lane had been; he ached for the safety of crowds, people and cars, so that at least he would lose the awful sensation of being alone, with feet pounding after him in implacable pursuit.

Down the side road, round the corner and along the wall of the churchyard, faster, faster; Simon's heart sank as he ran. His legs were stiff after the cramped pause in the bushes, and his whole body was very tired. He knew that he would not be able to last very much longer.

A car passed him, travelling fast in the opposite direction. Wild thoughts flickered through Simon's mind, as he felt the road beating hard through his thin rubber soles: he could shout and wave at a car, perhaps, or run for refuge into one of the little houses that were fringing the road as he neared the village. But the boy Bill had a man with him now, and the man could tell some story to any stranger Simon approached, and the stranger would probably believe that instead. . . .

"Stop!" a deep voice called behind him. Desperately Simon tried to fling himself forward faster. Everything would be over if they caught him. They would have the manuscript, they would have the

85

whole secret. There would be nothing left to do. He would have broken the trust, he would have let Gumerry down. . . .

His breath began to come in great painful gasps, and he staggered as he ran. There was a crossroads ahead. The fast decisive footsteps behind him sounded louder and louder; almost he heard his pursuers breathing in his ears. He heard the boy call, on a note of triumph: "Quick . . . *now* . . ." The voice was farther away than the footsteps. It must be the man who was behind him, almost at his heels, his feet thudding nearer, nearer. . . .

Simon's ears were singing with the fight for breath. The crossroads loomed ahead, but he could hardly see it. He heard half consciously the noisy roar of a car's engine, very near, but it barely registered in his weary brain. There was a rattle and a squeal of brakes, and half-way across the crossroads he almost collided with the rusting hood of a big car.

Simon slithered to a halt and made to dodge round it, aware only of the danger at his heels. And then, as if the darkening twilit sky were once more suddenly flooded with sunlight, he realized Great-Uncle Merry was leaning from the window of the car.

The car's engine revved up again with a thunderous roar. "The other side! Get in!" Great-Uncle Merry yelled at Simon through the window.

Sobbing with relief, Simon stumbled round the back of the big estate car and wrenched at the handle of the door on the other side. He collapsed into the creaking seat and pulled the door shut as Great-Uncle Merry let in the clutch and slammed his foot down on the accelerator. The car leapt forward, jerking round the corner, and then they were down the road and away.

• *Chapter Eight* •

"But how did you know where to come?" Simon said, as Great-Uncle Merry changed gear noisily at the foot of the hill up to the Grey House.

"I didn't really. I was just driving round the village hoping I should find you. I left as soon as Jane and Barney came tumbling back into the house. Poor mites, they were in a dreadful state—they rushed into the drawing-room and grabbed me bodily. Your parents were rather amused. They seem to think we're playing some great private game." Great-Uncle Merry smiled grimly.

"Gosh, it was lucky you chose that road to drive along," Simon said. "I've never been so glad to see anybody in my life."

"Well, you must remember I know Trewissick. When the children said they hadn't been able to find you on the path back to the house I knew there was only one way you could have gone. You came out into Pentreath Lane, didn't you?"

"There was a lane," Simon said. "All shut in by trees. I didn't really have time to see what it was called."

Great-Uncle Merry chuckled. "No, I dare say not. Anyway I gambled on your turning out of that lane on to the main Tregoney road, which in fact you did. Good job you didn't go the other way."

"Why?" Simon said, remembering the blind choice he had made in the lane, with the boy scrambling over the stile behind him.

"In the other direction that lane is a dead end. It leads up to Pentreath Farm. If you can call it a farm—it's been hopelessly neglected for years. Mrs. Palk's no-good brother lives there— young Bill Hoover's father. So does the boy himself when he bothers to go home, which I gather isn't very often. But on the whole it wouldn't have been a very healthy place for you to run to."

"Golly!" Simon felt cold at the thought.

"Well, never mind. You didn't anyway." Great-Uncle Merry stopped the car with a final rattle and roar and heaved at the hand-brake. "Here we are. Safe home. Now you run along in and clean yourself up before your mother sees you. There's some friend of hers come to supper, luckily, so she'll be shut up in the drawing-room. Out you get. I'll put the car away. And Simon—"

Simon, half-way out of the door with the manuscript clutched to his breast, paused and looked back. He could only just see Great-Uncle Merry's face, his ruffled white hair turned to a dark tangle by the shadow, and light from a street lamp up the hill reflecting eerily back to make his eyes two glinting points in the dark.

"It was very well done," Great-Uncle Merry said quietly.

Simon said nothing, but slammed the door feeling suddenly more grown-up than he ever had before. And when the car had coughed on up the hill he forgot all his weariness and crossed the road holding his back very straight.

Jane and Barney were at the door before he had one foot on the step. They hustled him inside and towards the stairs.

"Did he catch you?"

"You've still got it! Oh well done . . ."

"We thought you'd get all beaten up. . . ." This was Barney, wide-eyed and solemn.

"You didn't get hurt, did you? What happened?" Jane ran her eyes critically over Simon like a doctor.

"I'm all right. . . ."

There was a sudden bright streak of light in the hall as the drawing-room door opened. Mother called, over a murmur of voices from inside. "Is that you, children?"

"Yes," Jane called across the banisters.

"Supper's nearly ready, don't be long. Come straight down when you've washed."

"All right, Mother." The door closed again. "They're all talking like anything in there," Jane said to Simon. "Mother and Father met some long-lost friend in the harbour and it turns out she lives in Penzance. I think she paints too. She's staying to supper. She seems quite nice. Did he chase you for *miles?*"

"Hundreds of miles," Simon said. He yawned. "Hundreds and hundreds . . . and then Great-Uncle Merry turned up just when I was going to get caught."

"We sent him out after you," Barney said eagerly. They went on up the stairs.

"We didn't send him," Jane said reprovingly. "He went. Like a rocket, as soon as he heard what had happened."

"Well, he wouldn't have gone if we hadn't told him, and then Simon wouldn't have got rescued." Barney was glowing with excitement. He would have given his ears to have been the hero of the chase. "We didn't know which way you'd gone. We tailed Miss Withers for a bit, but she just went down the headland and sat down on the grass at the bottom *looking out at the sea*." His voice rose to an incredulous squeak. "So we rushed home, and Great-Uncle Merry was just back from fishing. We were jolly glad to see you getting out of the car," he added unexpectedly.

"Not half so glad as me," Simon yawned again, and rubbed his forehead. "I do feel mucky. It must have been when I hid in those bushes . . . come on, I can tell you while I wash."

* * *

First they were too busy eating to talk, and then towards the end of supper, too busy trying not to fall asleep; so all three children were grateful that Miss Hatherton was there. She was a small. bright, bouncy person, quite old, with cropped grey hair and twinkling eyes. She was a sculptress—a famous one, Great-Uncle Merry told them afterwards—and had taught Mother when she was a student at art school. She also seemed to have a passion for catching sharks, and at the supper-table she alternated between enthusiastic discussions of art with Mother and fishing with Father. The children listened with interest, but were relieved when Mrs. Palk brought the coffee in and Mother, who had not missed their yawns, sent them to bed.

"Nothing like Cornish air to send you to sleep," Miss Hatherton said cheerfully as they pushed back their chairs and said good night. "If any of these follows in your footsteps," she added to Mother, "it'll be that one." She pointed disconcertingly at Barney.

Barney blinked at her.

"What do you want to do when you grow up, young man?" she asked him.

"I'm going to be a fisherman," Barney said promptly. "With a big boat, like the *White Heather*."

Miss Hatherton roared with laughter. "You tell me that in ten years' time," she said, "and I shall be very surprised. Good night. I'll buy your first picture."

"She's dotty," Barney said as they went upstairs. "I don't want to be a painter."

"Never mind," Simon said. "She's nice. Don't go, Jane, come in our room for a minute. I think Gumerry's coming up, he made a sort of face at me as I closed the door."

They waited, and in a few moments Great-Uncle Merry appeared in the doorway. "I can't stay more than a minute," he said. "I am engaged in the beginnings of what promises to be a long and heated discussion with Miss Hatherton and your mother over the relative merits of Caravaggio and Salvator Rosa."

"Coo," said Barney.

"As you say, Barnabas, coo. I rather think I am out of my class with those two. However—"

"Gumerry, we found it," Jane said eagerly. "We found the second step, and we've started properly now. It's one of the standing stones on Kemare Head. The boys did it between them really," she added honestly. "Come on, Simon, get the manuscript out."

Simon got up and retrieved the telescope case, grubbier and more battered now than it had been, from the top of the wardrobe. They laid the scroll out on the bed and showed Great-Uncle Merry the rock where it had all begun, and the small rough sketch of the sun, and how they had worked their way to the standing stone.

"But we can't tell which standing stone it is on the map," Simon said. "Because they don't look the same here as they actually do on the headland."

They all bent over the drawing that they still could not help calling a map. Great-Uncle Merry looked at it in silence.

"Gumerry," Jane said tentatively, an idea that she could not quite grasp beginning to chase about her brain, "would he have done the whole thing on the same system, do you think?"

"Whatever do you mean?" Simon said, bouncing flat on his back on the bed.

"Well, you remember when we were trying to work out the first bit, and I said that it ought to be the way all treasure maps start— six paces to the east, or something. And you said, no, it might be done by getting one thing in line with another as a sort of pointer."

"Well?"

"Well, does that mean that you have to get everything in line with something else, at every step? Are all the clues going to be the same kind of clue?"

"You mean, next we shall have to get something else in line with the standing stone?"

Great-Uncle Merry was still gazing down at the map. "It's possible. What makes you think so?"

"That," Jane said. She pointed at the map. Everyone peered.

"I can't see anything," Barney said querulously.

"Look, there. Over the end of Kemare Head."

"But that's just another of those blodges," Simon said in disgust. "How can that mean anything?"

"Doesn't it remind you of anything else?"

"No," Simon said. He lay back again, and yawned.

Great-Uncle Merry looked from one to the other, and smiled to himself.

"Oh really," Jane said, exasperated. "I know you've done jolly well today and I know you're tired, but honestly—"

"*I'm* listening," Barney said at her elbow. "What about the blodge?"

"It's not a blodge at all," Jane said. "At least I don't think so. It's a bit smudged, but it's a circle, a properly drawn one, and I think it means something. It looks just like the other one, the one over the standing stones that turned out to be the setting sun."

Simon propped himself up on his elbows and began to take an interest again.

Jane went on, thinking aloud: "The way the first clue worked, we had to find the stone that was in line with the sun and the rock we started from. And then we had to go to the stone and check that it was the right one by the shadow. Well, perhaps now we have to do the same thing. Find something that's in line with the stone, and then go to it and see if its shadow points back to the stone."

Great-Uncle Merry said softly. "The signs that wax and wane but do not die . . ."

Jane turned to him eagerly. "That's it. That's what he said, isn't it, in the manuscript? There must be all sorts of clues in the writing, as well as in the drawing. Only they're even more buried and we don't know how to get at them."

"This shadow business," Simon said doubtfully. "Couldn't it be simpler than the way you just said? Perhaps all we have to do is find out what the shadow of our standing stone points at."

"But it points back at the place we started," Barney said. "Because he didn't use it as his first clue. His first clue was 'Look and see what's between you and the setting sun.' The shadow was just our way of proving it."

"Well, it doesn't have to be a shadow made by the setting sun this time."

"That's where my blodge comes in," Jane said.

Barney said sleepily: "Perhaps it's the rising sun. Only it can't be, it isn't in the right place."

"No," Simon said. "Of course it isn't. It's just a blodge."

Jane spluttered with impatience and glared at him. "Oh . . . why does it have to be the sun at all?"

Great-Uncle Merry was still sitting silent and statuesque on the edge of the bed. He said again lovingly to himself: "The signs that wax and wane but do not die. . . ."

Simon gazed at him blankly.

"Don't you see?" Jane almost howled at him. "It isn't the sun—it's the moon!"

Simon's face began to change like the sky on a windy day, different expressions chasing one another across it. He looked from Jane, to the map, to Great-Uncle Merry. "Gumerry," he said accusingly, "I believe you knew all the time. Is she right?"

Great-Uncle Merry stood up. The bed creaked as he rose, and his height seemed to fill the room; the light, swinging from the ceiling behind his head, cast his face into shadow and brought back once more to all three of them the old sense of mystery. His great dark figure, with a mist of light faintly silver round his head, left them silent and awed.

"This is your quest," he said. "You must find the way every time yourselves. I am the guardian, no more. I can take no part and give you no help, beyond guarding you all the way." He turned slightly so that the light shone on his face and then his voice was ordinary again. "I imagine you'll need some guarding on this next stage, too. You know what it is now, don't you?"

Simon said slowly: "We have to find which way the shadow of the standing stone points at night. Under the moon."

Barney said, matter-of-fact: "The full moon."

"The full moon?"

"Jane's blodge—he drew it round, not crescent-shaped, so it must mean the full moon."

"What's it like now?"

"You are *not* going up on the headland to look at the moon tonight," Great-Uncle Merry said firmly.

"No, I didn't really mean that. I don't think I could manage it anyway." Simon stifled another yawn. "I wondered whether the moon was full or not now. We should have to wait for ages if it were all thin and new."

"It's full tonight," Jane said. "I could see it shining in through my bedroom window. So that means it will be almost as bright tomorrow. Would that do, Gumerry? I mean, could we go and look tomorrow night?"

Before their great-uncle could answer Simon was sitting up again, looking thoughtful. "There's one thing wrong with all this. If we've got a moon that's only just past full, then we've got all the light we ought to have. But the moon changes, doesn't it? I mean, it rises and sets at different times, and in different places, according to the time of year. Well—we're in August now, but how do we know that the Cornishman wasn't working out his clues in the middle of January or April or something, when the moon wouldn't look the same as it does to us?"

"You're just being awkward," Barney said.

"No," said Great-Uncle Merry. "He's right. But I will say just one thing. I think you will find that this *is* the right time of the year. Call it luck, call it anything you like. But since you were able to follow the first clue, I think you'll find you're able to follow the rest as well. And yes, Jane, tomorrow night would do very well for looking at the moon and the standing stones. Especially well, for a reason you don't know yet—just after you came up, Miss Hatherton was asking your parents to go and see her studio in Penzance tomorrow, and to stay the night."

"Ooh! Will they go?"

"Wait and see. Go to bed. And try not to put all your faith in the moon. There may be greater problems still waiting for you than you think."

* * *

Mother stood with her hand on the door of Miss Hatherton's small beetle-like car. "Now you're sure you'll be all right?" she said doubtfully.

"Oh Mother, of course we shall," Jane said. "What could possibly happen to us?"

"Well, I don't know, I'm not altogether happy about leaving you . . . what with that burglary . . ."

"That was ages ago now."

"So long as you don't set the place on fire," Father said cheerfully. Miss Hatherton had promised to take him shark-fishing the next day, and he was as excited as a schoolboy.

"Don't let them go to bed too late, Uncle Merry," Mother said, getting into the car.

"Now don't worry, Ellen," Great-Uncle Merry said paternally from the doorstep, looking like an Old Testament patriarch with the children clustering round him. "I shan't have a chance to lead them astray with Mrs. Palk living in. We shall all probably die of overeating instead."

"Are you sure you won't all come too?" Miss Hatherton leant across the steering-wheel, blinking in the morning sun. The car lurched slightly as Father squeezed himself into the back. Simon handed in his fishing-rods after him.

"No, honestly, thank you," he said.

"It's no good, you can't tear these three away from Trewissick," Father said. "I've never seen anything like it. Even trying to get them as far as the next village is like prising a limpet off a rock. I daren't think what's going to happen when the time comes to go home."

"Well, well, they know their own minds. And I can't tempt you away, Professor Lyon?"

"Oh dear," Mother said. "I'm sorry you're stuck with them, Merry." She made a face at the children.

"Nonsense," Great-Uncle Merry said. "This is my element. Disgusting place, Penzance, anyway." He scowled horribly at Miss Hatherton, who grinned amiably back. "Trippers, ice-cream and little brass piskies. Commercialised. You can keep it."

"Well," Miss Hatherton said with a grin, starting the engine, "off to the piskies. We'll send you a stick of rock, Professor. Good-by. Good-by, children." The car moved off, a ragged chorus of farewell following it.

"Good-by!" Mrs. Palk shrilled, appearing suddenly behind them on the doorstep and waving a tea-cloth. The little car chugged up the hill and out of sight.

"Well now, idn' that nice, the two of them going off together?" Mrs. Palk said sentimentally. "Quite like old times, I'll be bound, before their troubles began." She wagged her tea-cloth at the children.

"Do you mean us?" demanded Barney indignantly.

"That I do. Proper 'eadache, you be . . . still, you'll do, I dare say." She vanished, beaming, back to the kitchen.

"Jolly useful, that Miss Hatherton," Simon said with satisfaction. "Of course I hope they have a lovely time and all that, but it does leave the coast clear, doesn't it?"

"That moonlight shadow . . ." Jane said thoughtfully. "You know, I've been thinking . . ."

"No thinking today," Great-Uncle Merry said firmly. "We can't do anything until tonight. I haven't been in the sea since I came down here this year, I think you should all take me down for a bathe."

"For a *bathe*?" Barney's voice rose in amazement.

"That's right." Great-Uncle Merry glared down at him through bristling white eyebrows. "D'you think I'm too old to swim, is that it?"

"Er—no, no, not at all, Gumerry," Barney said, confused. "I just never thought of you in the water, that's all."

"But what about the map?" Jane wailed.

"We've just got going," Simon said reproachfully.

"Well, and we shan't stop. We'll spend a nice quiet day on the beach in the sunshine." Great-Uncle Merry grinned at them. "And who knows, perhaps there'll be a moon tonight."

* * *

And there through the windows of the Grey House the moon hung, in the late August evening, when they were back from their day and washing before Mrs. Palk called them down to supper. The sun had flamed down on the beach all day, and they were all tanned—Barney's fair skin was burning an angry red. But now the moon dominated the sky: a sky deepening after the sunset to a strange grey-black, with all but the brightest stars dimmed by the milky luminous sheen that flowed over sky and sea without seeming to come from the moon at all.

Simon said, low and excited: "It's a perfect night."

"Mmm," Jane said. She had been outside to look at the sky, and to study nervously the black outline of Kemare Head rising dark and impenetrable behind the house. Like Simon, she was excited, but the old uneasiness was back as well.

It would be better, she told herself severely, not to think about the dark, or at least to think of it as the same dark in which the long-ago Cornishman worked out the clues that they were following now. But perhaps in this darkness too there still lurked the evil which had been creeping up on him then, from the unfriendly east, threatening the grail as he sought urgently for a hiding-place . . . perhaps it was waiting for them, out there . . . why was there no light burning on the Witherses' yacht . . . ?

"Oh, stop it," Jane said aloud.

"What?" said Simon in surprise.

"Nothing . . . I was talking to myself. . . . Oh good, there's the bell. Come on."

Mrs. Palk, in the intervals of carrying heaped plates from the kitchen and empty ones back out again, was in a very firm motherly mood. Great-Uncle Merry told her that they were going night-fishing off the outer harbour, and at once she began laying great plans for filling thermos flasks with hot coffee, and leaving plates of sandwiches ready in the kitchen for their return. But she would not hear of Barney going too.

"You'm not goin' anywhere wi' sunburn like that, midear, twouldn' be sensible, now. You stay here wi' me and have a nice early night, that'd be the best thing by far. If you go out you'll be rubbin' and blisterin' quick as anything, and then you'd find yourself in bed tomorrow when you could be out in the sunshine, and you wouldn't like that, would you?"

"I should be perfectly all right," Barney said, halfheartedly. Mrs. Palk had painted calamine on his sunburned legs, but they were very sore and tender, and although he tried to hide the pain he winced every time he took a step.

And he was very sleepy after the day spent running and swimming in the open air.

Great-Uncle Merry said, "I think it would be best, Barney. If you're awake we'll come and report to you when we get in."

"That 'ee won't," Mrs. Palk said. She treated Great-Uncle Merry, for all her respect for "the Professor," with exactly the same indulgent strictness that she did Simon and Barney and Jane. "He'll have a good long sleep, undisturbed, till mornin', and then he'll wake up fresh as a daisy with all that soreness gone. And he can hear all about everything then."

"Mrs. Palk," Great-Uncle Merry said meekly, "you are a good

soul and you remind me overwhelmingly of my old nanny, who would never let me go outside the door without taking my galoshes. Well, young Barnabas, I think . . ."

"Oh, all right," Barney said sadly. "I suppose so. I'll stay here."

"That's right," Mrs. Palk beamed. "I'll go and make 'ee a nice hot drink before bed." She bustled out of the room.

"You lucky things," Barney said enviously to Simon and Jane. "I bet you find all sorts of marvelous clues, just because I can't come. It isn't fair."

"As a matter of fact you'll have the most important job of all tonight," Simon said impressively. "And the most dangerous too. We decided it would be too risky to take the map with us, so you'll be in charge of it here. You might have to guard it with your life— suppose the burglars came back again."

"Oh don't," Jane said in alarm.

"That isn't very likely, don't worry," Great-Uncle Merry said, getting to his feet. "But it's a responsibility all the same, Barney, so you aren't altogether out of things."

Barney was not sure whether to feel important or pathetic, but he went obediently to bed. Looking back as they set off into the dark, they saw his face pressed white against one of the upstairs windows, and a dim hand waving them good-by.

"Gosh, it's cold," Jane said, shivering slightly, as they went up the road away from the village.

"You'll be all right once we've been walking for a bit," Great-Uncle Merry said. He had insisted before they went out that they should wear sweaters and scarves under their coats, and they were grateful now.

"Everything seems terribly big," Simon said suddenly. They all spoke softly by instinct, for there was no sound in the dark night but the soft tread of their own feet. Only, occasionally, they heard a car humming past in the village, and, very faint, the wash of the sea and the creak of boats at their moorings in the harbour below.

Jane looked round at the silver roofs and the patches of black shadow cast by the moon. "I know what you mean. You can only see one edge of everything, there's always one side in shadow. So you can't see where it ends . . . and the headland looks awfully sinister. I'm glad I'm not on my own."

This was a confession she would never have made in daylight.

But somehow in the dark night it seemed less shameful. Simon said unexpectedly: "So am I."

Great-Uncle Merry said nothing. He walked along beside them in silence, very tall, brooding, his face lost in the shadows. With every long stride he seemed to merge into the night, as if he belonged to the mystery and the silence and the small nameless sounds.

Round the corner of the road, away from the harbour, they turned off and climbed over a fence on to the headland. The road curved round inland again, and above them stretched the dark grassy sweep of the slope, up towards the standing stones. In a little while they found the foot-path, and began the long to-and-fro climb to the top.

"Listen!" Jane said suddenly, stopping in mid-stride.

There was no sound as they stood there, but only the sigh of the sea.

"You're hearing things," Simon said nervously.

"No—I'm sure—"

Above their heads, from the top of the headland still out of sight, there came drifting down a faint ghostly call. "Whoo-oo."

"Oh, Jane said in relief. "Only an owl. Horrible, I couldn't think what it was."

Great-Uncle Merry still said nothing. They began to climb again. Then all at once they hesitated, as if by some unspoken agreement. A dark curtain seemed to have come down all round them.

"What is it?"

"A cloud's come over the moon. Look. It's only a little one."

Like a puff of smoke the cloud drifted away from the face of the moon as suddenly as it had come, and the land and sea were silver again.

"You said there wouldn't be any cloud."

"Well, there isn't much, only a few little ones."

"The wind has changed," Great-Uncle Merry said. His voice, out of his long silence, sounded very deep. "It comes from the south-west, Cornwall's wind. It brings cloud sometimes, and some-times other things." He went on up the hillside, and they did not like to ask him what he meant.

As they climbed after him more clouds came up, ragged and silver-edged in the moonlight; scudding swiftly across the sky as if another wind were up there, stronger and more purposeful than the gentle breeze blowing down into their faces over the slope.

And then, looming over the dark brow of the headland, they saw the outline of the standing stones. Magnified by the darkness, they towered mysteriously against the silverwashed sky, and vanished unnervingly into shadow whenever a cloud rushed over the face of the moon. In the daylight the stones had seemed tall, but now they were immense, dominating the headland, and all the dim moonlit valleys that stretched inland from the lights of the village twinkling faintly below. Jane clutched at Simon's arm, suddenly overawed.

"I'm sure they don't want us here," she said unhappily.

"Who don't?" Simon demanded, bravado making his voice louder than he intended.

"Ssh, don't make such a noise."

"Oh, grow up," Simon said roughly. He did not feel happy in the dark emptiness of the night, but he was determined not to think about it. Then he felt a coldness at the pit of his stomach, as his great-uncle's deep voice came back to them in a way that seemed to confirm all that Jane felt.

"They don't mind," Great-Uncle Merry said softly. "If anything, we're welcome here."

Simon shook himself slightly, pretending not to have heard. He looked round at the stones, surrounding them now, rearing up against the sky. "This was the one." He crossed to the stone they had found the day before. "I remember this funny sort of hole in the side."

Jane joined him, calmed by his matter-of-fact tone. "Yes, that's it. When we looked across from here we were absolutely in line with the sun, and that rock we started from. Over on that other headland. Funny you can't see it now. I'd have thought the moon would shine on it like the sun did."

"The moon's in another direction, out over the sea," Simon said. "Look at the shadow, come on, that's what we've got to follow."

"Oh bother," Jane said, as another cloud crossed the moon and they were left in the dark again. "The clouds are getting much thicker, I wish they'd go away. There seems to be much more wind up here too." She clutched her duffle coat round her, and tucked her scarf in more tightly.

"Don't be long," Great-Uncle Merry said suddenly out of the darkness. He was standing against another of the stones, swallowed up in its outline so that they could not even make out his shape. Jane felt a shiver of alarm return.

"Why? Is anything wrong?"

"No, nothing . . . look, here's the moon again."

The night became silver again; looking up, it was as if they saw the moon sailing through the clouds instead of the other way round; racing smoothly across the sky, passing puffs and wisps of cloud on either side, and yet never moving from its place.

Simon said, in flat, dull disappointment: "It doesn't point at anything!" He stared at the ground beside the towering stone. Dark on the silvered gloom of the grass lay the shadow cast by the high bright moon; and it pointed like a blunt finger away from Kemare Head, towards the long dark inland horizon of the Cornish moors.

"Perhaps it points to some landmark we haven't noticed," Jane said doubtfully, gazing in vain over the shadow-masked hills.

"More likely the Cornishman used a landmark that's fallen down, or been destroyed, or just crumbled away. There's always been that risk. And it would mean we could never get any further than this."

"But he wouldn't have done that, I know he wouldn't." Jane looked wildly round her into the night, into the wind gusting over the bleak headland; and then suddenly she stood still, and stared. From her place beside the great stone that was their only sure mark, she had turned her head to the moon that raced motionless high over the top of Kemare Head, over the sea; and she saw, as if for the first time, the pathway of light that it laid down.

Straight as an arrow the long white road of the moon's reflection stretched towards them across the surface of the sea, like a path from the past and a path to the future; at its edges it danced and glimmered as the waves rose beneath the wind. And where it ended, at the tip of Kemare Head, a clear dark silhouette stood against the shining sea-carried light.

She said to Simon, huskily. "Look."

He turned to see, and she knew that in a moment he was as certain as she that this was what they were supposed to find.

"It's those rocks on the end of the headland," she said. "Outlined there. It must be. And we weren't supposed to use the shadow as a pointer this time—we had to stand here by this stone and let the moonlight itself show us the next clue."

"And that's what it does." Simon's voice rose as the familiar excitement of the chase came flooding back. "And if that's what he meant by the signs that wane but do not die, then the grail must be hidden somewhere in that clump of rocks. Buried on the end of Kemare Head. Gosh—Gumerry, we've found it!" He turned back towards the silent dominating circle of the standing stones, and then hesitated. "Gumerry?" he said uncertainly.

Jane came quickly to stand close to him. Out of the shelter of the rock the wind blew her pony-tail round across her face. She called more loudly, "Gumerry!" Where are you?"

There was no answer but the rise and fall of the sighing wind, loud enough now to drown the distant murmur of the sea. Jane, feeling very small indeed under the ghostly group of great stones, took hold of Simon's sleeve. Her voice quavered in spite of itself. "Oh Simon—where's he gone?"

Simon called into the growing wind: "Great-Uncle Merry! Great-Uncle Merry! Where are you?"

But still there was nothing but the darkness, and the high white moon sailing now dark, now light, and the noise of the wind. They heard the husking wail of the owl again, nearer this time, over the headland in the opposite valley; a friendless, inhuman, desolate sound. Jane forgot everything but the loneliness of the dark. She stood speechless with fright, as if she knew a great wave were bearing down on her and she could not move out of its path. If she had not been there Simon would have been as paralysed by fright himself. But he took a deep breath, and clenched his fists.

"He was over here before," he said, swallowing. "Come on." He moved in the direction of the other standing stones, barely visible now in the blackness.

"Oh no—" Jane's voice rose hysterically, and she clutched at his sleeve. "Don't go near them."

"Don't be stupid, Jane," Simon said coolly, sounding much braver than he felt.

Another owl hooted, unexpectedly, on their other side, towards the end of the headland. "Oh," Jane said miserably. "I want to go home."

"Come on," Simon said again. "He must be over here. I expect he can't hear us, this wind's getting up like anything." He took Jane's hand, and unwillingly she moved with him towards the dark looming shapes of the standing stones. The moon dimmed and disappeared into the depths of a bigger cloud, so that only a dim luminous glow from the stars gave shape to anything at all. They went gingerly through the darkness, feeling that at any moment they might collide with something unseen; panic suppressed only by the desperate hope of finding their great-uncle suddenly at their side. He seemed a very strong and necessary refuge now that he was not there.

They were right among the standing stones now, and they could feel rather than see the black rock pillars rearing up around them. The wind blew gustily, singing through the grass, and again they heard the owl cry below them out of the dark. They moved slowly together, straining their eyes to peer ahead. Then the ragged cloud turned silver again, and the moon came sailing out through the flying wisps at its edge; and in the same moment they became aware of a tall dark shape looming up before them where no stone had been before.

It seemed to swell as the wind blew, so that suddenly they saw that it was no stone, but the tall figure of a man all in black, with a long cloak that swirled in the wind as he turned towering over them. For an instant the moonlight caught his face as he turned, and they saw eyes shadowed under dark jutting brows, and the flash of white teeth in what was not a smile. Jane screamed, terrified, and hid her face in Simon's shoulder.

And then at once the moon was covered again by cloud, and the threat and roar of the darkness seemed to rear up all around them. Without a word they swung round and ran, stumbling, driven by panic, away from the silent standing stones and down the hill, until with an enormous flooding of relief they heard the call of a familiar deep voice. As they looked ahead, gasping, they saw Great-Uncle Merry silhouetted against the lighter background of the sea, standing before them on the path.

They rushed to him, and Jane flung her arms round his waist and clung to him, sobbing with relief. Simon had just enough self-possession left to stand on his own. "Oh Gumerry," he said breathlessly, "we couldn't find you anywhere."

"We must go down from here quickly," his great-uncle said low and urgently, holding Jane to him and stroking the back of her quivering head. "I was looking for you. I knew there was something in those cries that was not like an owl. Come quickly."

He bent down and picked Jane up in his arms in one swift movement as if she had been a baby, and with Simon close at his heels he strode off down the hill, keeping to the path that they could just see as moonlight flashed through the racing clouds.

Simon said, panting as he trotted along, "There was a man up there. We saw him, all of a sudden, out of the dark. He was all muffled up in a big coat like a cloak, all in black. It was horrible."

"I went to find them," Great-Uncle Merry said. "He must have got past me. Then there were others. I shouldn't have left you alone."

Jane, shaken in his arms as he loped down the hill, opened her eyes and looked back over his shoulder at the top of the headland, where the dark fingers of the standing stones still pointed up into the sky. And in the moment before they disappeared over the horizon she saw that there were twice as many shapes as there had been before, with other black figures standing among the stones.

"Gumerry, they're coming after us!"

"They dare not follow while I am here," Great-Uncle Merry said calmly, and he went down the slope at the same long easy stride.

Jane swallowed. "I think I'm all right now," she said in a small voice. "Could you put me down?"

Hardly pausing, Great-Uncle Merry set her on her feet again, and like Simon she half ran beside him to keep up. They reached the bottom of the slope, and crossed the field to the road, feeling it a reassuring place after the vast bleak emptiness of the headland. The wind no longer whined round their ears down here, and they heard again the friendly soft murmur of the sea.

"That man," Simon said. "That man we saw. It was him, Gumerry, the one we'd never seen before. It was the man you rescued me from. The man who chased me, with the boy."

Jane said in a small frightened voice, looking straight ahead of her at the twinkling village lights as she walked, "But I recognised him straight away, when moonlight shone on his face. That's why I was so scared. It was the vicar of Trewissick. And he's the man who saw my outline of the map in the guide-book."

• *Chapter Nine* •

Barney, left behind, flattened his nose against the window of Jane's bedroom. He saw Simon and Jane glance up and wave, but Great-Uncle Merry was marching along without looking to right or left, a tall thin figure vanishing into the dark. Barney smiled to himself. He knew that determined stride very well.

He peered after them until he could see nothing in the darkness but the lights of the village dancing in the black rippled water, among the ghostly boats. From the Witherses' yacht, there was no light at all. He turned away from the window, sighing a little at the frustration of being left out. To comfort himself he took a firmer hold on the telescope case which Simon had solemnly handed over to him when they came up to say good-by. At once he felt better. He was a knight entrusted with a sacred mission, he had been wounded in battle but had to guard his secret just the same . . . he bent each leg gently in turn, and winced at the burning tightness of the skin over his knees. The enemy were all round, hunting the secret which he held in his charge, but none of them would be able to get near. . . .

"Now then, back 'ee come to bed," Mrs. Palk said behind him, unexpectedly. Barney swung round. She was standing massive in the doorway, with the light from the landing streaming round her, watching him. Barney's fingers instinctively curled tighter round the cool metal case, and he came towards her, padding softly on his bare feet. Mrs. Palk backed out on to the landing to let him through the door. As he passed close to her she reached out her hand curiously.

"What's that 'ee got there?"

Barney jerked the case out of her reach, and then quickly forced a laugh. "Oh," he said as casually as he could, "it's a telescope of the captain's I borrowed. It's jolly good. You can see all the ships going past out in the bay. I thought I might be able to watch the others go down to the harbour with it, but it's not much good in the dark."

"Oh ah." Mrs. Palk seemed to lose interest. "Fancy that, I never seen the captain use any telescope. Still, there be all sorts of strange things in this house, more than I shall ever know about, I'll be bound."

"Well, good night, Mrs. Palk," Barney said, making for his own room.

"Good night, midear," Mrs. Palk said. "Just give me a shout if 'ee want anything. I reckon I'll be going to bed myself soon, my days of waitin' up for fishermen are over." She disappeared downstairs, and the landing light went out.

Barney switched on the lamp at the side of his bed and quietly closed the door. He felt unprotected, and rather excited still, without Great-Uncle Merry in the house. He thought of pushing a chair against the door, but changed his mind when he remembered that Simon would fall over it when he came back. The last thing he wanted was for anyone to think he had been worried at being alone.

He took the manuscript out to have one last look, and to guess what Simon and Jane might find from the shadow of the standing stone. But he could see nothing in the rough picture of the stones and the moon. Suddenly sleepy, he slipped the roll back and turned out the light; snuggled down into the bed-clothes with the case clutched to his chest, and fell asleep.

* * *

He never knew exactly what it was that woke him. When, through the confusion of half-dreams and imagined noises, he realised that he was awake, the room was quite dark. There was no sound but the constant murmur of the sea, very faint on this side of the house but always in the air. But from the way all his senses were straining to catch something, he knew that a part of him which had not quite gone to sleep at all was warning him of some danger very near. He lay very still, but he could hear nothing. Then there was a very faint creak behind him, from the direction of the door.

Barney felt his heart begin to thump a little faster. He was used to hearing noises at night; their flat in London was part of a very old house which creaked and muttered all the time at night, as if the

105

walls and floors were breathing. Although he had never been awake here long enough to find out, he guessed that the Grey House probably did the same. But this noise, somehow, was not as friendly as those. . . .

Barney did what he did at home whenever he woke up and heard a noise that sounded more like a burglar than an ordinary creak of the floor. He made the small grumbling, yawning whimper that people give sometimes in their sleep, and turned over in bed as if he were settling himself down without waking up. As he turned, he half opened one eye for a quick look round the room.

At home when he did this there was never anything to see at all, and he fell asleep again feeling rather foolish. But this time it was different. By a faint line of light he could see that the door was standing open, and near it the glow of a small torch was moving across the room. The light of the torch stopped quite still as he moved. Barney snuggled into his new position, lay still and breathed deeply for several minutes with his eyes closed. Gradually he heard the small noises begin again. He lay listening, more perplexed than frightened now. Who was it? What were they doing? It can't be someone who wants to knock me on the head, he said to himself, or they'd have knocked me on the head before this. They don't want to wake me up, and they don't want to make a noise. *They're looking for something.* . . .

He groped under the bed-clothes, careful not to show any movement or make a noise. The telescope case was still there, and he kept tight hold of it.

Then he heard another sound. The person moving noiselessly about his room in the dark sniffed, very slightly. The noise was almost imperceptible, but Barney recognised it as a sniff he had heard before. He grinned to himself in relief, feeling his muscles relax. Very slowly he edged his hand out from under the bed-clothes towards the bed-side table, and switched on the light.

Mrs. Palk jumped, dropped her torch with a clatter and clapped her hand to her heart. For some seconds Barney was completely dazzled by the sudden light flooding the room, but he blinked his eyes clear in time to see disappointment and surprise on her face. Quickly she pulled herself together, and gave him a broad reassuring smile.

"There now, and I thought I hadn't waked 'ee up. What a pity. I'm so sorry, midear. Did I frighten 'ee?"

Barney said bluntly: "Whatever are you doing, Mrs. Palk?"

"Came up to see if 'ee was all right and sleepin' properly. And I thought while I was up here I'd pick up your dirty cup to wash up wi' the rest of the things downstairs. Had your Horlicks up here, remember? Bless the boy," she added fondly, "he's half asleep still."

Barney stared at her. He did feel sleepy, but not too sleepy to remember Jane coming into his room when he had first gone up to bed and saying, "Mrs. Palk said would I pick up your cup if you'd finished, or do you want any more?"

"Jane took my cup down."

Mrs. Palk looked vaguely round the room, and gazed wide-eyed at his empty bed-side table. "So she did then, it quite slipped my mind. What a silly old thing I be. Well, I'll leave 'ee to go back to sleep, my love, I'm so sorry to have waked 'ee." She bustled with almost comical speed out of the room.

Barney had almost fallen asleep again when he heard low voices outside the door, and Simon came in. He shot up in bed. "What happened? Did you find anything? Where did you go?"

"Nothing happened much," Simon said wearily. He peeled off his windbreaker and sweater and dropped them on the floor. "We found where we've got to go next. Where the next clue leads. It's those rocks at the end of Kemare Head, right over the sea."

"Did you go and look? Is there anything there?"

"No, we didn't." Simon was abrupt, trying not to remember the nastiness of the moments when he and Jane had been alone in the dark.

"Why not?"

"The enemy were up there, that's why. All round us in the dark, and one of them was the man who chased me that day with the boy. Only Jane says it was the vicar. I don't know, it's all awfully complicated. Anyway, we ran away and nobody followed us. Funny, they all seem scared of Gumerry."

"Who were *they*?"

"Dunno." Simon yawned hugely. "Look, I'm going down to have some cocoa. We can talk in the morning."

Barney lay down again, sighing. "All right. Ooh—" He jerked up again. "Wait a minute. Shut the door."

Simon looked at him curiously and pushed the door shut. "What is it?"

"You mustn't say anything in front of Mrs. Palk. Not a word. Tell Jane."

"We shouldn't. She wouldn't understand anyway."

"Ho," Barney said importantly. "That's what you think. I woke up just now and she was snooping around the room in the dark with a torch. Good job I had the map all safe. She's after it. I bet you she's after it. I think she's *bad*."

"Hmmm," Simon said, sceptically, looking at him. Barney's hair was ruffled, and his eyes shadowed with sleep. It was very easy to believe that what he was describing had been no more than a dream.

* * *

When they went downstairs in the morning Mrs. Palk was bustling energetically about the kitchen beating eggs in a bowl with her elbow flicking up and down like a machine. "Breakfast?" she said brightly. Barney watched her closely, but he could see nothing but good humour and beaming honesty. And yet, he said insistently to himself, she looked so guilty when I turned on the light. . . .

"It's a wonderful day again," Jane said happily as they sat down. "The wind's still quite strong, but there isn't a cloud anywhere. It must have blown them all away."

"Ah well, let's hope it doesn't blow the marquee away as well," Mrs. Palk said, putting an enormous jug of creamy yellow milk on the table.

"What marquee?"

"What!" Mrs. Palk opened her eyes. "Haven't 'ee seen the posters? Why, 'tis carnival day today. People come in from all round, even from St Austell. All sorts of things go on . . . there's a swimming gala in the harbour, then the band comes out, and there's dancing all the way up the street from the sea. They play the 'Floral Dance.' You know the tune, surely." She began to sing lustily.

"I know it," Simon said, "but I thought they only danced it somewhere else."

"Helston," said Jane. "The Helston Furry Dance."

" 'Es, so they do," Mrs. Palk said. "I reckon they copied it from us myself. Everyone knows Trewissick's Floral Dance, it was danced in my grandmother's time. Everyone dressed up gay and fancy in costume, and there's a great crowd in the street all dancin' and laughin'. No one goes out fishing today. There's a great marquee in the field behind the village, and all kinds of stalls and games, and wrestling. . . . Then when the sun begins to go down

108

they crown the carnival queen, and they stay round the harbour long after it gets dark, and dance in the moonlight . . . 'tis a long time before anyone wants to go to sleep in Trewissick, carnival day."

"What fun," Jane said.

"Hmmm," said Simon.

"Oh, you mustn't miss it," Mrs. Palk said earnestly. "I shall be there every minute, 'tis like the old days all over again. Eh, but now here I stand talking and your scrambled eggs will be getting hard on the stove." She turned and sailed out of the room.

"It does sound fun," Jane said reproachfully to Simon.

"I dare say. We've got other things to do. Of course if you'd rather go to the carnival than find the grail. . . ."

"Sssh!" Barney looked nervously at the door.

"Oh, don't worry about her, she's all right. Great-Uncle Merry's a long time coming down, isn't he?"

"I didn't mean it," Jane said meekly. "Actually what I want to do more than anything is get back up on the headland, so we can go and find that rock."

"We can't go without Gumerry. I wonder if he's awake?"

"I'll go and see." Barney slipped from his chair.

"Hey, where be off to?" Mrs. Palk nearly collided with him, carrying her tray through the door. "Sit down and eat this now, while 'tis hot."

"I was going to call Great-Uncle Merry."

"Now you leave him be, poor old gentleman," Mrs. Palk said firmly. "Gadding about in the middle of the night, tidn' natural at his age, no wonder he's having a good long sleep. Night-fishin', indeed. And not a fish to show for it after all that traipsin' about. You proper wearied him last night, I reckon. You remember we aren't all as young as you three." She wagged her finger at them. "Now you get along into the sun after your breakfast, and let him have his sleep out." She departed again, shutting the door behind her.

"Oh dear," Jane said, abashed. "She's right, you know. Great-Uncle Merry is quite old really."

"Well, he's not doddering," Simon said defensively. "He doesn't seem old at all sometimes. He went like a rocket last night—*and* carrying you. It was all I could do to keep up with him."

"Well, perhaps this is the after-effect." Jane's conscience was beginning to nag. "Last night must have been an awful strain on him, what with one thing and another. I don't think we should wake him up. It's only nine o'clock, after all."

"But we haven't made any plans or anything," said Barney.

"Perhaps we just ought to wait here till he does wake up," Simon said despondently.

"Oh no, why should we? He wouldn't mind if we went on to the headland. He can follow us when he's had his sleep."

"Didn't he say we shouldn't go anywhere without him from now on?" Barney said doubtfully. "Or anyway, not without telling him?"

"Well, we can leave a message for him with Mrs. Palk."

"No, we can't!"

"Barney thinks Mrs. Palk is one of the enemy," said Simon sceptically.

"Oh, surely not," Jane said vaguely. "Well anyway, we don't really have to leave a message. He's bound to guess where we've gone. There's only one place any of us would want to go, and that's to the rocks on Kemare Head."

"We can say to Mrs. Palk that he'll know where we've gone. Just like that. And then she'll tell him and he'll understand."

"We can say we've taken Rufus for a walk," said Barney hopefully.

"That's not a bad idea. Where is he?"

"In the kitchen. I'll go and get him."

"Tell Mrs. Palk while you're there. And tell her we'll see her at her beloved carnival. We probably will anyway."

Barney bolted the last of his scrambled egg and went out to the kitchen, munching a piece of toast.

Simon suddenly had an idea. He got up and crossed to the window, and peered out down the hill. He turned back quickly to Jane. "We might have known. They're watching us already. That boy's at the bottom of the road, sitting on the wall. Not doing anything, just sitting there, looking up here. They must be waiting for us to come out, because they don't know whether we found a clue last night that will lead us somewhere."

"Oh, gosh." Jane bit her lip. Their night on the headland had left her more deeply nervous than ever before. It was as if they were fighting not people, but a dark force that used people as its tools. And could do what it liked with them. "Isn't there a back way out of the house up to the headland?"

"I don't know. How funny, we've never looked."

110

"Well, we've been doing other things. I suppose even if there was one, they'd be watching it."

"Well . . . the only person who'd be likely to know about a back way is that Bill, and he's at the front. There's no harm in looking."

Barney had come back, with Rufus lolloping joyfully at his side. "There is a way," he said. "You can get through the hedge at the top of the back garden. I found it one morning before you were up. Rufus showed me, actually—he was dashing about and suddenly he disappeared, and then I heard him barking miles away outside, half-way up the headland. You come out into a lane and then you're out on Kemare Head before you know it. It's a good way out because they wouldn't expect us to go through—there's no gate or anything."

"Gumerry won't know about that way," Jane said suddenly. "He'll come out the front way, and they'll follow him, and it'll be just as bad as if they'd followed us in the first place."

"No fear," Barney said confidently. "He'll shake them off somehow. I bet you this is one time they won't have the slightest idea where we are."

* * *

When the children were gone and the house lay silent, Mrs. Palk spent two brisk hours working downstairs. She took care not to make a noise. Then she sat down in the kitchen to drink a leisurely cup of tea.

She made the tea very strong, using one of the captain's best cups: very large, and made of thin, almost translucent, white china. She sat at the kitchen table sipping from it, a look of great secret satisfaction on her face. After a while she went to a cupboard under the sink, pulled out her big shopping-bag and took from it a brilliant jumble of coloured ribbons, with an elaborate feathery structure not unlike a Red Indian head-dress. She set this on her head, looked at herself in the mirror, and chuckled. Then she carefully put it aside and poured out some more tea in a fresh cup. She put this on a tray and sailed out into the hall and up the stairs, a great smiling mysterious galleon of a woman.

Without knocking, she opened the door of Great-Uncle Merry's room, went in, and set down the tray by the bed. Great-Uncle Merry was buried in the bed-clothes, breathing heavily. Mrs. Palk pulled back the curtains to let the light pour into the dim room, bent down and shook him roughly by the shoulder. As he stirred she drew back quickly and stood waiting, beaming down at him with her usual doting motherly smile.

He yawned, groaned and clutched his head sleepily, running his fingers back through the untidy white hair.

"Time to get up, Professor," said Mrs. Palk brightly. "Nice long rest I let 'ee have, after all that gadding about last night. Done 'ee good, I'll be bound. Not all as young as we used to be, are we now?"

Great-Uncle Merry looked at her and grunted, blinking himself awake.

"Drink 'ee's tea now, and I'll go and get 'ee's breakfast." Mrs. Palk's rich voice flowed on as she turned to twitch the curtains tidy. "Can have it in peace and blessed quiet for once. They children have been out for hours."

Suddenly Great-Uncle Merry was very wide awake. He sat up straight-backed, a startling sight in his bright red pyjama jacket. "What time is it?"

"Why, 'tis gone eleven." Mrs. Palk beamed at him.

"Where have the children gone?"

"Now don't 'ee worry about them. They can look after themselves well enough for one day."

"Little idiots—where are they?" His forehead creased.

"Now, now, Professor," Mrs. Palk said chidingly. "Gone off to save 'ee a journey, they have, as a matter of fact. Thoughtful, well-brought-up little things, they are, for all their mother's a bit higgledy-piggledy, begging your pardon. Gone off to Truro for 'ee.

"Truro!"

Mrs. Palk smiled innocently. " 'Es, that's right. Young Simon answered the telephone this morning. Nasty machine," she added confidingly, shuddering slightly. "Near scared me out of my life, screeching away. Talked to the man on the other end for a long time, he did. And after, he came to me and said, all serious, bless his heart—'Mrs. Palk, he says, that was a friend of Great-Uncle Merry's on the telephone from the museum at Truro, saying he's got to see us all very urgently about something.' "

"Who was it?"

"Wait a minute now, Professor, I'm not finished. . . . 'I reckon we ought to go off at once if our great-uncle's still asleep,' young Simon says to me, 'and catch the bus. Then he can come on after us when he wakes up.' "

"Who was it?" Great-Uncle Merry insisted.

"Simon didn't give me no name . . . very important he made it sound. So off they all went, the three of them, and got the bus into St Austell. 'Don't you worry, Mrs. Palk,' they said, 'just you tell our great-uncle for us.' "

"You should never have let them go alone," Great-Uncle Merry said curtly. "If you'll excuse me, Mrs. Palk, I should like to get up."

"'Course," said Mrs. Palk indulgently, still smiling and unruffled, and she sailed out of the room.

Within minutes Great-Uncle Merry was downstairs, fully dressed, frowning to himself and occasionally muttering anxiously. He waved away his breakfast, and went striding out of the Grey House. Mrs. Palk, watching from the doorstep, saw his big battered car appear on the road and roar off, leaving a great black smear of smoke hanging in the air as it disappeared out of the village.

She smiled to herself, and went back into the Grey House. A few moments later she came out again, the small secret smile still hovering round her mouth; locked the door behind her and went off with her shopping-bag down the hill to the harbour. A few bright red and blue feathers nodded over the top of the bag as it swung at her side.

• *Chapter Ten* •

"This isn't nearly as simple as I thought it would be," Simon said, frowning. He looked about him at the jagged grey rocks. "From the standing stones last night it looked as if there was just one lump of rock here, sticking out on its own. But there are so many of them, and they're all so big."

The wind blowing in from the open sea tossed Jane's pony-tail to and fro on the back of her neck. She looked back inland. "It's just like being out at sea. As if we were cut off, and looking at the land from the outside."

The end of Kemare Head was a more desolate place than any they had yet seen, even with the sunlight glittering on the water far below, and the smell of the sea in the wind. They stood in the midst of a bleak patch of rocks, rising bare out of the grass almost at the headland's tip. The ground fell away before them in a steep grassy slope, and from there the sheer edge of the cliff dropped to meet the other rocks, two hundred feet below, where the white waves endlessly grunted and sighed. They could see no sign of life or movement anywhere around.

"It's lonely," Barney said. "It feels lonely itself, I mean, somehow. Different from us feeling lonely. I wonder what the next clue is, if there is one."

"I don't think there is," Jane said slowly. "This is so much an end of a place. It doesn't lead anywhere, everything leads towards it. . . . Funny how we didn't see anybody at all on the way up. There are usually one or two people wandering about, even on the headlands."

"There certainly were last night," Simon said.

"Oh don't, I keep trying not to remember. But there just isn't a living thing up anywhere near here. I think it's odd."

"Mr. Penhallow says the locals keep away from the end of the headland," Barney said, clambering to perch above their heads on one of the rocks. Rufus tried to climb up beside him, slithered back again and licked his ankle, whining. "They don't like the standing stones much either, but they never come up here at all. He wouldn't talk about it much. He said people thought the rocks were haunted, and unlucky, and he sounded as if he believed it himself. He said they call them the Gravestones."

"They call the standing stones that?"

"No, these rocks here."

"Funny, I should have thought it would be the other way round. The others do look rather like gravestones in a kind of way. But these are just rocks, like any other rocks."

"Well, that's what he said." Barney shrugged his shoulders and nearly overbalanced. "Just that people didn't like them."

"I wonder why." Jane gazed up at the nearest crag of rock, rising just above her head. Simon, next to her, tapped idly at its surface with the old brass telescope case, the manuscript safely rolled up inside; Barney had ceremonially handed it back that morning. Then suddenly he stopped tapping and stood stock-still.

"Whatever's the matter? Have you found anything?" Jane peered at the rock.

"No . . . yes . . . Oh, it's all right, I'm not looking at anything. Don't you remember, in the manuscript? I can hear Great-Uncle Merry saying it now. Where the Cornishman said he hid the grail. Over sea and under stone."

"That's right, and the same when they buried the strange knight, what was his name . . ."

"Bedwin," Barney said. "Golly, I see what you mean. Over sea and under stone. *Here!*"

"But—" Jane said.

"It must be!" Simon hopped distractedly on one foot. "Over sea—well, we couldn't be anywhere that was much more obviously over the sea, could we? And under stone. Well, here are the stones."

"And this must be where they buried Bedwin as well!" Barney hastily slithered down from his rock. "And that's why they call it the Gravestones, and think it's haunted. They've forgotten all the real story, because it's hundreds and hundreds of years ago. But they remember that bit, or at least they remember people being

115

frightened to come here, and so they don't come either."

"Perhaps they're right," Jane said nervously.

"Oh come off it. Well, anyway, even if Bedwin's ghost was floating about somewhere, he wouldn't want to scare us because we're on the same side as he was."

"Great-Uncle Merry said something like that last night." Jane screwed up her forehead to remember.

"Oh never mind, don't you realise what this means? We're *there*, we've found it!" Barney spluttered with delight. Rufus, catching his mood, pranced joyfully round them barking into the wind.

Simon looked at him. "All right then. Where is it?"

"Well," Barney said, pausing a little. "Here. Under one of the rocks."

"Yes, well, just stop rushing about like a madman and think for a minute. What do we have to do, dig them all up? They're part of the headland. It's all rock. Look." Simon took out his penknife, a hefty steel weapon with two big blades and a marlinspike, and went down on his knees to dig away the earth at the foot of one of the crags. He tore away tufts of grass, dug a hole, and three inches from the surface came to solid rock. "There. You see?" He scraped at the rock with his knife-blade, making a depressing grating sound. "How can there be anything buried there?"

"It doesn't all have to be like that," Barney said rebelliously.

"Perhaps there's a different bit somewhere," Jane said hopefully. "If we all three divide up and search every inch we're bound to find something. We ought to have brought spades with us really. Come on."

So Barney went to one end of the rocks and Jane, twenty yards away, to the other. Simon, glancing nervously down at the steep edge of the headland, went round to the seaward side and began working his way in from there. They clambered up and down, over the sharp-edged granite, searching the patches of wiry grass between the rocks, tugging at boulders to see if they would move and show a place where something could be buried underneath. But no stone ever shifted an inch, and they found nothing but granite and grass, with no hint of a hiding-place.

Jane was holding something carefully in her hand as they came together again. "Look," she said, holding it out. "Don't you think it's peculiar finding a sea-shell up here? I mean how on earth could it have got up from the beach, specially if no one ever comes up here?"

"It's more like a stone than a shell," Simon said curiously, taking it from her hand. It was a cockle-shell, but its hollow was solid and hard, filled with what looked like rock; and the surface of the shell was not white and roughened like those they found on the beach, but smooth and dark grey.

"A visitor must have dropped it," Barney said easily. "Visitors wouldn't be frightened of coming up here, they wouldn't know anything about what the Trewissick people say."

"I suppose so." They all thought of visitors, scornfully. "Oh well." Jane put the shell in her pocket and looked around helplessly. "This is awful. We're stuck. What can we do now?"

"There must be something up here, there must."

"We don't really know . . . perhaps it's just another step on the ladder after all."

"But there's nothing else marked to follow. Let's have a look at the map again."

Simon squatted down on the grass and unscrewed the telescope case, and they peered at the manuscript, its words and lines faint brown in the sun.

"I'm certain he meant this to be the end of the quest," Barney said obstinately. "Look at the way the end of the headland stands all on its own. There's nothing to lead anywhere else."

Simon stared pensively at the map. "Perhaps it just leads back where we started from. He might have been pulling our legs all the while. A sort of insurance policy, to make it difficult for anyone to find the grail."

"Perhaps he hid it somewhere we shall never find."

"Perhaps he took it with him after all."

"Perhaps it doesn't exist."

They sat round in a gloomy group, ignoring the sunshine and the magnificent sweep of coast and sea. There was a long despondent silence. Barney glanced up idly. "Where's Rufus got to?"

"Dunno," Simon said morosely. "Fallen over the cliff, I expect. Sort of stupid thing that animal would do."

"Oh no!" Barney scrambled to his feet in concern. "I hope he's all right. Rufus! Rufus!" He put two fingers in his mouth and let out an ear-splitting whistle. Jane winced.

They saw nothing, and heard nothing but the wind, and then they became aware of a curious noise just above their heads; a kind of snuffling, scrabbling whine.

"He's up there!" Barney clambered round the side of the rocks, and they saw the top of his fair head appear behind a jutting grey hump as he stood up. Then he suddenly vanished. His voice came over the rocks to them on the wind, muffled but tense with excitement. "Hey! Come over here, quick!"

The rocks made a kind of fortress, rising one after the other like rows of battlements. They found him in the middle, crouching beside one of the peaks, watching Rufus. The dog stood quivering and intent, his nose close against the rock, one paw scraping feebly as he whined and sniffed.

"Quick," Barney said without turning round. "I don't know what he's trying to do, but I think he's found something. I've never seen him like this before. If it's rats or rabbits he just goes mad and barks and rushes about, but this is different. Look at him."

Rufus seemed to be standing in a trance, unable to tear himself away from the rock-face.

"Let me look," Simon said. He stepped carefully past Barney and put one arm round Rufus's neck, fondling him under the chin as he drew him away from the rock. "There's a tiny gap here." His voice came back to them. "I can get my fingers inside—ow! I say, this top rock moves! I felt it shift, I'm sure I did. It nearly caught my hand. It's terrifically big, but I think . . . Jane, can you get round on my other side?"

Jane squeezed herself between the rocks next to him.

"Now get hold there," Simon directed her. "That jutting out bit . . . when I tell you, push as hard as you can away from you, towards the sea. Wait a minute, I've got to get a grip on my side . . . I don't know if this'll work . . . now, *heave!*"

Obediently, but without any idea of what she was supposed to be doing, Jane pushed with all her might at the rock-face, with Simon panting and heaving beside her. For a long strained moment nothing happened. Then just as their lungs seemed about to burst, they felt the rock move beneath their hands. It gave a very slight tremor, and then a grinding, grating lurch. They staggered back, and the great rough round rock rolled away from their hands and down into the nearest hollow. They could feel the crunching thud of its fall shake the rock where they stood.

Where the boulder had been there was a dark, shapeless hole about two feet across.

They stood still, gaping. Rufus pattered forward across the rocks, bent his head to sniff delicately at it and then turned back, his tail waving and his tongue hanging out over his teeth as if he were grinning.

Simon moved forward at last and pulled away a couple of smaller rocks from the edge of the hole. He knelt down by it and peered inside, then put his arm in to see how deep it was.

His arm disappeared up to his shoulder, until he was lying flat, and he could feel nothing but rough rock at the sides. He blinked up at Barney and Jane. "I can't feel any bottom to it," he said, hushed.

His voice brought back their own, and they found they had been holding their breaths.

"Get up, let's have a look."

"This must be it, mustn't it? It must be where he hid the grail!"

"How deep d'you think it goes?"

"Gosh, this is terrific! Clever old Rufus!"

Rufus waved his tail faster.

"That chunk of rock," Jane said, looking at it reverently where it lay tumbled on its side. "It must have been there for nine hundred years. Imagine . . . nine hundred years . . ."

"Well, it wasn't exactly loose, was it?" Simon flexed his strained arm muscles tenderly. "Though it must have been fairly delicately balanced, or we shouldn't have been able to shift it at all. Anyway, we've got to find how deep this goes before we know if there's anything there."

He looked thoughtfully at the gaping dark mouth in the rock. Jane sighed to herself and stopped thinking about the centuries.

"Drop a stone down, then you can hear how deep it is. Like thunderstorms. You know, counting the seconds between the lightning and the thunder to see how far away the storm is."

Simon picked up a loose chunk of rock from the edge of the hole and poised it over the blackness. He let go, and it dropped out of sight. They listened.

After a long time Jane sat back on her heels. "I couldn't hear anything."

"Nor could I."

"Try again."

Simon dropped another stone into the hole, and again they strained their ears to hear it strike the bottom. Nothing happened.

"There wasn't anything then either."

"No."

119

"It must be *bottomless!*"

"Don't be an idiot, it can't be."

"Perhaps it comes out in Australia," Barney said. He looked nervously at the hole.

"It just means the noise was too far away for us to hear," Simon said. "But it must be tremendously deep. I wish we'd brought a rope."

"Look in your pockets," Jane said. "They're always full of junk. So are Barney's. At least Mother's always saying so when she has to empty them. You might have some string or something."

"Junk yourself," Simon said indignantly, but he turned out his pockets on to the rock.

The results, though interesting, were not very much help. Simon laid out an array of belongings including his knife, a very dirty hand-kerchief, a little scratched glass-covered compass, two and sevenpence-ha'penny, a stump of candle, two screwed-up bus tickets, four toffees in battered cellophane wrappings and a fountain pen.

"Well," he said, "we can have a toffee each anyway." He handed them round solemnly. The toffees were slightly furry at the edges where the cellophane had come loose, but tasted none the worse for that. Simon gave the fourth to Rufus, who made a few grimacing attempts to chew it and then swallowed it whole.

"What a waste," Barney said. He emptied his own pockets, in a shower of sand: a green glass marble with an orange pip in the middle; a small white pebble, a sixpence and four farthings, a headless lead sailor, a handkerchief miraculously much cleaner than Simon's, and a thick piece of wire curved round at both ends.

"Whatever do you carry that around for?" demanded Jane.

"Well, you never know," Barney said vaguely. "It might come in useful. Come on, let's have a look at yours."

"Nothing in them," Jane said, a trifle smugly. She pulled both pockets of her jeans inside out.

"Well, you brought your duffle coat," said Simon. He crossed the rocks, climbed down to the grass of the headland where they had been standing, and brought the jacket back. "Here we are. One handkerchief. Two hair-grips. Just like a girl. Two pencils. A box of matches. Whatever d'you want those for?"

"Like Barney—they might come in useful. A lot more useful than that old bit of wire anyway."

Simon felt in the other pocket. "Money, a button . . . what's this?" He brought out a spool of cotton. "Now that's an idea. Pretty daft thing to carry about, but it might help us find how deep the hole is."

"I'd forgotten I had that," Jane said. "All right, you win, I carry junk round too. But you must admit it's sensible junk." She took the cotton-reel from him. "It says there's a hundred yards of cotton on this. Well, no hole could be that deep, surely?"

"I wouldn't be surprised, with this one," Simon said. "Tie something to the cotton, and lower it down."

"Have to be something pretty light," Barney said. "Or it'll break."

Jane unwound a length of cotton and pulled on it. "Oh, I don't know, it's pretty strong. Here, I know, give me that bit of wire."

Barney looked at her doubtfully, but handed it over. Jane tied one end of the cotton to its curved end. "There. Now we just lower away and wait till it hits bottom."

"I know a better way." Simon took the reel back. and put one of Jane's pencils through the hole in the middle. It was just long enough to protrude at either side. "See, you hold on to both ends of the pencil and the reel unwinds of its own accord, because of the weight. Like playing a fish."

"Let me do it." Jane knelt down beside the hole and dropped the wire into its dark mouth. The cotton-reel spun round as the thread disappeared, and they held their breath. Then suddenly the reel slowed, turned wearily and came to a halt. Just as they were thinking that the wire had reached firm ground, they saw the end of the cotton blowing loose.

"Bother," Jane said in disappointment. 'It's broken." She looked down into the blackness in a vain attempt to see where the cotton had gone. Simon took the reel from her and examined it.

"Half the cotton's gone, anyway, and it still hadn't hit anything. That means the hole must be at least fifty yards deep. That's a hundred and fifty feet. Good grief!" He tapped Jane on the shoulder. "Come on, dopey, you won't see anything down there."

Jane flapped her hand at him, still bending over the hole. "Shut up."

They waited patiently until she straightened herself, red in the face. "I can hear the sea," she said, blinking in the sunlight.

"Of course you can hear the sea. So can I. It's just over the edge of the headland."

"No, no, I mean you can hear it down there."

Simon looked at her, tapped his head and sighed.

But Barney lay down close to the hole and put his head inside. "She's right, you know," he said eagerly, looking up. "Come and put your ear down here."

"Hmmm," said Simon sceptically, and lay down beside him. Then he heard very faintly, coming up from the depths of the hole, a hollow booming sound. It faded and then rose again, slow and regular. "Is that the sea?"

"Of course it is," Jane said. "That deep gonging sort of noise, don't you recognise it? The sort of noise waves make when they wash into a cave. And think what it means . . . the hole must go all the way down through the cliff to the sea, and there must be an entrance down there. *And that's where the Cornishman hid the grail.*"

"But it can't go all that way." Simon sat up slowly, rubbing his ear. "Couldn't this be vibration or something, coming through from the edge of the rocks down below?"

"Well, I ask you, does it sound like it?"

"No," Simon admitted. "It doesn't. Only . . . how could anyone have made such a narrow little hole so deep?"

"Goodness knows. But he did, didn't he? Perhaps that little shell I found was thrown up through it somehow."

"Then if the grail is down there, we have to get at it from the entrance where the sea comes in. There must be a cave. I wonder if we can climb round from the harbour?"

"Listen!" Barney suddenly scrambled to his feet and stood upright, his head cocked. "I heard something. Like an engine."

Simon and Jane stood up, and listened to the distant waves and the wind. They could hear sea-gulls crying, the plaintive yelping calls blown gustily towards them from below. And then the noise Barney had heard; the low thrumming of an engine from the direction of the harbour.

It was Simon who caught sight of the long white bow of the yacht moving out round the curve of Kemare Head. He crouched low. "Get down, quick!" he said hoarsely. "It's them! It's the *Lady Mary*!"

Barney and Jane dropped to the ground beside him. "They can't see us if we keep behind the rocks," Simon said quietly. "Don't move, anyone, until they've gone out of sight."

"I've got a gap here," Barney whispered. "I can just see them through the rock. . . . Mr. Withers is on deck, and his sister with him. Their skipper's not there, he must be in the cockpit . . . they're looking this way, not up here, they seem to be looking at the cliffs. . . . Mr. Withers has got binoculars . . . now he's put them down, and he's turned to his sister to say something. I can't see the expression on his face, they aren't near enough. I wish they'd come closer."

"Oh!" Jane swallowed, husky with agitation. "Suppose there is a cave down there, where the grail is, and they see it!"

The idea was paralysing, and they lay rigid, three minds wishing the boat away. The noise of the *Lady Mary*'s engine grew louder, passing the end of the headland close below them.

"What are they doing?" Simon hissed urgently.

"I can't see, there's a rock in the way now." Barney wriggled with frustration.

The noise of the engine filled the air. But it did not stop. As they listened, breathless. it grew gradually less, moving away across the sea.

"I can see them again now, there's another gap . . . he's still looking at the coast through the binoculars. I don't think he's seen anything, it looks as if he's still hunting . . . now they've gone round the corner." Barney rolled over and sat up. "If they are looking for a cave, how did they know?"

"They *can't* know, they haven't seen the map," Jane said in anguish. "They couldn't possibly. I mean even if the vicar is in league with them, and they know about the outline I drew in the guide-book, it hasn't got any sort of clue. I didn't put any of the clue marks in."

"But if they don't know where to look, why are they looking in the right place?"

"I think," Simon said reassuringly, "it's just part of their routine. I mean, they don't know where to look, so they look everywhere. Great-Uncle Merry said something like that the very first day we talked. It's like the way they searched the house—all at random, without any sort of plan. Perhaps they've thought of the idea of a cave, vaguely, and they're scouring the whole coast in case they find one. Not just this part, but all the way up and down. They don't *know* there is one."

"Well, we do. If it's there, why didn't they see it?"

"Perhaps they did," Barney said gloomily.

"Oh no, they can't have done. They'd have stopped. At any rate they wouldn't have gone on looking like you said they were. You did say that, didn't you?" Jane looked at him nervously.

"Oh yes—old Withers was still squinting hard through his glasses when they went out of sight."

"Well then."

"There's one other thing it might be," Simon said reluctantly. He paused.

"What?"

"We heard the sea, so the mouth of the cave might be covered. It might be under water. That could be why they didn't see it. There are lots of underwater caves in Cornwall, I remember reading about them somewhere. It might not have been like that when our Cornishman hid the grail, but perhaps the land's sunk a bit in nine hundred years."

"Well, that's good," Barney said. "They'd never be able to find it then."

Simon looked at him, and raised his eyebrows, "Nor should we."

Barney stared. "Oh. Oh, surely we could. You can dive pretty well."

"We wouldn't have a chance. I can dive, but I'm not a fish."

"I suppose the whole thing would be full of water," Jane said slowly. "And the grail would be under the sea, and all eaten away like wrecks of ships."

"Covered in barnacles," said Simon.

"It can't be. It mustn't be. He said over the sea, and it must be over the sea."

"We shall just have to find out. Great-Uncle Merry will know."

They stared at one another in consternation.

"Gumerry! I'd forgotten all about him."

"Where is he?"

"We've been up here for ages. He must have woken up hours ago."

"Barney, what exactly did you ask Mrs. Palk to tell him?"

"I said would she say we'd gone for a walk with Rufus, he'd know where. She looked at me a bit funny, but she said she'd give him the message. I tried to make it sound like a game," said Barney, very serious.

"I do hope nothing's happened to him," Jane said anxiously.

"Don't worry, I expect he's still snoring," Simon said. He looked at his watch. "It's half past eleven. Let's get down quickly before the yacht comes back. We might not be so lucky next time—if they came back under sail we shouldn't hear them. I wonder why they didn't last time, there's more than enough wind." He frowned.

"Oh never mind," Barney said. "Let's go and find Gumerry. Round the back again—that boy might still be watching the front."

"No, we shall have to go the front way, Gumerry might be coming up. I've got a feeling we haven't much time left. We shall just have to risk getting caught. Come on."

• *Chapter Eleven* •

But as soon as they came down within sight of the harbour they saw that there was no question either of passing unseen or of being caught.

The streets round the harbour were thronged with people; fishermen and shopkeepers in their Sunday suits, wives in their best summer dresses, and more gay crowding tourists than the children had ever seen in Trewissick before. All the boats, swaying level with the quays on the high tide, were moored at one side, leaving a clear rectangle of water marked out with strings of bobbing white floats. As they came down the road they heard the faint thud of a starting-pistol, and six brown bodies flung themselves into the water and began thrashing in a white flurry of spray across the marked course. The crowd began to cheer.

"It must be the end of the swimming gala," Jane said eagerly, caught up in the carnival atmosphere below them. "Let's go and watch for a minute."

"For heaven's sake," Simon said in despair. "We're on a mission. We've got to find Great-Uncle Merry before we do anything else."

But there was no answer to the doorbell of the Grey House, as they stood on the doorstep with knots of shirtsleeved visitors chattering past them up and down the hill. And when Simon had gone round to the back and retrieved the front-door key from its secret place in the toolshed, they went inside to find the house quite deserted.

Great-Uncle Merry's bed was neatly made, but there was no sign, in his bedroom or anywhere else, to tell them where he had gone. Mrs. Palk was nowhere to be found. There were three plates of cold mackerel and salad covered up on the kitchen table, left for their lunch. But that was all. The house was spotless, silent and neat—and empty.

"Where can he have gone? And where's Mrs. Palk?"

"Well, that's easy enough. She'll be outside watching the swimming with everyone else. You know how she was drooling about carnival day."

"Let's go and find her. She must know where he is."

"Tell you what," Barney said. "You two go down to the harbour and I'll run up to the top of the hill and see if Gumerry has gone up there after all. I'd be able to see him if he's climbing the headland, it takes quite a time to get to the top."

Simon thought for a moment. "All right, that seems sensible enough. But for goodness' sake keep out of sight of the yacht if you see it coming back. And come down to us as quick as you can, we don't want to get separated. We'll be down there on the quay where the start of the swimming is."

"Righto." Barney made off, but then turned back. "I say, what are you going to do with the manuscript? If we don't find Gumerry and we're all on our own, d'you think it's safe to go on carrying it about?"

"A lot safer than I'd feel if we left it anywhere," Simon said grimly, looking down at the case in his hand. "I'm going to hang on to it whatever happens."

"Oh well," Barney said cheerfully. "Don't drop it in the harbour, that's all. Cheerio. Shan't be long."

"I'm glad he's so bright about it all," Jane said, as the front door slammed. "I wish I were. It's as if there's someone waiting behind every corner to pounce on us. I only feel safe when I'm in bed."

"Cheer up," said Simon. "You're still suffering from last night. I was scared then too, but I'm not now. Try and forget about it."

"That's all very well," said poor Jane miserably, "but everyone seems to be turning out to be bad now, and it isn't even as if we knew what sort of badness it is. Why do they all want the manuscript so much?"

"Well"—Simon wrinkled his forehead, trying to remember what Great-Uncle Merry had said on the first day—"it's the grail they want, isn't it? Because it stands for something, somehow. And that's why Gumerry wants to find it as well. It's like two armies fighting in history. You're never quite sure what they're actually fighting about, but only that one wants to beat the other."

127

"Great-Uncle Merry's like an army sometimes, all in one person. Those times when he goes all peculiar and distant and you feel he's not quite there."

"Well, there you are, then. It's the same with the others. They're a kind of bad army. Up on the standing stones last night, even before we knew they were there, you could still feel the badness."

"I know," Jane said fervently. "Oh dear. I should feel much better if we knew where Great-Uncle Merry was."

"We shall know as soon as we find Mrs. Palk. Buck up, Jane." Simon patted her awkwardly on the shoulder. "Come on, let's go down to the harbour. Barney'll get there before us at this rate."

Jane nodded, feeling a little better. "Oh—Mother and Father will be coming back this afternoon. D'you think we ought to leave a note?"

"No, we'll be back long before them."

* * *

They went out of the Grey House, leaving it to its silence, and walked down the hill to the harbour. Unfamiliar children were running all over the place, ignoring their anxious calling parents; and the sleepy little shop which sold ice-cream down on the quay was festooned with flags and posters and doing a roaring trade.

Simon and Jane threaded their way along the side of the harbour, through the wandering crowds, to the course marked out for the swimming gala. But they felt as if they were paddling against a current; all the crowds were moving towards them, and when they reached the right place they found everything was over. Only a few boys and girls dodging wet through the crowds in swim-suits, and the bobbing lines of floats on the empty water, showed that there had been a swimming gala at all.

One of the swimmers brushed past Simon, and as he glanced up at the wet brown body he recognized the face below the dark water-flattened hair. It was Bill.

The boy's mouth opened and he paused belligerently; but then in an instant, changing his mind, he scowled and disappeared, running barefoot through the crowds towards the front quay.

"Hey, Jane! Jane!" Simon called urgently. She was a few paces ahead of him, and had not noticed Bill.

A deep voice said in Simon's ear, "Your young friend lost un's race. He'm not in a very good temper. They 'Oovers be all the same."

128

Simon looked round, and saw the beaming wrinkled brown face of the old fisherman they had met on the day they first encountered the boy Bill.

"Hallo, Mr. Penhallow," he said, reflecting how odd the greeting sounded. "Was he in the swimming gala, then?"

"Aye, that he were, the race for the championship. Be'aved 'isself badly as usual too, lost by a few yards and turned 'n's back on the winner when the lad went to thank'n for a good race." He chuckled. "The winner were my youngest."

"Your son?" said Jane, who had turned back at Simon's call.

She looked at Mr. Penhallow's weather-beaten face; he looked much too old to have a son young enough for a swimming race.

" 'A's right," said the fisherman equably. "Tough little lad. He'm sixteen now, on leave from the Merchant Navy."

"I say," said Simon, impressed. "Could I join the Merchant Navy when I'm sixteen, d'you think?"

"You wait awhile," said Mr. Penhallow, twinkling at him. " 'Tis a hard life at sea."

"Barney says he wants to be a fisherman like you now," Jane said. "With a boat like the *White Heather*."

Mr. Penhallow laughed. "That's an idea won't last long neither. I'd take 'n out with us one night if he were a bit bigger, then he'd soon change his tune."

"Are you going out tonight?"

"No. Havin' a rest."

Jane, suddenly feeling one of her shoes damp, looked down and found she was standing in a pool of water. She moved hurriedly. "Those swimmers must have splashed about a lot. There's puddles all along the quay."

"Not just the swimming, my love," Mr. Penhallow said. " 'Tis the tide. It came right over there this morning—spring tides be higher than usual this month."

"Oh yes," said Simon. "Look—there are bits of seaweed right at the back of the path. It must have washed right up to the wall. Does it often come as high as that?"

"Not often. Once or twice a year, usually—March and September. 'Tis strange to have such big tides in August. I reckon 'tis because of these strong winds we been havin'."

"How low will it go down?" Jane said, fascinated.

"Oh, a long way. Th 'arbour don't look pretty at any low tide, but

129

it do look worse at the biggest springs. Lot of stinkin' old mud and weed that 'ee don't normally see. You wait till about five o'clock today. Still, I dare say you'll be watching the carnival like everyone else then."

"I expect so," Simon said vaguely. He was thinking furiously; it was as if the fisherman's words had touched a spring in his brain. "Mr. Penhallow," he said, carefully casual, "I suppose when you get a really low tide like that there's a lot more rocks than usual uncovered outside the harbour?"

"Oh, a good old lot," the fisherman said. "They do say 'tis possible to walk all the way round from Trewissick harbour to the Dodman, that's two-three bays beyond Kemare Head. But that be nothing more'n a tale—I dessay the rocks be uncovered, but the tide'd be coming up again before you was half-way there."

Jane was only half listening. "Mr. Penhallow, we were looking for Mrs. Palk, she's the lady who keeps house for us. Do you know her?"

"Know Molly Palk?" said Mr. Penhallow, chuckling. "I should say I do. Nice lass, she used to be—still is, but she turned a bit miserly when old Jim Palk died. Costing your mum and dad a pretty penny, I'll be bound. Do anything for a few extra pound, would old Moll. Now I come to think of it, course, she'm your young friend Bill's auntie, too."

"Mrs. Palk is?" Jane said, amazed. "That awful boy?"

"Ah," Mr. Penhallow said, placidly. "The two sides of the family don't have much to do with each other, mind. Most of Trewissick forgets they'm even related. Don't suppose Moll likes people to know."

"I think Great-Uncle Merry told me once," Simon said. "I'd clean forgotten. He said Bill was Mrs. Palk's no-good brother's son."

Jane said thoughtfully: "I wonder whether. . . . Oh well, it doesn't matter now. Have you seen her anywhere about?"

"Let me see, now, I did pass the time of day with her. Oh ah, up on the front quay. She were all dressed up for the carnival, some funny affair on her head, helping with the procession, most like. I reckon you'll still find her up by there, unless she've popped in to have her dinner."

The crowds had thinned round them now, milling about instead on the front quay, with here and there groups of bandsmen in bright blue uniforms, clutching large curly silver instruments and wearing ill-fitting blue peaked caps. Simon and Jane peered across the harbour, but they were too far away to be able to distinguish faces.

"Well, I must be off to find my young Walter. Real cock-a-hoop he'll be. Remember me to our liddle fisherman, midears." Mr. Penhallow toddled off along the quay, grinning to himself. Jane, who had been wondering what it was about him that seemed different, realized for the first time that instead of the blue jersey and long thigh-boots, he was in a stiff black suit, and shoes that squeaked.

"I don't think he should have talked like that about Mrs. Palk," she said, troubled.

"You don't know, it might be important," Simon said. "Anyway, what are we going to do now? We've got to find Mrs. Palk to know where Great-Uncle Merry's gone. But Mr. Penhallow says he saw her on the other side of the harbour, and we told Barney we'd meet him here."

"I wonder where Barney is? He's surely had time to get up to the top of the road and back by now. Look, you go and see if Mrs. Palk is over there, and I'll wait here till he comes."

Simon rubbed his ear. "I don't know, I don't like all this splitting up. We haven't got Great-Uncle Merry, we haven't got Barney for the moment, and if you and I split up, nobody will have anybody else at all. Any one of us could get nobbled and the others not know. I think we ought to keep together."

"Well, all right," Jane said. "We'll wait a bit longer. Let's go back to the corner of the front quay and we can cut him off. That's the only way down here, he'll have to pass it."

As they walked back they saw the Trewissick band forming up across the harbour, with the crowd bobbing and weaving round them and children darting excitedly to and fro on the edge. One or two strange figures stood out among the white shirts and summer dresses; tall, fantastically coloured, decked with ribbons and leaves, with monstrous false heads set on their shoulders.

"They must be part of the carnival procession."

"I think it's starting. Listen, what a horrible noise."

The band had begun a wavering brassy tune that resolved itself gradually into a recognisable march.

"Oh come on, it's not that bad," Jane said. "I expect they're more used to fishing then playing trumpets. Anyway, it's very cheerful-sounding. I like it."

"Hmmf. Let's sit on the wall here at the corner, we can catch Barney when he passes." Simon crossed into the road and looked up the hill. "I can't see any sign of him. But there's so many people about it's difficult to see properly."

"Oh well." Jane hoisted herself up on to the wall, wincing as the rough slate rubbed the skin behind her knees. "We'll just wait. Hey listen, the music's getting louder."

"Music!" said Simon.

"Well, it is. . . . Oh look, the procession's started! And they're coming this way!"

"I thought Mrs. Palk said they would go straight up the hill."

"Perhaps they go up from this corner of the harbour instead of the other. Or perhaps they go all round the village first . . . look, they're all dressed up. And they're playing that thing Mrs. Palk was singing this morning, the 'Floral Dance.'"

"We've got a good view, anyway." Simon hopped up to sit on the wall beside her.

Slowly the crowd drew near them along the front quay, children running and jumping about in front of the red-faced puffing band. Behind them, edged by delighted pushing throngs of visitors, came a dancing file of the fantastic figures they had seen from across the harbour, the monstrous heads lurching and hopping in a slow parody of dance, and others, masked and disguised, weaving in and out of the crowds. Here and there they swooped on the bystanders, taking pretty girls by the hand, pretending to strike squealing old ladies with a ribboned wand, guiding the visitors and villagers to join hands and dance with them in rows across the width of the street. "Pom . . . pom . . . di-pom-pom-pom . . ." the music boomed in the children's ears where they sat on the wall, and the crowds eddied all round them on the corner, overflowing up the hill as well as down.

Jane, beaming round her in delight at the tops of the giant grinning heads, suddenly stared across the crowd. She pointed, and shouted something in Simon's ear.

Simon could hear nothing but the music, thrumming round him till the wall seemed to shake. "What?" he shouted back.

Jane ducked her head close to his ear. "There's Mrs. Palk! Look! Just over there, with feathers on her head, behind the man covered in leaves. Quickly, let's catch her!" And before Simon could stop her she had slipped down from the wall and was on the edge of the crowd.

Simon jumped down after her and caught at her arm just as she was about to push her way across the crowd between two dancing, laughing files. "Not now, Jane!" But he too was swept along for several yards by the dancing crowd before he could draw her back into a clear space. They stood pinned against the far wall of the road, away from the harbour, hemmed in by others standing watching the carnival procession dance by.

And that was why they did not see Barney, who had been threading his way down the hill-road past the Grey House, dodge between people's legs to slip round the corner of the wall, ignoring the procession; and run as fast as he could along the inner quay to the place where they had agreed to meet.

• *Chapter Twelve* •

It took Barney a long time to make his way down the hill past the house. There had been no sign of Great-Uncle Merry on the headland. On the road, knots of wandering people were scattered maddeningly about in his path, and three times he had to stand aside as a car came grinding up the steep narrow slope. Barney dodged impatiently to and fro, in and out, with Rufus at his heels.

Half-way down the hill he heard music from the other side of the harbour, and through the heads he caught sight of the dancing procession moving forward along the quay. Slipping his finger inside Rufus's collar, he side-stepped through the thickening crowd and down the hill as fast he could, darting through every visible gap like a shrimp in a pool.

But when he reached the corner of the harbour the procession was upon him, and he could see nothing at all but an impenetrable wall of legs and backs. He wriggled through behind them, the din of the music thumping in his ears, until he was out of the crowd at last and on the quay. With a sigh of relief he let go of Rufus's collar, and ran with him towards the deserted corner where he had arranged to meet Simon and Jane.

There was nobody there.

Barney looked round wildly. He could see nothing to give him the slightest hint of where the others had gone. Reasoning with himself, he decided they must have caught sight of Mrs. Palk. She had been very keen on the idea of the carnival and the dancing; she must be in the procession. And it had been Simon's and Jane's job to go and find her, as it had been his to go and scout on the headland. They must have gone chasing her, knowing that he would guess where they had gone.

Satisfied, Barney went off to find the carnival. He followed the last of the crowd still drifting up the road. Even down in the sheltered harbour the wind was blowing in from the sea, but now and again it dropped for a moment, and Barney heard a tantalizing snatch of music come wafting over the roofs from somewhere in the village. "Pom . . . pom . . . di-pom-pom-pom. . . ." All round him people were wandering aimlessly about, idly talking . . . "Where've they gone?" . . . "We can meet them at the ground" . . . "But they dance through the streets for ages yet" . . . "Oh, come *on*."

Disregarding them, Barney set off down a little side turning, with Rufus still loping patiently at his heels. He wandered from one winding lane into another, down narrow passages where the slate roofs almost touched overhead, past neat front doors with their brass knockers gleaming golden in the sun, through the cobbled alleys where front doors opened not on to a pavement but straight on to the street. For a small place, Trewissick seemed to be an extraordinary endless maze of winding little roads. Straining his ears all the time, Barney followed the sound of the music through the maze.

He made one or two false turns, losing the sound. Then gradually the band grew louder, and with it he began to hear the hum of voices and the rasping shuffle of feet. He snapped his fingers to Rufus, and broke into a trot, swinging from one quiet deserted little alley into the next. And then suddenly the noise burst on him like a storm, and he was out of the muffling narrow street and among the crowds, out in the sunshine filling a broad road where the procession jogged and danced by. "Come on, my white-headed boy," someone called to him, and the people nearby turned and laughed.

Barney could not see Simon and Jane amongst the dancers, and there seemed little chance of being able to get to them even if he did. He gazed fascinated round him at the bobbing giant heads, the bodies beneath them fantastic and gay in doublets and red, yellow, blue hose. Everywhere he saw costumed figures: a man dancing stiff as a tree, a solid flapping mass of green leaves; pirates, sailors, a hussar in bright red with a tall cap. Slave-girls, jesters, a man in a long blue silk gown made up as a pantomime dame; a girl all in black, twirling sinuous as a cat, with a cat's bewhiskered head. Little boys in green as Robin Hood, little girls with long fair hair as Alice; highwaymen, morris-men, flower-sellers, gnomes.

135

It was like nothing he had ever seen before. The dancers whirled in and out of the crowd on the edge of the street where he stood; and then suddenly, before Barney knew what was happening, they were dancing round him.

He felt someone catch at his hand, and he was drawn out into the centre of the dancing crowd, among the ribbons and feathers and bright bobbing heads, so that his feet fell into step with the rest.

Breathless, grinning, he glanced up. The black-gloved hand holding one of his own belonged to the figure of the cat, twirling in the skin-close black tights with a long black tail swinging out behind, and whiskers bristling long and straight from the head-mask fitting over the cheeks. He saw the eyes glint through the slits, and the teeth flash. For a moment, among the dancing figures all round, he saw close to him one in a great feathered Red Indian head-dress, with a face startlingly like Mrs. Palk's. But as he opened his mouth to call, the black cat seized both his hands and wheeled him round and round in a dizzy spiral through the ranks of the crowd. People glanced down at him and smiled as he passed, and Barney, giddy with the music and the speed and the twisting black limbs of the cat before his eyes, flung himself laughing round where it swung him. . . .

. . . Until he came up with a sudden halt against the long white robes of a figure dressed as an Arab sheikh, moving with the rest so that the robes were swung wide and billowing by the breeze. And glancing up through a world swaying with his own giddiness, Barney had time only to glimpse a slim figure and a dark-skinned lean face, before the cat swung him by the hands straight into the out-swung muffling folds of the man's white robes.

The robe twisted round him as he staggered, still laughing, in the sudden gloom. And then, so quickly that he had no time even to feel alarmed, the man's arm came round him like an iron band and lifted him from the ground, and the other hand muffled his mouth in the folds of the cloth, and Barney felt himself being carried away.

Before he could struggle, he was swung in a scuffling moment through the roaring music and the crowd. Pushing ineffectually against the man's chest, he felt him run a few steps and heard the noise of the voices and the band suddenly grow fainter. He kicked out blindly and felt his toes hit the man's shins. But he was only wearing sandals, and could do no great harm: the man gave a muffled curse but did not pause, jolting him along for a few more steps until Barney felt himself swung higher into the air and dropped on to a padded seat that protested with the noise of springs.

The robe fell loose from his mouth. He yelled, and went on yelling until a hand came back and pressed hard against his face.

A girl's voice said urgently: "Quickly! Get him away!"

A voice almost as light as a girl's, but masculine, said curtly: "Get in. You'll have to drive."

Barney suddenly lay quite still, all his senses alerted. There was something familiar about the second voice. He felt a coldness at the back of his neck. Then the pressure of the hand over his mouth relaxed a little through the cotton folds, and the voice said softly, close to his ear, "Don't make a noise, Barnabas, and don't move, and nobody will be hurt."

And suddenly Barney knew the black-masked figure of the cat, and the dark man in sheikh's robes. He felt the seat shudder slightly as the noise of a powerful car's engine coughed and then rose in a throbbing howl. Then the note deepened, and he felt a lurch, and knew that he was being driven away.

* * *

Rufus jumped nervously back from the shuffling, dancing feet that had enclosed Barney in the crowd. Tentatively he put his nose forward to follow, once, twice, but always a heel came up in the way with an accidental kick, and he had to dodge away.

From a safer distance, he barked, loudly. But the sound was lost at once in the booming music and the clamour of the crowd. Alarmed by the shattering noise and bustle suddenly filling his small world, he put his ears back flat against the side of his head: his tail was down between his legs, and he showed the whites of his eyes.

He retreated further from the noise, waiting hopefully on the corner of the street for Barney to reappear. But there was no sign of him. Rufus moved uneasily.

Then as the band drew directly opposite, blowing and banging only a few yards away, rocking every corner with the rise and fall of music that to a dog's ears was a menacing roaring noise, Rufus could suddenly stand it no longer.

He gave up all hope of Barney, and turning his back on the clamour of the carnival, he padded away down the alley with the tip of his tail sweeping the ground and his nose lowered, sniffing his way home.

137

* * *

Simon and Jane rejoined one another at the corner of the harbour, quiet again now in the sunny afternoon.

"Well, I've been back to where we said. He isn't there."

"I had a good look in the house. He hasn't been there either."

"D'you think he could have gone off after Mrs. Palk?"

"I keep telling you, it couldn't have been Mrs. Palk you saw."

"I don't see why not. If only you hadn't stopped me I could have grabbed her."

"How could we meet Barney here if you—" Simon began.

"Oh all right, all right. But we haven't met him."

"Well then, he can't have come down from the headland yet."

Jane's expression changed. "Oh dear. Perhaps he's got into trouble up there."

"No, no, don't worry when we don't need to. More likely he's found Great-Uncle Merry after all and they're both up there still."

"Well, come on then, let's go and look."

* * *

The car swayed and growled as if it were alive. Barney lay wrapped up like a parcel in the robe which Mr. Withers had slipped from his own shoulders as he dropped him in the car. He decided that it must be a sheet; the smell of it under his nose was like clean laundry on the beds at home. But he wasn't at home. He muttered peevishly under his breath, and kicked at the side of the car.

"Now, now," said Mr. Withers. He took hold of Barney's legs and swung him none too gently round into a sitting position, at the same time pulling the sheet clear of his face. "I think perhaps we might let you emerge now, Barnabas."

Barney blinked, dazzled by the sudden sunlight. Before he could open his eyes properly to look at the road the car swung squealing through a gap in a high wall, and slowed down, its wheels crunching on gravel, along a tree-lined drive.

"Nearly there," Mr. Withers said placidly.

Barney twisted his head to glare up at him. He could still barely recognise Mr. Withers' face through the dark-brown stain that turned him into an Arab; the eyes and teeth glinted unnaturally white, and behind the make-up the man seemed withdrawn and pleased with himself, almost arrogant.

"Where are we? Where are you taking me?"

"Don't you know? Ah no"—the dark head nodded wisely—"of

course, you would not. Well, you will know soon, Barnabas."

"What do you want?" Barney demanded.

"Want? Nothing, my dear boy. We're just taking you for a little ride, to meet a friend of ours. I think you'll get on very well together."

Barney saw, through the trees, that they were coming to a house. He looked down at the sheet still twined round him, and wriggled to move his arms free. Mr. Withers turned quickly.

"Take this stupid thing off me. I feel silly."

"Just a little joke of ours," Mr. Withers said. "Where's your sense of humour, Barnabas? I thought you were enjoying yourself."

He leaned over and began pulling the sheet free as the car drew up outside the peeling front door of a big, deserted looking house. "You'll have to hop out, if you can. I can't loosen it properly in here." He spoke casually, easily, with no trace of menace in his voice, and as Barney glanced up at him suspiciously the white teeth shone briefly again in a smile.

The girl slipped out of the driving seat, moving like a snake in her black tights, and came round to open the door at Barney's side. She helped him out, and spun him round to pull the sheet away. Barney staggered, his arms and legs so stiff with cramp that he could hardly move.

Polly Withers laughed. Her head was still a fantastic sight in the close-fitting black cat's mask, covering all her face but the eyes and mouth. "I'm sorry, Barney," she said companionably. "We did overdo it a bit, didn't we? You danced jolly well, I thought. I was almost sorry to stop. Still, never mind, now we'll go and have some tea, if it isn't too early for you."

"I haven't had any lunch," Barney said irrelevantly, suddenly remembering.

"Well, in that case we must certainly get you something to eat. Good gracious, no lunch? And it's all our fault, I expect. Norman, ring the bell, we must feed the poor boy."

Mr. Withers, making a concerned clicking noise with his tongue, crossed from the car and pressed the bell next to the big door. He was all in white still, but in shirt-sleeves and white flannels without his Arab robe. His bare arms were stained the same dark brown as his face.

Barney, following him slowly with the girl's hand resting lightly on his shoulder, was puzzled by their friendliness. He began to

139

wonder whether he had been seeing everything in the wrong light. Perhaps this was after all only a joke, part of the fun of carnival day. Perhaps the Witherses were perfectly ordinary people after all. . . . They had never actually done anything to prove beyond doubt that they were the enemy . . . perhaps he and Simon and Jane had got things all wrong. . . .

Then he heard footsteps echoing faintly within the house, clumping gradually nearer, and the door was opened. At first he did not recognize the figure in tight black jeans and a green shirt. Then he saw that it was the boy Bill Hoover, who had chased Simon for the map. And in a moment he remembered the scene on Kemare Head that day, and the greed on Miss Withers' face when she had looked at the map, and he knew that they had not been wrong after all.

Bill's face lit up out of its down-turned sullenness as he saw Barney, and he grinned across at Miss Withers.

"You got'n, then?" he said.

Mr. Withers cut in quickly, stepping forward and almost pushing the boy out of the way. "Hallo, Bill," he said smoothly, "we've brought a young friend of ours on a visit. I don't think anyone will mind. We could all do with something to eat, run and see if you can manage to rustle anything up, will you?"

"Mind?" the boy said. "I should say not." He looked at Barney again with the same eager, unpleasant grin, then turned and disappeared down the long corridor, calling something into an open doorway as he passed.

"Come along in, Barney," the girl said. She propelled him gently through the door and shut it behind her. Barney looked round him in the long empty passage, at the marks of damp on the fading wallpaper; and he felt very small and lonely. He heard a deep voice call from somewhere inside the house: "Withers? Is that you?"

Mr. Withers, who had been standing surveying Barney with a slight smile, jumped and put his hand half-consciously up to his collar. "Come," he said curtly. He took Barney by the hand and led him down the corridor, their footsteps echoing on the uncarpeted wooden floor, to the doorway of a room at the far end.

It was a big room, dark after the blazing sunlight outside. Long windows stretched from floor to ceiling in one wall, with long shabby velvet curtains half pulled across, and the light that shafted in between them fell on a big, square desk in the centre of the room, its top littered with papers and books. The room seemed empty.

Then Barney jumped as he saw a tall man move in the shadow beyond the sunlight.

"Ah," said the deep voice, "I see you have brought the youngest of them. The white-haired child. I am most interested to make his acquaintance. How do you do, Barnabas?"

He held out his hand, and Barney, bemused, took it. The voice was not unpleasant, and rather kind.

"How do you do?" he said faintly.

He looked up at the tall man, but in the half-light he had only a vague impression of deep-shadowed eyes under dark, heavy brows,and a clean-shaven face. The smooth edge of a silk jacket brushed his hand.

"I was about to have a cool drink, Barnabas," the man said, as courteously as if he were talking to someone older than himself. "Will you join me?" He waved his hand towards the shadows, and Barney saw the glint of silver and a white cloth on a low table beside the desk.

"The boy has had nothing to eat, sir," Miss Withers said behind Barney, in a peculiarly hushed, reverent voice. "We thought perhaps Bill could fetch something. . . ." Her voice died away. The man looked at her, and grunted.

"Very well, very well. Polly, for goodness' sake go and change into some normal clothes. You look ridiculous. The necessity for fancy dress is over, you are not at the carnival now." He spoke sharply, and Barney was astonished at the meekness with which Miss Withers answered him.

"Yes, sir, of course. . . ." She slipped away into the passage, sleek and inhuman in the black cat's skin.

"Come in, my boy, and sit down." He spoke softly again, and Barney came slowly forward into the room and sat down in an arm-chair. It creaked with the crackling rustle of wicker-work, and he suddenly felt for an instant that he had been in the room before. He glanced round, his eyes growing accustomed to the dim light, at the dark walls and the shelves of books rising to the ceiling. There was something . . . but he could not place it. Perhaps it was just that the room reminded him a little of the Grey House.

As if he read his thoughts, the man said: "I hear you are on holiday in the Grey House, above the harbour."

Barney said, surprised at his own daring, "It must be a very interesting house. That seems to be the only thing anyone ever says to us."

The man leant forward, resting his hand on the edge of the desk. "Oh?" The deep voice rose a little with eagerness. "Who else has asked you about it?"

"Oh, no one important," Barney said hastily. "After all, it's a nice house. Do you live here, Mr.—?"

"My name is Hastings," the big man said, and at the sound of the name Barney again felt the flicker of familiarity, vanishing as soon as it came. "Yes, I do. This is my house. Do you like it, Barnabas?"

"It's rather like the Grey House, as a matter of fact," Barney said.

The man turned back towards him again. "Indeed? Now what makes you say that?"

"Well—" Barney began; but then the door opened again and the boy Bill came in carrying an enormous tray with a big jug of milk and some bottles of lager, glasses, and a plate piled with sandwiches. He crossed the room to where the tall man stood and put the tray down on the desk; nervously, just within reach, as if he were frightened to come too near. "Mis' Withers said for someth'n to eat, sir," he said, gruffly, already backing towards the door. The man waved him away without speaking.

The sight of the sandwiches made Barney realize how long it was since breakfast, and he felt more cheerful. He sat back in the creaking chair and glanced round him. It could have been worse, he thought. The mysterious Mr. Hastings seemed to mean him no harm, and he was beginning to enjoy the sight of all their enemies cringing in terror before someone else. He took a sandwich from the plate held out to him and bit into it cheerfully. The bread was soft and new, with plenty of butter, and in the middle there was some delicious kind of potted meat. He began to feel better still.

Mr. Withers moved silently across to the desk and poured him out a glass of milk, then began opening the bottles of lager. The big man called Hastings sat down in the chair behind the desk and swung gently from side to side, regarding Barney thoughtfully from beneath his heavy brows. He said softly, conversationally, "Is it buried under the Grey House, Barnabas, or one of the standing stones?"

Half-way through a gulp of milk, Barney suddenly choked. He groped for the desk and put his glass down with a bang, and leaned forward, coughing and spluttering. Mr. Withers, soft-footed, crossed to pat him on the back. "Dear me, Barnabas," he murmured, "has something gone down the wrong way?"

Barney, his mind working furiously, went on coughing for rather longer than he needed to. When he looked up he took refuge instinctively in innocence. "I'm sorry, I caught my breath," he said. "Did you say something?"

"I think you heard perfectly well what I said," Mr. Hastings said. He stood up again, towering very tall over Barney in the low chair, and walked over to the window with a glass of lager in his hand. The light fell on his face for the first time, and watching, Barney felt a slight chill of uneasiness at the flat permanent scowl of the brows and the grim lines running down to the mouth. It was a strong, far-away face, something like his great-uncle's, but with a frightening coldness behind it that was not like Great-Uncle Merry at all. Barney found himself wishing very much that there was somebody to tell Great-Uncle Merry where he had gone.

Mr. Hastings held up his glass to the window. The sunlight shone through it clear and golden. "An ordinary glass of beer," he said, abstractedly, "until you hold it against the light. And then it becomes quite transparent, you can see right through it. . . ." He swung round on Barney so that he was silhouetted dark and menacing against the window again. ". . . As transparent as every single thing that you children have been doing, these past days. Do you think we have not seen through it all? Do you think we have not been watching?"

"I don't know what you mean," Barney said.

"You may be a stupid little boy," Mr. Hastings said, "but not, I think, as stupid as all that . . . come along. We know that you have found a map, and that with the help of your esteemed great-uncle, Professor Lyon"—his mouth twisted on the words as if he were tasting something unpleasant—"you have been attempting to trace the place to which it leads. We know that you have come very near the end of that track. And since, my dear Barnabas, we cannot afford to risk your reaching the end of it, we have decided at last to draw in the net and put a stop to your little quest. That is what you are doing here."

Barney shivered at the menace in the cold deep voice. His mouth felt very dry. He reached forward and picked up the glass of milk again, and took a long drink. "I'm sorry," he said, blinking wide-eyed at Mr. Hastings over the rim of the glass and licking a moustache of milk away from his upper lip. "I don't know what you mean. Could I have another sandwich, please?"

Behind him, he heard Mr. Withers' sharp shocked intake of breath, and for a second a very small voice deep inside his brain crowed with triumph. But he watched the tall figure by the window apprehensively. It seemed to grow for a moment and loom still more menacingly over him. And then it moved abruptly, back into the dim shadow of the rest of the room.

"Give him another sandwich," Mr. Hastings said. "And then you can go, Withers. You know what you have to do. We haven't much time. Come back when I ring."

Mr. Withers, his dark-stained face scarcely visible in the gloom, pushed the plate of sandwiches across to Barney's elbow. He said obsequiously, "Yes, sir," and ducking his head in a bow he went out of the room.

Barney took another sandwich, feeling fatalistically that whatever was likely to happen, he might as well eat. "Why do they all call you 'sir'?" he said curiously.

The tall man came and sat down at the desk again, playing with a pencil between his fingers. "Who is there that you would call 'sir'?"

"Well, nobody really. Only the masters at school."

"Perhaps I am one of their masters," Mr. Hastings said.

"But they aren't at school."

"I think you would not really understand, Barnabas. In fact there are a great many things that you do not understand. I wonder what stories that great-uncle of yours has put into your head. He has told you that we are bad and wicked, no doubt, and that he is a good man?"

Barney blinked at him, and took another bite of his sandwich.

Mr. Hastings smiled grimly. "Ah, but of course you do not know what I am talking about. You haven't the slightest idea." The heavy irony in the deep voice made Barney wrinkle his nose. "Well, let us forget that, just for a moment, and pretend, just pretend, that you do know what I mean. You have been led to believe, I think, that my friends and I are everything that is evil. That we want to follow up the clues in the map because we can do bad things with what we find. You have nothing to go on but your great-uncle's word, and perhaps one or two strange things that Polly or Norman Withers may seem to have done."

The voice dropped until it was silky and very gentle. "But just think, Barnabas, of the strange things your great-uncle does.

144

Coming out of nowhere and vanishing again . . . he has vanished again today, has he not? Well no, of course, you can't answer me, because we are only pretending that you know what I am talking about. But this is not the first time he has unexpectedly disappeared, I think, and it will not be the last."

He stared at Barney, dark eyes penetrating and level from beneath the overhanging brow. Barney ate his sandwich a little more slowly, unable to take his own gaze away. "As for our being evil . . . well, now, Barnabas, do I strike you as being a bad man? Have I done you any harm? There you sit, eating and drinking quite happily, certainly not looking alarmed. Are you frightened of me?"

"You had me kidnapped," Barney said flatly.

"Oh come now, that was just a little joke of Polly's. I wanted to talk to you, that's all."

Mr. Hastings sat back in his chair and spread his arms wide, with the tips of his fingers just touching the edge of the desk. "Now look, my boy. I will make a bargain with you. I will tell you what is actually behind everything that has been going on these last days, and you will stop playing this game of not having seen the map."

He did not wait for Barney to say anything. "We are indeed hunting the same thing that your great-uncle is hunting, my friends and I. But whatever story he has spun you about us is, quite frankly, a lot of moonshine. Your great-uncle is a scholar, and an outstanding one. Nobody would dispute that, and I probably know it better than you. The trouble is that he himself knows it, and thinks about it much too much."

"What d'you mean?" said Barney indignantly.

"When a man is famous for being a very great scholar he wants very much to go on being famous. You found this old manuscript, you and your brother and sister, and when you told your great-uncle about it he realised, as you did not, how important it was. When he saw it he was even more certain. Now I, Barnabas, am the curator, that means the director, of one of the most important museums in the world. I have been hunting the manuscript that you found, and especially what it leads to, for a very long time. They are both very important to the people who study such things, and could make a lot of difference to the total of knowledge there is in the world. And your great-uncle knew that I was hunting them.

"But when you found the manuscript he saw that he had a chance of achieving the quest himself. The more he thought about this, the

145

more attractive an idea it seemed. He has always been famous as a man who knows a great deal about the part of history these things are connected with. If he were to find them, he would know more than anyone else in the world. People would say, what an amazing man Professor Lyon is, to know so much, there's no one like him anywhere. . . ."

"To know *how* much?" Barney said.

"You would not understand the details," Mr. Hastings said shortly. Then his voice dropped again to the same deep persuasive note. "Don't you see, Barnabas? Your great-uncle is concerned only with his own fame. Do you think for one moment that when you have ended the hunt, any of the credit will go to you children? It will all go to him. . . . Whereas I and my museum, and the people I employ, believe that all knowledge should be shared, and that no one man has the right to it alone. And if you were to help us, we should take care that you had whatever credit was due to you. The whole world should know what you had done."

In spite of himself Barney had forgotten his sandwich and milk. He sat listening, troubled; trying to understand the truth for himself. Yes, Great-Uncle Merry was strange, often, not like other men; but all the same. . . .

He said, slow and perplexed, "Well, I don't know—all this just doesn't sound like Great-Uncle Merry. Surely he couldn't do anything like that?"

"But I assure you—" Mr. Hastings jumped to his feet and began walking to and fro between the desk and the door. He seemed unable to keep still any longer. "Many people one knows well, often most excellent people, can prove capable of the most curious acts. I do realise that you may be surprised, and shocked. But this is the truth, Barnabas, and it is very much more simple than you have been led to believe."

Barney said: "So we ought to give the map to you, and let you find the—" Just in time he caught back the word "grail." Through the whole conversation there had been no mention of what the map led to. Perhaps they knew less than they said they did. Perhaps that was one of the things they wanted to trap him into telling them.

Mr. Hastings paused for a second. "Yes?" he said.

"Well, and let you find whatever it leads to."

Barney picked up the glass of milk again and drank reflectively.

"Because then you would put whatever it is in your museum and everyone would be able to know about it."

Mr. Hastings nodded gravely. "There you have it, Barnabas. All knowledge is sacred, but it should not be secret. I think you understand. This is something you should do—that *we* should do—in the name of scholarship."

Barney looked down into his milk, swishing it gently round the glass. "But isn't that what Great-Uncle Merry's doing?"

"No, no!" Mr. Hastings swung impatiently on his heel, striding impatient and very tall up and down the room. "Whatever he does he is doing in the name of Professor Lyon, and that is all. What else would he do anything for?"

Barney never knew afterwards what put the words into his head; he spoke before he thought, almost as if someone else were speaking through him. He heard himself saying clearly, "In the name of King Arthur, and of the old world before the dark came."

The tall dark figure stopped abruptly, completely still, with its back still turned. For a moment there was absolute silence in the room. It was as if Barney had pressed a switch that would any moment bring an avalanche thundering down. He sat motionless and almost breathless in his chair. Then very slowly the figure turned. Barney gulped, and felt a prickling at the roots of his hair. Mr. Hastings was at the darker end of the room, near the door, and his face was hidden in shadow. But he seemed to loom taller and more threatening than he had ever done before, and when he spoke there was a different throb in the deep voice that paralysed Barney with fright.

"You will find, Barnabas Drew," it said softly, "that the dark will always come, and always win."

Barney said nothing. He felt as if he had forgotten how to speak, and his voice had died for ever with his last words.

Mr. Hastings did not take his eyes off him. He reached out beside him and tugged twice at a cord hanging down from the ceiling beside the door. Within seconds the door swung open and Mr. Withers slipped noiselessly inside. He had washed the dark brown stain from his arms and face.

"Is everything ready?" said the deep voice.

"Yes, sir," Mr. Withers hissed obsequiously. "The car is at the side door. The girl has changed. She will drive again."

"You will drive with her. I shall follow in the closed car with the boy. Bill has it ready?"

147

"The engine is running already. . . ."

"Where are you taking me?" Barney's voice rose shrill in fright, and he jumped down from his chair. But he could not run out of the room, past the tall figure that still held his gaze.

"You are coming with us to the sea," said the voice behind the dark intent eyes. "You will cause no trouble, and you will do whatever I say. And when we are on the sea, Barnabas, you are going to tell us about your map, and show us where it leads."

• *Chapter Thirteen* •

The Grey House was as calm and empty as it had been when they left. "Barney!" Simon shouted up the stairs. "Barney?" His voice dwindled away uncertainly.

"He can't be inside," Jane said. "The key was still in its hiding-place. Oh Simon, what can have happened to him?" She turned back anxiously to the open front door, and stared down the hill.

Simon came back down the dark, shadowy hall to join her in the pool of sunlight. "He must have missed us in the harbour."

"But surely he'd have come back here after that? There isn't a soul about down there now, they've all gone after the band. That awful Bill passed us—you don't think—"

"No," Simon said hastily. "Anyway Barney's got Rufus with him. He can't get into much trouble. You wait, he'll be back soon. I expect he's found Gumerry and they're looking for us."

He was turning back into the house when Jane suddenly shouted joyfully: "Look! You're right!"

Rufus was loping up the hill towards them, a swift streak of red on the grey road. But they could see no-one behind him. Jane called, and he raised his muzzle and trotted more quickly, up the steps, between their legs and into the house. Then he stood facing them, his long ribbon of a tongue dangling over his jaws. But his tail was down, and there was none of the bouncing, barking delight with which he usually came home.

"No sign of Barney." Jane came slowly in from the doorstep. She looked down at Rufus. "What is it, then? What's happened?"

The dog took no notice of her. He stood there apathetically, his eyes blank. Even when they had given him a drink of water and

149

taken him into the room overlooking the harbour, he still gave no sign that he knew he was home. It was as if he were thinking of something quite different.

"I expect it's the heat," Simon said. He sounded unconvinced. "Come on, there's nothing we can do except wait. The yacht's still down in the harbour, anyway."

"That doesn't mean anything," Jane said miserably.

"Well, it does mean—" But Simon had no chance to explain. Jane had clutched his arm nervously. He saw that she was staring at Rufus.

They could never explain it afterwards. It was as if Rufus had been lying there listening for something, and had at last caught the thing he was waiting for: though they knew that they had heard no sound at all. He raised his head, his eyes so wide open that the whites were showing, and stood up slowly in a way more like an old man than a dog. His ears were pricked and his muzzle raised high, pointing straight at something they could not see. He began to walk, very slowly and deliberately, towards the door.

Mesmerised, Simon and Jane followed. Rufus went out into the hall until he reached the front door, and stood waiting. He did not turn his head. He simply stood there rigid, looking ahead at the door, as if quite certain that they knew what he wanted them to do.

Simon reached forward, glancing nervously down at the long, straight red back, and opened the door; and they stood on the step watching in complete bewilderment as Rufus stalked with the same ageless confidence straight ahead across the road. When he reached the other side he leapt up with a quick light flurry to stand erect on the wall which kept the road from the sheer sixty-foot drop down to the harbour side. He seemed to be looking out at the sea.

"He's not going to jump?" Jane jerked in alarm, but found that she was whispering.

And then they heard the noise that they never afterwards forgot.

* * *

Barney knew, dimly, that he had been taken out of the big silent house and driven away in a car; and that now they were walking in a group with the noise of the sea somewhere near. But he was not certain how many of them there were, or where they were taking him. Since the moment in the shadowy room when those blazing dark eyes had glared into his face, he had been conscious of nothing except that he was to do what he was told. He no longer had any

150

thoughts of his own; it was a strange, relaxed feeling, as if he were comfortably half asleep. There could be no argument now. No fighting. He knew only that the tall dark figure walking at his side, wearing a wide-brimmed black hat, was his master.

Master . . . who else had used the word that day?

"Come, Barnabas," said the hypnotic deep voice above him. "We must hurry. The tide is going out, we must reach the yacht."

Reach the yacht, said Barney dreamily to himself, we're going on the sea . . . that was the sea he could smell, the water lapping beside them at the edge of Trewissick harbour.

Far away, as if it came from a great height, he heard Polly Withers' voice say urgently: "Anyone could see us from the road up by the house. They'll see us, I know they will—"

"Polly," said the deep slow voice, "I am the one who sees. If our old Cornish friend has done her work well, there will be no one there. And if the other two children have been let slip . . . well, are they a match for us?"

Somewhere Mr. Withers laughed, soft and sinister.

Barney walked on, like a machine. The air was warm and thick; he could feel the sun fierce on his face. He had heard them talking ever since they left the house, but nothing they said seemed to have meaning for him any more. He was not frightened; he had forgotten Simon and Jane. He was somehow floating outside himself, watching with mild interest while his body walked along, but feeling nothing at all.

And then, like the sudden snapping of a bow, the noise came.

Into the air over their heads, a dog howled: a long weird note so unexpected and anguished that for a moment they all stopped dead. It echoed slow through the harbour, a freezing inhuman wail that had in it all the warning and terror that ever was in the world. Even Mr. Hastings stood listening, paralysed.

And the Barney who was outside Barney, floating half detached in the air, felt the noise wake him up with a savage jolt. He looked up, and saw Rufus standing above him, outlined red against the sky, with the sound still throbbing from his throat. And suddenly he knew where he was, and that he must get away.

He swung round on his heel, ducked under the arms that grabbed too late to catch him, and raced along the quay towards the road. The hill was empty, drained of people by the carnival procession, and he was twenty-five yards clear of the confused group on the quay before they could properly begin to give chase. He heard the shouts and pounding feet behind him, and flung himself up the hill towards the Grey House.

Simon and Jane stared in amazement from the steps. Suddenly there had been Rufus's blood-chilling howl; now suddenly Barney, with four threatening figures at his heels. They ran instinctively down the steps towards him, and then swung back in alarm at the worst sound of all. Behind them, the door of the Grey House had slammed; and the key was inside.

Barney staggered up to them, and Rufus came bounding down from the wall. Jane said, panic-stricken: "Which way?"

Simon turned frantically to the great wooden door in the wall which was the Grey House's side entrance; often it was kept locked. He pressed the latch, his heart thumping. Relief flooded over him in a wave as the door opened, and he pushed it wide. "Quick!" he yelled.

The four figures pounding grim and intent at Barney's heels were only a few steps behind. Jane and Barney shot inside the door, with Rufus a swift red flurry among their feet. The wall itself seemed to shake as Simon slammed the door shut and hurriedly pushed home the three big iron bolts. They ran up the cold, narrow little alley between the side of the Grey House and the house next door, and paused at the far end. Outside, footsteps skidded up to the door. They saw the latch rise as someone on the other side pressed it. It rattled angrily, and there was a thump against the door. Then there was silence.

"Suppose they climb over the wall?" Jane whispered fearfully.

"They couldn't possibly," Simon whispered back. "It's too high."

"Perhaps they'll break the door down!"

"Those bolts are jolly strong. Anyway people would see them and get suspicious. . . . Listen. They've gone away."

They all strained their ears. There was no sound from the door at the other end of the alley. Rufus looked up at them inquiringly and whined, whistling plaintively through his nose.

"What are they doing? They must be up to something. . . ."

"Quick!" Simon said decisively. "We've got to get away from the house before they have time to get round the back. They'll have it surrounded soon."

In panic they ran into the little back garden, and up through the knee-high grass to the hedge at the top. Rufus bounded round them

152

cheerfully, jumping to lick Barney's face. He seemed to have forgotten the uncanny impulse that had made him utter that one long,
lost howl, and now he was behaving as if everything were just a
great game.

"I hope that dog's going to keep quiet," Jane said anxiously.

Simon peered through the gap in the hedge.

"He will," Barney said. He bent down and cupped one hand
gently over Rufus's long red muzzle, murmuring to him under his
breath.

Simon straightened. "It's all clear. Come on."

One by one they slipped out of the garden into the road that
curved round behind the houses from the harbour, along the edge of
Kemare Head.

"Oh," Jane said in sudden anguish, "if *only* we knew where
Gumerry had gone."

Barney said, horrified, "Didn't you find him? What about Mrs.
Palk?"

"No, we didn't find him. We did see Mrs. Palk, but we couldn't
get to her through the crowd. Didn't you see him? Why were they
chasing you? Where did you come from? We thought something
awful must have happened when Rufus came back on his own, but
we didn't know where to look for you."

"Wait a minute," Barney said. The shock of waking from his
bewitched daze was turning into an enormous sense of urgency. A
dozen things that he had heard in the last hour were dodging about
in his mind; and as he began to see their meaning he was feeling
more and more alarmed.

"Simon," he said earnestly, "we've got to get the grail. *Now*.
Even without Great-Uncle Merry. There isn't time to look for him,
or wait, or anything. I think they're very nearly on to it. Only not
quite, that's why they wanted me."

"First thing is to get away from here." Simon looked about him
wildly. "They could come up either way from the harbour. We'll
have to get off the road and hide in that field at the back of the headland. The land doesn't slope there, we ought to be able to keep hidden."

They crossed the road and came out into the fields at the bottom
of Kemare Head. The sun blazed high up in the sky still, beating
down with a heat that pressed on them like a giant hand. But not
even Jane was worrying about the chances of sunstroke now.

As they reached the hedge on the far side of the first field, they heard voices. They scrambled hastily through the hedge, without pausing to look round, and flattened themselves in the long grass on the other side. Barney slid his arm apprehensively over Rufus's back, but the dog lay quiet, with his long pink tongue lolling out.

Nobody saw quite where they came from, but suddenly the figures were standing there on the road. Mr. Withers, slight and stooping a little, darting his head about like a weasel; the boy Bill, walking wary and belligerent in his bright shirt; and towering over them both, the tall menacing figure in black, a dark gash across the heat-wavering summer day. Watching, Simon thought suddenly of the desperate day when threatening feet were pounding after him, down a lonely road; and he turned his eyes away from the man.

"The girl's not there," Barney hissed. "She must be watching the front, in case we tried to come out that way again."

Down on the road the little group stood for a moment irresolute. Bill turned and peered across the field, straight towards the hedge. The three children flattened themselves closer to the ground, hardly daring to breathe. But Bill looked away again, apparently satisfied. Withers looked across the field as well, and said something to him. The boy shook his head.

The tall figure in black had been standing a little way apart, motionless. It was difficult to tell which way he was looking. All at once he raised his arm, pointing seaward to the rising bulk of Kemare Head. He seemed to be talking earnestly.

"What are they going to do?" Jane whispered. Cramp was beginning to gnaw agonisingly at her right leg, and she was longing to move.

"If they're going to the end of the headland we're sunk," Simon said, low and strained.

"How many more of them are there, for goodness' sake? That tall man . . ." Jane stared at him through the erratic leaf-starred gaps in the hedge. She could not see his face, but a cold sense of familiarity was beginning to grow in her mind. Then, as she gazed, he took off his wide black hat for a moment to brush his hand across his forehead, and suddenly she knew the shape of the head with the thick dark hair. The pattern of twigs and grass and sunlight swirled before her eyes, and she clutched at Simon's arm.

"Simon! It's him again! It's—"

154

"I know that," Simon said. "The moment he came round the comer I knew. I thought you did."

"He's the boss of all of them," Barney whispered in the same urgent undertone. "His name's Hastings."

"That's right," Jane said faintly. "Hastings. The vicar."

Barney wriggled a little in the grass to stare at her. "He's not the vicar."

"He is. I saw him at the vicarage. Oh, you remember. . . ."

"Is it a big rambling sort of house, all neglected?" Barney said slowly. "With a long drive, and a room full of books?"

It was Jane's turn to stare. "I remember saying about the books, but not about the drive. How did you—"

Barney said, with the utmost conviction: "I don't care what you say, he isn't the vicar. I don't know what he is, but it isn't that. He can't possibly be. There's something perfectly beastly about him. He's like everything Gumerry said about the other side, you can sort of feel it, looking at him. And he says things . . ."

"Keep down!" Simon said abruptly. They all dropped their heads into the grass, and lay silent for a long moment while the sun beat down on their backs and scorched the skin behind their knees, and the cool long grass along the edge of the hedge tickled their cheeks. Rufus stirred and grunted and was quiet again. He had fallen asleep.

In a little while Simon nervously raised his head a few inches from the ground, hearing nothing but the call of one far-away gull high up in the sky. He had seen the three figures turn and move across the field and for a moment he had thought they were caught in a trap. But there was no one now on the road where they had stood, and no one in the silent stretch of the field.

"They've gone!" he whispered exultantly. Barney and Jane raised their heads too, slowly and cautiously.

"Look!" Jane propped herself on one elbow, and pointed out to the coast. There they were, the tall black striding figure and the two smaller ones, one on either side, bobbing out of sight along the side of Kemare Head.

"Oh!" Barney rolled over on his back and groaned with despair. "We're cut off! How can we get out on the headland now?"

Jane sat up, wincing as she stretched her cramped legs. She said despondently, " I don't see what there is to get worked up about. We can't do anything. We found where the grail is, but we can't get at it anyway. If there is a bottom entrance, it's under the sea, and the hole we found at the top is too narrow to get through even if we had a rope."

Barney said, yelping, "But they'll be able to. I know they will. That man can do anything, he seems to have things planned before he even knows they're going to happen. And if they find the hole in the rocks. . . ."

"But they couldn't go down any more than we could," Jane said reasonably. "And they couldn't get in from the bottom either, unless they've got diving suits on the yacht. Anyway," she added without much conviction, "we aren't really absolutely sure the grail's there at all."

"But we are, you know we are!" Barney's anxious frustration was mounting unbearably. "We've got to stop them. Even if we can't do anything ourselves, we've got to stop them!"

"Don't be a silly little boy," Jane said, irritated by disappointment. "We'll just have to let them go, and keep out of their way till we find Great-Uncle Merry. There isn't a thing we can do."

"There is one thing," Simon said. His voice sounded muffled and rather gruff, as it always did when he was trying not to be excited. They looked at him, and Jane raised an eyebrow sceptically. Simon said nothing. He was sitting hugging his knees, frowning out across the field.

"Well, go on then."

"The tide."

"The tide? What d'you mean?"

"The tide's out."

"Well, what's so marvellous about that? I know it is," Barney said, wonderingly. "You could see the mud down in the harbour."

But Simon was not listening. "Jane, you remember what Mr. Penhallow said down in the harbour. About the tide being low."

"Oh yes." Jane began to look less gloomy. "Yes, that's right. It goes very low today, he said . . . spring tide . . . right round the rocks . . ."

"You can walk right round the rocks," Simon said.

"So what?" demanded Barney.

"If we could walk right round the rocks," Simon said with careful patience, "we could walk right round the bottom of Kemare Head."

Jane interrupted, catching him up, "And the cave, the underwater entrance—when we heard the noise of the sea coming up the hole this morning, the tide was high. So the waves were still coming over the entrance. But don't you see, Barney, with this special low tide—if it uncovers all the rocks down there, it may uncover the entrance as well, and we should be able to get in."

Barney's face was a comical mixture of expressions; blankness dissolving into excitement, and then into alarm. "Gosh! Come on then, let's get down there!" He jumped to his feet, and then wailed. "But we can't! There's one of them watching the harbour, and the other three out on the headland—how can we get down there without being seen?"

"I've thought of that too." Simon was pink with importance. "Just a minute ago. There's the other side. The bay on the other side of the headland, where we bathe from. We can get across the fields to it from here without them seeing us, unless they're actually up by the standing stones looking down in that direction. If they look down we've had it, but it's the only way I can see."

"They won't be," Jane said confidently. "They wouldn't expect us to go down there. They'd be watching the harbour side."

"Come on, we've got to be quick. Quicker than ever now. The tide was still going out when we were up over the harbour, I think, but it may turn any moment. I wish we knew exactly when."

Barney, with Rufus roused and leaping round him again, was already several yards across the field. He halted suddenly, looking troubled, and turned slowly back. "There's still Great-Uncle Merry. He'll never find us now. He'll be worried stiff."

"He didn't bother much about worrying us stiff when he disappeared this morning," Simon said shortly.

"Oh, but all the same—"

"Look," Simon said, "I'm the oldest, and I'm in charge. It's got to be Gumerry or the grail we look for, Barney, there isn't time for both. And I say we go after the grail."

"So do I," Jane said.

"Oh well," said Barney, and he went on over the field, secretly relieved to be able to accept commands. He felt he had had enough of being the lone hero that day to last him for years—so that his private dreams of solitary bold knights in shining armour would never be quite the same again.

* * *

They were all three hot and breathless by the time they reached the beach in the next bay from Trewissick, on the other side of Kemare Head. But they saw to their relief that the tide had obviously not yet begun to come back in.

The sea seemed to be miles away, over a vast stretch of silver-white sand unscarred by footprints under the sun, and as they looked eagerly along the side of the headland they could see rocks uncovered at its foot. Before, the waves had always washed up against the cliff, even at the lowest tide.

Their feet sank into the soft dry sand at the top of the beach. Barney flopped down and began to unstrap one sandal. "Wait a minute, I want to take my shoes off."

"Oh come on," Simon said impatiently, "you'll only have to put them back on again when we get to the rocks."

"I don't care, I'm taking them off now all the same. Anyway I'm tired."

Simon groaned, and whacked the telescope case against his knee in exasperation. More than ever now he was determined to carry the manuscript wherever they went, and the case was hot and damp in the palm of his hand.

Jane sat down on the sand beside Barney. "Come on, Simon, have a rest just for five minutes. It won't hurt, and I'm jolly hot as well."

Not altogether unwillingly, Simon let his knees give way and collapsed to lie flat on his back. The sun blazed down into his eyes, and he turned over quickly. "Golly, what a day. I could do with a swim." He looked longingly out at the sea; but his eyes swivelled at once back to the rocks.

"There's even more uncovered than I thought there would be. Look, it's going to be easy as anything to walk round the cliff. It looks pretty wet in places, where the tide's left some water behind, but we can get through that easily enough."

"So you'll have to take your shoes off as well," said Barney triumphantly. He hung his sandals round his neck by their straps and wiggled his toes luxuriously in the sand, looking up at the gulls wheeling and faintly calling high over the beach. Then he stiffened. "Listen!"

"I heard that too," Simon said, looking up curiously. "Funny, it sounded like an owl."

"It was an owl," Barney said, peering up at the towering side of the headland. "It came from up there. I thought you only heard owls at night."

158

"You do. And if they come out in the day-time they get mobbed by all the other birds, because they eat their young. We studied it at school."

"Well, the gulls don't seem to be taking any notice," Barney said. He looked up at the dark specks lazily sailing to and fro over the sky. Then he glanced round the beach. "Hey, where's Rufus?"

"Oh, he's around somewhere. He was here just a minute ago."

"No, he isn't." Barney stood up. "Rufus! Rufus!" He whistled, on the long lilting note that the dog always answered to. Behind them they heard a bark, and they looked up the beach towards the sloping field to see Rufus on the edge of the grass, facing away from the sea but with his head turned to look back at them.

Barney whistled again, and patted his knee. The dog did not move.

"What's the matter with him?"

"He looks frightened. Has he hurt himself?"

"I hope not." Barney ran up the beach and took Rufus by the collar, fondling his neck. The dog licked his hand. "Come on, boy." Barney said softly. "Come on, then. There's nothing wrong. Come on, Rufus." He tugged gently at the collar, moving back towards Simon and Jane. But Rufus would not move. He whined, straining away from the beach; his ears were pricked uneasily, and when Barney pulled more impatiently at his collar he turned his head and gave a low warning growl.

Puzzled, Barney relaxed his grip. As he did so, the dog suddenly jerked as if he had heard something, growled again, and slipped out of his grasp to trot swiftly away over the grass. Barney called, but he went on without a pause, head bent, tail between his legs, loping away in a straight line until he disappeared round the side of the headland.

Barney came slowly back down the beach. "Did you see that? Something must have frightened him—I bet he's run all the way home."

"Perhaps it was that owl," Simon said.

"I suppose it might have been—hey, listen, there it is again!" Barney looked up. "It *is* up on the headland."

This time they all heard it; the long husking wail drifting softly down: "Whooo-oo. . . ."

As she listened, Jane felt all her warning instincts mutter deep in her mind. For a moment she could not understand. She looked up,

159

troubled, at the looming mass of Kemare Head, and the tops of the standing stones outlined against the sky.

"Stupid bird," Simon said idly, lying down on his back again. "Thinks it's night-time. Tell it to go back to bed."

As if something exploded inside her head, Jane remembered. "Simon, quick! It's not a bird at all. It's not an owl. It's them!"

The others stared at her.

Jane jumped to her feet, the lulling warmth of sun and sand forgotten in a sudden new panic. "Don't you remember—that night, up on the headland, by the standing stones. We heard some owls hoot, and that was why Gumerry went off to look, because he thought they didn't sound right. And it wasn't owls, it was the enemy. Oh quick, perhaps they've seen us! Perhaps that was a signal from one of them to tell the others we're here!"

Simon was up on his feet before she had finished. "Come on, Barney. Quick!"

Away from the revealing emptiness of the beach they dashed towards the rocky side of the headland, the sand squeaking against their feet as they ran. Barney's sandals bounced about on his chest, kicking him. Jane lost the hair-ribbon from her pony-tail, and her hair flowed loose, tickling the back of her neck. Simon ran clutching the telescope case grimly like a relay-runner's baton. They made straight for the cliff, and paused under its great grey height to look fearfully back at the grassy slope rising behind the beach. But there was no sign of anyone coming after them, and they heard no owl cry.

"Perhaps they didn't see us after all."

"I bet they can't really see this beach from anywhere on the top of the headland."

"Well, we've got to hurry all the same. Come on, or the tide will turn and beat us to it."

They were still running on sand, along the side of the cliff, towards the end of the headland and the sea. Then they came to the rocks, and they began to climb.

The rocks were perilous to cross. At first they were dry, and fairly smooth, and it was easy to scramble from one grey jagged ridge to the next, skirting the small pools where anemones spread their tentacles like feathered flowers among seaweed leaves, and shrimps darted transparent to and fro. But soon they came to the rocks that were uncovered only at the lowest spring tides. Great

160

masses of seaweed grew there, shining, still wet in the sun; slippery brown weed that squelched and popped under their feet, giving way sometimes without warning to drop them into a pool.

They came to a long stretch of water left trapped in the rocks. Barney, still determinedly barefoot, was trailing some way behind the other two. They waited at the edge of the water as he picked his way gingerly towards them. "Ow!" he said, as he trod on a winkle.

"Do put your sandals on," Jane said imploringly. "It doesn't matter about getting them wet, ours are sopping already. You might step on anything in this pool and cut your feet to bits."

Barney said, with surprising meekness due to having stubbed three toes, "All right." He perched on a jutting rock and unhooked his sandals from round his neck. "Seems silly to put your shoes on to go paddling, instead of taking them off."

"You can call it paddling," Simon said darkly. "There might be all sorts of ravenous deep-sea fish left in here. Mr. Penhallow says the sea's terrifically deep just off the headland." He gazed into the mass of bulbous brown seaweed floating on the surface of the pool. "Oh well, here goes."

They splashed through the weed, keeping close to the cliff and catching nervously at the rock to keep their balance. Simon, first in line, reached out warily with his forward foot, stirring the water so that the seaweed swirled cold and clammy against his skin. The bottom of the pool seemed fairly smooth, and he went more confidently, with the others following behind. Then suddenly his probing foot met no resistance, and before he could throw his weight backwards he had slipped down waist-deep in water. Jane, last in line, squealed involuntarily as she saw him drop. Barney held out a hand to Simon, suddenly a much shorter figure than himself.

"It's all right," Simon said, more surprised than damaged. After the first shock the water felt pleasantly cold on his sunbaked legs. He moved carefully forward, and after a couple of steps felt rock against his knees under the water of the pool. He hauled himself up, splashing like a stranded fish, and in a few moments was only ankle-deep in water again.

"It's a sort of underwater trough. It goes right up to the cliff. Be careful, Barney. Feel with your toes a bit further out and see if there are any footholds there. There might be some sticking up under the water, like stepping-stones. I went down before I had a chance to

161

feel. If there aren't any you'll just have to come across the way I did. Only slower."

Barney prodded carefully about with one foot beneath the water and its swaying carpet of seaweed, but even farther away from the cliff he could feel only the edge of the underwater ridge, and beyond it nothing. "I can't feel anything to tread on at all."

"You'll have to go down, then. Lower yourself into it."

"We might as well have gone swimming after all," Barney said nervously. He crouched with both hands on the bottom until he was sitting in the water with his legs dangling over the hidden crevasse, and let himself slip down.

The water was almost over his shoulders when he felt his feet on firm rock; he had forgotten how much taller Simon was. He waded across and Simon hauled him out into the shallow water. Barney's shorts, wet and dark, clung heavily to his thighs, and he bent to detach odd fronds of seaweed that had twined themselves round his legs. Almost at once he felt the heat of the sun begin to dry his skin, leaving behind only the rasp of salt. Jane followed in the same way, and together they splashed across the last few shallow feet of the pool to where the rocks jutted out dry among the brown mounds of seaweed again.

"I do wish we knew about the tide," Simon said anxiously to Jane. Barney had gone eagerly slipping and slithering over the rocks ahead of them.

Jane looked towards the sea. It lapped mildly against the edge of the rocks a few yards away, leaving a natural pathway all round the bottom of the cliff.

"It certainly hasn't moved. It might even be going out still. I shouldn't worry yet, we must be nearly there."

"Well, keep an eye on it. It's that deep bit I'm worried about. When the water does start coming in it'll come into the pool first of all, and it wouldn't have to fill up far for us not to be able to get back the way we came. It'd be over Barney's head in no time."

Jane blanched, and looked ahead at her younger brother now scrambling on all fours. "Oh Simon. D'you think we should have left him behind?"

Simon grinned. "I'd like to have seen you try. Don't worry, it'll be all right. Just so long as we watch the tide."

Looking back, Jane suddenly realised how far they had come. They stood now on the rocks at the very tip of the headland. The small distant sounds of the land no longer drifted out from the beach, and there was nothing but the gentle sigh of the sea. It was almost as if they were cut off already.

Then Barney yelled in excitement. "Hey look! Quick! Come here! I've found it!"

He was standing close to the cliff, some yards ahead, almost hidden by a rock. They could see him pointing towards the cliff-face. In an instant they had forgotten the tide, and they jumped and slithered over pools and rocks towards Barney, bladder wrack popping under their feet like machine-gun fire.

"It's not very big," he called as they came up. Simon and Jane saw the deep cleft in the rock only when they were very close. It was not the kind of cave they had pictured in their minds. Narrow and triangular, it rose barely high enough for Barney to stand upright inside, and they themselves would certainly have to crouch to go in. Rough boulders lay heaped round the entrance, and water dripped from wet green weed coating the roof. They could not see very far inside.

Jane said doubtfully, "Are you sure this is it?"

"Of course it is," Barney said positively. "There couldn't be more than one."

"I don't see why not."

"Neither do I," Simon said, "but I think this is the one all right. Look up above—you can just see a sort of green triangle at the top of the cliff where the grass grows over the edge by the rocks. We must be almost directly in line with the place where that hole comes out up there."

Jane looked, and looked down again quickly, shaken by the unnerving height of the cliff leaning over them out of the sky. "I suppose so."

Barney peered into the darkness. "It isn't a cave at all really, just a hole, like at the top. Pouf"—he sniffed critically—"it smells all seaweedy and salty. And the sides are all wet and green and dripping. Good job we're wet already."

"I don't like it," Jane said suddenly, staring hard at the dark entrance so small in the vast mass of the cliff.

"What d'you mean, you don't like it?"

"It gives me the creeps. We can't go in there."

"You can't, you mean," Simon said. "You'll have to keep watch in case the tide turns. But I can."

"What about me?" Barney demanded indignantly. "I found it."

"D'you *want* to?" said Jane in horror.

"With the grail in there? Who wouldn't? Be much better if I tried," he said persuasively to Simon, "I'm the smallest, and it's jolly narrow. You might get stuck, and never get out again."

"Oh don't," said Jane.

"If you go in, I'm going in after you," Simon said.

"Okay," Barney said cheerfully. He had been so unutterably relieved ever since he found himself free of the clutches of the sinister Mr. Hastings that nothing else, in comparison, seemed frightening at all. "I wish we'd brought a flashlight, though." He gazed speculatively into the cave. Within a few feet of the entrance it was black and impenetrable.

"I wish we'd brought a rope," Jane said unhappily. "Then if you did get stuck I could pull you out."

Simon put his hands in his pocket looking up at the sky, and began to whistle nonchalantly. They stared at him.

"Well?"

"What's the matter with you?"

"Good job someone in the family's got brains," Simon said.

"Who? You?"

"I don't know what you'd do without me."

"Oh come on," Jane said impatiently, "you haven't got a rope or a flashlight, so don't pretend you have."

"I jolly nearly have." Simon delved into the pocket of his shorts. "You know when we went through our pockets up there this morning to see if we had some string, and we only had that cotton of yours—well, I thought we ought to be a bit better equipped just in case. So when we were back at the house I pinched some of Father's fishing-line. He didn't take it all with him." His hand emerged from his pocket clutching a tight-wound wad of thin brown line. "That's as tough as any rope."

"I never thought of that," Jane said, with new respect.

"I've still got that old bit of candle too. But I bet you haven't still got your matches."

Jane groaned. "No, I haven't. They were in my duffle, and I left it at home. Oh bother."

"I thought you would," Simon said, and with the smug flourish of a conjuror he produced a box of matches and the candle stump from his shirt pocket. Then his face fell. "Oh gosh, they've got wet.

They must have been splashed when I slipped in that pool. The wick of the candle's soaking, it won't be any good. Still, the matches are all right."

"They'll do fine," Barney said encouragingly. "That's smashing. Come on."

Simon took the telescope case from where he had tucked it under his arm and handed it to Jane. "You'd better take charge of the manuscript, Janey. If I dropped it in there we'd never find it again."

He looked out again at the sea. The rocks where they stood were even more like a causeway here, stretching out almost flat from the base of the cliff into the water. Only one hump of grey rock stood alone near the entrance of the cave.

The water still lapped gently at the edge six or seven yards away, no nearer and no further than it had been when they first left the beach. Simon wondered nervously how much time was left before the tide would turn. "I reckon we've got about half an hour," he said slowly. "After that we shall have to get away quick before the tide catches us. Come here, Barney, and hold still."

He found the loose end of the roll of fishing-line and tied it securely round Barney's waist. "If you're going to go first I can hold on to the line behind you."

"D'you think he ought to?" Jane said.

Barney turned round and glared at her.

"Well, I'm not awfully keen on the idea," said Simon, "but he's right about its being narrow, and he may be the only one who can get properly inside. It's all right, I won't lose him. Here—" He handed Jane the roll of line. "Don't let it go slack."

"And don't keep it too tight," said Barney, making for the entrance, "or you'll cut my middle in half."

Jane looked at her watch. "It's nearly five o'clock. When you've been in there ten minutes I'll pull on the line twice to tell you."

"*Ten minutes!*" said Barney in scorn. "We may have to go in for miles."

"You might suffocate," said poor Jane.

"That's a good idea," Simon said quickly, glancing at her face. "You pull twice, and if I pull back twice, it means we're all right but we're staying in there. If I pull three times, it means we're coming out."

"And if I pull three times it means you've got to come out, because the tide's turned."

"Fine. And four pulls from either end means a distress signal—not," Simon added hastily, "that there's going to be any need for it."

"All right," Jane said. "Oh dear. Don't be long."

"Well, we shall have to go slowly. But don't get in a flap, nothing's going to go wrong." Simon patted her on the back, and followed as Barney, straining eagerly at the line round his waist like a dog on a leash, waved one hand briefly and disappeared into the mouth of the cave.

• *Chapter Fourteen* •

Barney blinked at the darkness. As his eyes grew accustomed to being out of the sunlight, vague objects took shape in the dark. He realized that the light from the entrance penetrated further inside than they had realised; and for the first few yards at least he could see the faint shine of the slimy green weed covering the walls and roof of the cave, and the glint of water lying along the bottom in a shallow unmoving stream.

He moved warily forward, one hand up touching the roof and the other stretched out to one side. He could feel a slight steady pull on the line round his waist from Simon holding it behind him. Very loud in the enclosed silence of the cave he could hear the splash of their feet through the water, and his brother breathing.

"Go carefully," Simon said, behind him. He spoke softly, almost in a whisper, but the cave echoed his voice into a husking mutter that filled the space all around them.

"I am."

"You might bump your head."

"You might bump yours. Mind this bit here, it comes down lower. Put your hand up on the roof and you'll feel it."

"I can," Simon said fervently. His neck was bent uncomfortably downwards; taller than Barney, he had to stoop slightly all the while to avoid hitting his head on the slimy rock above. Occasionally a large cold drop of water dripped down inside his shirt collar.

"Isn't it cold?"

"Freezing." Barney's shorts were clinging clammily to the tops of his legs, and he felt the air chill through his shirt. He was finding it more and more difficult to make out any shapes around him, and soon he paused uneasily, feeling the darkness close in as if it were pressing on his eyes. Groping upwards, his fingers could no longer feel the roof. Ahead of him it rose out of reach, and he clutched at air.

"Wait a minute, Simon." His voice came eerily back at him from all sides. "I think it gets higher here. But I can't see a thing now. Have you got those matches?"

Simon felt his way along the line to where Barney stood. He touched his shoulder, and Barney felt more comforted at the contact than he would have admitted even to himself.

"Don't move. I'm letting go of the line for a minute." Simon groped in his pocket for the matches and opened the box, feeling the edges carefully to make sure he had it the right way up.

The first two matches grated obstinately on the box as he tried to strike them, and nothing happened. The third flared up but broke as it did so, burning Simon's fingers so that he dropped it with an exclamation before they could blink away the dazzle of the sudden light. There was a small hiss as it dropped into the water around their feet.

"Buck up," said Barney.

"I'm going as fast as I can . . . ah, that's it."

The fourth match was dry, and rasped into flame, flickering. Simon cupped his hand to shelter it. "Funny, there must be a draught in here. I can't feel one."

"The match can. That's good, it means there must be an opening somewhere at the other end. So it is the right cave after all."

Simon's hand hid the dazzle of the little flame, and Barney peered hastily round in the wavering light. Their shadows danced huge and grotesque on the wall. He looked up, and took a few careful steps forward. "Hold it up . . . hey, come on, the roof does go up higher here, you'll be able to stand upright."

Simon stepped cautiously towards him, bent over the match, and straightened his back with a gasp of relief. Then the match burned his fingers, and he dropped it. At once the darkness wrapped them like a blanket again.

"Hang on, I'll light another one."

"Well, wait a minute, we don't want to waste them. I could see a bit of the way ahead when it went out, so we can go that far before you light the next."

Barney shut his eyes. Somehow, even though the cave was just as dark when his eyes were open, he found shutting them gave him a sense of being safer. Still touching the slippery wall with his finger-tips, he moved two or three paces forward. Simon followed him with one hand on his shoulder, staring ahead into the darkness but seeing as little as if a thick black curtain were hanging close before his face.

They went on into the cave for what seemed a long time. Every few moments Simon struck a match, and they moved forward while the dim light lasted, and for the few remembered paces after it flickered out. Once they tried to light the candle stump, but it only sputtered obstinately, so Simon put it back in his pocket.

The air was cold, but fresh on their faces. Although there was a smell all round them of salt and seaweed, as if they were under the sea, it was not difficult to breathe. The silence, like the darkness, seemed almost solid, broken only by their own footsteps, and an occasional echoing musical plop as water somewhere dripped from the roof of the cave.

As Simon was standing still, fumbling with the matchbox again, Barney felt the line round his waist jerk tight and dig into him; once, twice. "There's two pulls on the line. It must be Jane. Ten minutes. Gosh, I thought we'd been in here for hours."

"I'll signal back," Simon said. He struck a match and saw the line thin and taut in its light. Taking firm hold of it he gave two slow steady pulls on the direction from which they had come.

"Funny to think of Jane on the other end," Barney said.

"I wonder how much there is left?"

"Gosh—d'you think we shall run out? How much line was there?"

"Quite a lot," said Simon, more optimistically than he felt. "We've been going awfully slowly. Ow!" The match burned down to his fingers, and he dropped it hastily.

There was no hiss as it fell. As they moved on, groping, Simon suddenly realised that he had been listening for the noise.

"Stop a tick, Barney." He scuffed at the ground with one foot and peered down. "The floor's not wet any more."

"My shoes still squelch," Barney said.

"That's the water inside them, idiot, not outside." Simon's voice boomed hollowly round the cave, and he hastily dropped it to a whisper again, half afraid that the noise might bring the roof down on them.

"The sides aren't slimy here either," Barney said suddenly. "It's dry rock. It has been for some time actually, only I hadn't really taken any notice."

Another match fizzed alight as Simon held it to the one dying in his fingers. He held the flame close to the wall. They saw bare grey granite, veined here and there with a white sparkling rock, and no seaweed. The ground, when Barney stooped to touch it, was covered with a kind of dusty sand.

"We must be going uphill."

"The sea can't ever have come in this far."

"But we heard it booming about from up the top, this morning. Does that mean we've come past the opening of the chimney bit?" Barney craned his neck back to look at the roof.

"I don't think so," Simon said uncertainly. "The noise would carry a long way. Hey, look ahead quick, this match is going out."

Barney peered forward at the now-familiar picture that he was never afterwards to forget: of narrow shadow-swung walls tunnelling into the dark, holding them in a cramped, unfriendly grip. And in the second before the darkness came down on them again he thought he saw the curtain of shadow at the end nearer than it had been before.

He moved hesitantly forward, and then some instinct told him to stop. He put out his hand in the silent darkness. It met solid rock a few inches from his face. "Simon! It's a dead end."

"What?" Incredulity and disappointment rose in Simon's voice. He struggled with the matches; he could feel the bottom of the box through them now, and realised that there could not be many left.

In the flickering light it was difficult to tell shadow from darkness, but they saw that the cave had not actually come to an end. Instead it changed, just in front of them, to a far narrower passage: tall and thin, with a great boulder wedged between its sides about three feet from the ground. Above their heads, out of reach, the cleft was open to the roof: but there was no way of climbing up to it. The boulder blocked their path.

"We'll never get through that," Simon said in despair. "There must have been a fall of rock since the Cornishman went through."

Barney looked down at the forbidding dark gap that remained at the bottom of the cleft, jagged and sinister through the dancing shadows, and swallowed. He was beginning to wish very much that they were back in the sunlight again.

Then he thought of the grail, and then of Mr. Hastings' face. "I can get through underneath, if I crawl."

"No," Simon said at once. "It's dangerous."

"But we can't go back now." Barney gained confidence as he began to argue. "We've got this far, we may be just a few feet away from it. I'll come out again if it's too narrow. Oh come on, Simon, let me try."

The match went out.

"We haven't got many left," Simon said out of the darkness. "They'll run out soon. We've just got to make that candle light, or we shall be stuck in the dark. Where are you?"

Groping his way along the line towards Barney, he took his hand and put the match-box into it. Then he felt in his own pocket for the stump of candle, rubbing its wick hopefully on his shirt to dry it. "Now light one of the matches."

There was a noise behind them in the darkness, like a stone falling; a grating, rattling noise and then silence again.

"What was that?"

They listened nervously, but could hear only the sudden violent thumping of their own hearts. Barney struck a match, his hand shaking. The cave sprang into light again round them, with only the darkness pressing mockingly from the direction of the noise.

"It wasn't anything," Simon said at last. "Just a stone we must have brushed loose. Here." He held the candle stub to the flame. The match burned right down, but still the candle wick only sputtered as it had before. They tried again, holding their breath, and this time the wick caught, and burned with a long smoking yellow flame.

"Hold these," Barney said with determination. "I'm going in there." He gave Simon back the last few loose matches and took the candle. "Look," he said, shielding the smoking flame from the draught with his other hand. "It's not so low really, I can go on my hands and knees."

Simon peered at the entrance unhappily. "Well . . . for goodness' sake be careful. And pull at the line if you get stuck, I'll keep hold of it."

Barney went down on his hands and knees and crawled into the dark opening beneath the wedged rock, holding the dangerously flickering candle in front of him. The draught seemed to be stronger now. The rock brushed his body on all sides, so that he

171

had to keep his head down and his elbows in, and for a moment he almost panicked with the sense of being shut in.

But before the panic could take hold, the shadows looming round the one point of light changed their shape, and he raised his head without hitting the rock. He crawled a little farther, the floor rough and gritty under his knees; and found not only that he could stand upright but that the cave was much wider. The pool of light cast by his carefully guarded flame did not even show the walls on either side.

"Are you all right?" Simon's anxious voice came muffled through the opening behind him.

Barney bent down. "It's okay, it widens out again here, that must be an entrance. . . . I'm going on."

He felt the line at his waist tighten as Simon jerked an answer and he set off slowly across the cave. The darkness opened before him in the small light from his inch of candle, already burning down and dripping hot wax over his finger-nails. When he glanced back over his shoulder he could no longer see the entrance from which he had come.

"Hallo," Barney said tentatively into the darkness. His voice whispered back at him in a sinister, eerie way: not booming and reverberating round as it had in the narrow tunnel-like cave they had come through, but muttering far away, high in the air. Barney swung round in a circle, vainly peering into the dark. The space round him must be as big as a house—and yet he was in the depths of Kemare Head.

He paused, irresolute. The candle was burning down, soft between his fingers. The thought of the towering dark man in his strange empty house came back to him suddenly, and with it all the feeling of menace that surrounded their pursuers, the enemy, who so desperately wanted to keep them from finding the grail.

Barney shivered with fright and sudden cold. It was as if they were all round him in the silent darkness, evil and unseen, willing him to go back. His ears sang, even in the great empty space of the cave he felt that something was pressing him down, calling him insistently to turn away. Who are you to intrude here, the voice seemed to whisper; one small boy, prying into something that is so much bigger than you can understand, that has remained undisturbed for so many years? Go away, go back where you are safe, leave such ancient things alone. . . .

But then Barney thought of Great-Uncle Merry, whose mysterious quest they were following. He thought of all that he had said, right in the beginning, of the battle that was never won but never totally lost. And although he saw nothing but the shadows, and the blackness all around his small lonely pool of yellow light, he suddenly had a vivid picture of the knight Bedwin who had begun it all when he came fleeing to Cornwall from the east. In full armour he stood in Barney's mind, guarding the last trust of King Arthur, chased by the same forces that were now pursuing them.

And Barney remembered the story that Bedwin was buried on Kemare Head, perhaps directly above the cave where he stood, and he was not frightened. There was friendliness round him in the dark now as well as fear.

So Barney did not turn back. He went on, sheltering his small dying light, into the dark that gave back in whispering echoes the sound of his own steps. And then, above his head, he became aware of a noise stranger than anything he had ever heard.

It seemed to come from nowhere, out of the air; a husky, unearthly humming, very faint and far-away, yet filling the whole cave. It wavered up and down, high and then low, like the wind that sings in the trees and telegraph-wires. As the thought flickered through Barney's mind, he held the candle up and saw that over his head the roof opened into a kind of chimney, rising up and up and out of sight. He thought for an instant that he saw a point of light shining down, but his own light dazzled his eyes and he could never be sure. And he realised that the noise he could hear was the wind, far above, blowing over the hole in the rocks that they had found that morning. The singing down in the cave was the singing of the wind over Kemare Head.

It was almost by accident, as he was looking up, that he saw the ledge. It jutted out from the rocky side of the chimney at the end of the cave; a bump of rock beneath a hollow, like a kind of natural cupboard, just within his reach. Inside it, he saw the glint of candlelight reflected back from a shape that was not part of the rock.

Hardly daring to breathe, he reached up and found his hand touching the side of something smooth and curved. It rang beneath his finger-nail with the sound of metal. He grasped it and took it down, blinking at the dust which rose from the ledge as he did so. It was a cup, heavy and strangely shaped; swelling out from a thick stem into a tall bell-shape like the goblets he had seen pictured in his books about King Arthur. He wondered how the artists could have known. He could hardly believe that this, at last, must be the grail.

The metal was cold in his hand; dusty and very dirty, but with a dull golden sheen underneath the dirt. There was nothing else on the ledge.

The candle flickered suddenly. The wax felt soft and warm, and Barney guessed with a shock that it would burn for only a few moments more before he would be left alone in the dark. He turned away from the ledge to the direction from which he had come, and realised how lost he would have been without the line tied to his waist. The vast round chamber of the cave stretched out all round him into the dark; only the line, straight and thin, told him the way to go.

He walked towards it; the line dropped to the ground and then drew taut again. Simon must be pulling it in. Barney clutched the grail to him with one hand and held up the candle, now almost burned away, with the other. Excitement bubbled away any of the fears he had felt before. "Simon!" he called. "I've found it!"

There was no answer but his own voice, whispering back at him from the empty cave. "Found it . . . found it . . ." . . . a dozen voices, each his own, from every side.

And the light flickered, and went out.

The line stayed taut as Barney put his hand on it and walked slowly forward. "Simon?" he said uncertainly. Still there was no answer. For a moment he saw in his mind a terrible picture of Simon overpowered and helpless. And on the other side of the narrow passage in the rock, the tall sneering figure of Mr. Hastings, taking in the line as if he were playing a fish on a hook, and waiting. . . .

Barney's throat felt suddenly dry. He held the grail tighter to him in the darkness, his heart thumping. Then he heard Simon's voice, low down in the darkness before him and very muffled.

"Barney! . . . Barney?"

Barney put out his hand and felt the rock where the roof dropped suddenly to the narrow part of the cave. "I'm here . . . Simon, I've found it, I've got the grail!"

But all the muffled urgent voice said was, "Come on out, quick."

Barney went down on his hands and knees, wincing again at the pressure of the sharp edges of the rock. Carefully he crawled into the crevice that separated the two parts of the cave, bumping his head in the dark on the low uneven roof.

He held the grail upright before him, but it knocked against the side of the rock and rang out, to his surprise, with a long musical note as clear and true as a bell.

He saw a dim glow lighting the farther end of the crack, and then the bright star of a match, and Simon crouching low and pulling in the line with his free hand. The shadows made his eyes look big and dark and alarmed. He stared as Barney emerged, forgetting everything at the sight of the tall cup.

Simon had been growing more and more anxious, and only the feel of Barney still moving at the other end of the line had stopped him from squeezing through the narrow gap himself. He had stood alone in the dark, straining for every sound, longing for light but forcing himself to keep the six remaining matches in his pocket for the journey back. It had seemed a very long time.

He took the cup from Barney's hands. "I thought it would be a different shape, somehow . . . what's this inside?"

"Where?"

"Look—" Simon felt inside the cup and brought out what looked at first like a short stick, almost as dark with age as the cup itself. It had been wedged between the sides, and Barney had not seen it in his haste.

"It's very heavy. I think it's made of lead."

"What is it?"

"A kind of tube. Like the telescope case, only a lot smaller. It doesn't seem to unscrew, though. Perhaps it just fits together." Simon pulled experimentally at the tube, and suddenly one end of it came off like a cap: and wound in a roll inside they saw something very familiar indeed.

"It's another manuscript!"

"So that's what he meant when he said—" Simon broke off. He had taken hold of one end of the rolled parchment in an attempt to pull it out of the tube, and the edge had crumbled away at his touch. When sudden caution he jerked his hand away, and in the same instant remembered why he had called so anxiously for Barney to come out.

"We can't touch it, it's too old. And Barney, we've got to get out as quick as we can. Jane gave three pulls on the line just before you came back. The tide must be coming in. If we don't get out soon we shall be cut off."

* * *

As the boys disappeared into the mouth of the cave Jane had settled herself to lean against the lone standing rock, amongst the wet pillows of seaweed and the grey-green sweep of flat granite causeway round the cliff. She tucked the telescope case carefully under her arm. Even though she had always been with Simon when he was carrying it about, she felt a peculiar unnerving sense of responsibility at the thought of what was inside.

Gradually she paid out the thin fishing-line from the neatly wound wad in her hand. The pressure on it was uneven, as if inside the cave the boys were moving forward and then stopping every few moments. She had to concentrate to keep the line from either pulling too tight or drooping loose on the ground.

It was very hot. The sun beat down over the towering grey cliff, and she felt the heat prickling along her skin. Even the rock she leant on was baked by the sun, and she could feel the warmth of it through her shirt on her back. Behind her, the water swished gently as it washed the edge of the uncovered rocks. There was no other sound anywhere, at the lonely foot of the headland with the sea stretching all around, and without the line moving in her hands Jane could have believed that she was the only person in the world. The land, and the Grey House, seemed very far away.

She wondered idly if their parents had come back from Penzance yet, and what they would think when they found the house completely empty, with nothing to show where anyone had gone.

She thought of the three figures they had seen striding out over Kemare Head, led by the frightening Mr. Hastings, black and long-legged like some giant insect. Instinctively she looked up at the cliff. But there was no sound, no movement, only the great grey sweep of rock that leant over her in permanent unmoving menace, with the green cap of grass on the headland at the top, two hundred feet above.

And then Great-Uncle Merry followed them into her mind. Where was he? Where had he gone this time? What, so near the end of the quest, could possibly have been important enough to take him away? Never for one moment did Jane think that he could have come to any harm, or have been captured by the enemy. She remembered too clearly the utter confidence with which Great-Uncle Merry had swept her into his arms on the midnight headland: "They dare not follow if I am here. . . . "

"I wish you were here now," Jane said, aloud, shivering a little in

176

spite of the hot still air. She was not happy with Simon and Barney deep in a darkness where anything might be lurking, where they might get lost and never get out, where the roof might fall in. . . .

Great-Uncle Merry would have made sure that nothing like that could happen.

Jane looked at her watch. It was twelve minutes past five, and still the line in her hands was moving slowly and irregularly into the cave. She gave two strong deliberate tugs on the line. After a pause she felt it move twice in reply; but faintly. The line was two-thirds unwound; she wished she had measured it as she let it go. Time dragged by; still the line pulled insistently out of her hand, moving into the dark entrance more slowly now. The sun blazed down immovable out of the empty blue sky, and a small breeze sprang up from nowhere to lift the edges of Jane's long loose hair.

She leant against the rock and let her senses drift, feeling the heat of the sun on her skin, breathing the sea-smell of the wet rocks and seaweed, and listening to the gentle lap-lap of the sea. Then in a kind of sleepy daze, with only her fingers awake, she became aware that the sound of the sea had changed.

She jerked to her feet and swung round. To her horror, the piles of seaweed nearest the sea were swaying up and down in a swell that had not been there before. Waves were washing over what had been the edge of the rocks; nearer her, she thought, than they had been. The tide was on the turn.

Jane felt panic begin to rise within her. The last few loops of the line were loose in her hand now: the boys must be an alarming way inside the cave. She took firm hold of the line, winding part of the slack round her hand and going right up to the dark mouth of the cave, and jerked it hard one, two, three times.

Nothing happened. She waited, listening to the regular swash of the waves creeping in. Then just as tears of fright were beginning to prickle in her eyes she felt the answering signal; three faint tugs on the line pulling at her hand. Almost at once the strain lessened, and the line began to fall slack. Jane let out a great breath of relief. The line came towards her as she pulled at it; slowly at first and then more easily, faster than she had paid it out. Then at last, Simon and Barney, blinking at the daylight behind hands raised to shield their eyes, came stumbling out of the narrow entrance of the cave.

"Hallo," Simon said foolishly, sounding dazed. His matches had run out five full minutes before they reached the light, and the last

177

part of the way had been a nightmare journey in the pitch dark, walking blind and trusting to the feel of the line to tell them that the way ahead was clear. He had made Barney let him go first. All the time he felt that every next step might bring him crashing against rock, or face to face in the dark with some nameless Thing, and he would not have been surprised when they emerged to find that all his hair had turned white.

Jane only looked at him with a small wry grin and said as he had, "Hallo."

"Look!" Barney said, and held up the grail.

Jane felt her grin widen with delight. "Then we've beaten them! We've got it! Gosh, I wish Gumerry were here."

"I think it's made of gold." Barney rubbed at the metal. Out in the sunlight, the grail seemed far less magical than in the mysterious darkness of the cave; but a bright yellow gleam showed here and there through the dirt on its side. "There's a sort of pattern scratched all over it, too," he said. "But you can't see properly, without cleaning it up."

"It's terribly ancient."

"But what does it *mean*? I mean everyone's trying like mad to get hold of it, because it can tell them something, but when you look at it there doesn't seem to be anything it could possibly tell anyone. Unless that pattern's some sort of message."

"The manuscript," Simon said.

"Oh gosh, yes." Barney took the small, heavy lead tube from the cup, and showed Jane the manuscript inside. "This was wedged in the grail. It must follow on from where our manuscript leaves off. I bet it's tremendously important. I bet it explains everything. But it breaks up almost as soon as you look at it." He carefully fitted the cap back on the tube.

"We've got to get it home safely," Simon said. "I wonder if there's room . . . wait a minute." He took the telescope case from under Jane's arm and unscrewed it. Their own familiar manuscript stood up from the lower half, fitting it closely.

Simon took the dark leaden cylinder and dropped it carefully inside the centre of the parchment in the telescope case. "There. Got a hanky, Jane?"

Jane took her handkerchief from her shirt pocket. "What for?"

"Like that," Simon said, fitting the handkerchief in a tight ball inside the top of the parchment roll. "It'll keep the new one steady.

178

We'll have to run if we're going to get off before the tide catches up with us, and it'll get bounced about a lot."

Automatically Jane and Barney turned to look again at the sea. And at exactly the same moment each of them gasped, with a noise of pure strangled fright. Simon had bent his head to screw the two halves of the case back together. He looked up quickly. The waves were lifting the seaweed now within six feet of where they stood. But that was not what was wrong. Jane and Barney, arrested in mid-movement, were looking further out to sea.

For a moment, the one jutting rock obscured Simon's view. Then he too saw the tall sweeping lines of the yacht *Lady Mary*, under full sail, come round the end of the headland towards them. And he too saw the tall dark figure standing in the bow with one arm raised, pointing.

"Come on, quick!" He grabbed at Barney and Jane as they stood motionless with shock, and pushed them ahead of him.

They jumped and slithered over the seaweed-cushioned rocks, away from the cave and the pursuing yacht. Barney clutched the grail in one hand as he ran, his arms outstretched to keep his balance, and Simon held the manuscripts in their case grimly to his chest. He glanced back over his shoulder and saw the great white mainsail of the yacht crumpling down on to the deck, and a small dinghy being lowered over the side.

Barney slipped and fell, and nearly brought them both down on top of him. Even as he fell the grail did not leave his grip, but struck the rock once more with the same clear bell-like note as before. It rang out over the sound of their splashing hasty feet.

He struggled up again, biting his lip at the sting of salt eating into a graze on his knee, and they hurried on. They were splashing through water all the while now. The waves had grown, and were washing right over the rocks with every pulse of the rising tide. The water masked the pools and hollows with drifting brown weed, and glossed the bare rock with a swirling coat that would turn, soon, into a current strong enough to dislodge their quick desperate feet.

Barney slipped again, and fell with a splash.

"Let me take it."

"No!"

He scrambled for a foothold, Jane pulling him up by his free arm, and the frenzied nightmare of a race drove them faster, zigzagging in wild blind leaps over the wave-washed rocks. Simon glanced

179

back again. Two figures in a small dinghy were paddling fast towards them from the yacht. He heard the yacht's engines cough into life.

"Go on, quick!" he gasped. "We can still do it!" They hastened on, half stumbling, kept on their feet only by their own speed. Still there was no sight of the beach round the headland, but only the sea on one side and the great wall of the cliff rising on the other. And before them, dwindling into the tide, the long path of rocks and weed.

"Stop!" a deep voice rang out across the water behind them. "Come back! You stupid children, come here!"

"They won't catch us," Simon panted, catching Barney as he almost fell a third time, and jerking him back to his feet. Jane at his side was sobbing for breath at every step, but running and stumbling with the same desperate haste. Then round the headland in front of them something else came into sight, and dropped their hopes like stones to the bottom of the sea.

It was another dinghy, broad as a tub, breasting the waves like a barge. The boy Bill sat at a chugging outboard motor in the stem, and Mr. Withers was leaning eagerly forward in front of him, his long dark hair blowing in the wind. He saw them and shouted with triumph, and they saw an unpleasant grin break on the boy's face as he turned the boat's nose towards the rocks in their path.

They skidded to a halt, appalled.

"Which way?"

"They'll cut us off!"

"But we can't go back. Look! The others are going to land!"

With the edge of the water creeping round their feet they looked distractedly back and forth. Not ten yards ahead, the boat with Mr. Withers evilly smiling was heading to cut off their path, and behind them the other dinghy was bobbing almost at the edge of the rocks. They were caught, neatly, in a trap.

"Come over here!" the deep voice called to them again. "You will not get away. Come here!"

Mr. Hastings was standing up in his dinghy, a tall black figure, one arm flung out towards them. With his legs planted apart to keep him balanced, swaying with the boat's rise and fall on the swell, he looked as if he were straddling the sea.

"Barnabas!" The voice dropped lower, to a hypnotic monotone. "Barnabas, come here."

Jane clutched at Barney's arm. "Don't go near him!"

180

"No fear." Barney was frightened, but not bewitched into obedience as he had been before. "Oh Simon, what can we do?"

Simon stared up at the cliff, wondering for a wild moment if they could climb to safety. But the sheer granite face towered implacably up, far, far above their heads. They could never have found footholds there even to climb out of reach, and they would have fallen long before they reached the top.

"Barnabas," the voice came again, gentle, insidious. "We know what it is you have in your hand. And you too, Simon. Oh yes, Simon, especially you."

Simon and Barney each closed a hand instinctively tighter round the manuscripts and the grail.

"They are not yours." The voice rose, more roughly. "You have no right to them. They must go back where they belong."

Mr. Hastings was watching them intently, poised in the dinghy waiting for the right moment of the swell to jump across to the rocks. Only the heaving mounds of seaweed, masking the edge, made him hesitate. At the tiller, Polly Withers was struggling to control the boat in the rising waves.

Barney shouted suddenly: "You can't have them. They're not yours either. Why do you want them anyway? You haven't really got a museum, I don't believe all the things you said."

Mr. Hastings laughed softly. The noise echoed eerie and spine-chilling over the gentle murmur of the sea.

"You'll never win properly," Simon called defiantly. "You never do."

"We shall this time," a lighter voice said behind them. They swung round again. It was Withers. The outboard motor had cut out, and quietly the other dinghy was edging nearer to them as the boy Bill groped for the rock with an oar.

They drew closer together with their backs against the cliff, pressed as far away as they could; but on either side the boats crept closer towards them. The *Lady Mary* was edging slowly along off the headland. They could hear her engines thrumming faintly, though they could see no one on board.

"If only we had a boat," Jane said in despair.

"Couldn't we swim for it?"

"Where to?"

"There must be *something* we can do!" Barney's voice rose frantically.

"There is nothing at all you can do." Withers' light sneering voice came over the rocks to them. He was less than five yards away in the bow of the tossing dinghy. "Give us the manuscript. Give it to us and we will take you off safely. The tide is rising very fast now. You must give it to us."

"What if we don't?" Simon called rebelliously.

"Look at the sea, Simon. You can't get back now the way you came. Look at the tide. You're cut off. You can't get away unless you come with us."

"He's right,"Jane whispered. "Look!" She pointed. Further along the rocks the sea was already washing the foot of the cliff.

"Where's your boat, Simon?" called the mocking voice.

"We'll have to give in," Simon said, low and angry.

"Take your time, Simon. We can wait. *We've* got all the time in the world."

They heard the boy snicker on the other side of the boat.

"They've got us."

"Oh think—*think*—we can't give it up now."

"Think of Great-Uncle Merry."

"It's a pity we ever thought of him in the first place," Simon said fiercely. "It's no good, I'm going to say we give in."

"*No!*" Barney said urgently, and before they realized what was happening he had snatched the manuscript case from Simon and splashed forward over the wet rocks to the edge of the sea. He held up the long glinting case in one hand and the grail in the other, and gazed furiously at Mr. Hastings. "If you don't pick us up and let us take them home I shall throw them in the sea."

"Barney!" Jane croaked. But Simon held her back, listening.

Mr. Hastings did not move. He stood looking across with immense calm arrogance at Barney's small bristling figure, and when he spoke the deep voice was colder than any voice they had ever heard. "If you do that, Barnabas, I shall leave you and your brother and sister here to drown."

They had no doubt that he was speaking the truth. But Barney was carried away with a passionate indignation, and he was determined never again to believe anything that Mr. Hastings said. If once he did, he knew he would be under the spell again.

"I will, I will! If you don't promise, I will!" He raised the grail higher in his right hand, flexing his muscles to throw it. Simon and Jane gasped.

The whole world seemed to stop and centre round the towering black-clad man and a small boy: one will against another, with Barney saved by his own fury from the full force of the commanding glare driving into his eyes. Then Mr. Hastings's face twisted, and he let out a strangled shout. "Withers!"

And from that moment, for the children, the world cracked into unreality and there seemed no reason in anything that happened,

From either side, Norman Withers and Mr. Hastings made a dive for Barney. Simon shouted, "Barney, *don't*!" and dashed towards him to clasp his outstretched arm. Withers, nearer, made a great leap on to the rocks from his boat, setting it swaying wildly with Bill clinging frantically to the tiller. But as his lunging foot came down where the rock should have been, they saw the viciousness in his face change to alarm, and he flung up his arms and disappeared under the water.

He had jumped down on the masked pool among the rocks: the gap where the retreating sea had left deep water, and which now was filled far deeper by the incoming tide. Jane, cowering back against the cliff, chilled with horror as she realized that they would all three have gone headlong into it if they had run another yard further on.

Withers surfaced again, coughing and spluttering, and Barney hesitated, the grail still held over his head. Mr. Hastings had leapt across to the rocks without falling, and was coming at him from the other side with long loping strides, his dark brows a menacing bar across his face and his lips drawn back in a horrible unlaughing grin. Simon dived desperately, and was brushed aside by the sweep of one long arm; but in falling he grabbed at the man's nearest leg and brought him crashing down full length on the wet slippery rocks.

For all his height, Mr. Hastings moved like an eel. In a moment he was on his feet again, with one big hand clasped round Simon's arm, and in a swift cruel movement he pulled the arm round behind Simon's back and jerked it upwards so that he cried out with pain. The girl in the boat laughed softly. She had not moved since the beginning. Jane heard, and hated her, but stood transfixed by the look of concentrated evil cruelty on the face above her. It was as if something monstrous blazed behind Mr. Hastings' eyes, something not human, that filled her with a horror more vast and dreadful than anything she had felt before.

"Put it down, Barnabas," Mr. Hastings panted. "Put down the manuscript, or I'll break his arm." Simon wriggled in his grasp and kicked backwards, but then gasped and went limp as his arm was jerked savagely higher and pain shot through him like water boiling in his blood. But before Barney, his face twisted with concern, could even move, a great yell rang out over the water from the yacht. A rough voice shouted, in anguished warning, "*Master*!"

In the same moment they heard a new noise over the low throb of the yacht's waiting engines: a high-pitched drone that grew louder and nearer. Suddenly round the corner of the headland from Trewissick, they saw a glittering arc of spray shooting up from the bows of a big speed-boat. It was moving tremendously fast, swinging out round the seaward side of the yacht towards the place where they stood. And in a glimpse through the spray, they saw the only figure they knew that could tower as tall as Mr. Hastings, and above it the familiar blowing tousle of white hair.

Jane let out a shout high with relief. "It's Gumerry!"

Mr. Hastings snarled and released Simon suddenly, making a desperate lunge forward at Barney where he stood wavering on the edge. Just in time Barney saw him and ducked away backwards under his hand.

Bill, in his dinghy, ripped at the outboard motor and set it roaring; then jumped, slithering on the rocks but landing safe. Chunky and menacing beside the giant height of the man in black, he faced them, crouching slightly. Like dancers in a minuet the two moved forward, groping slowly for the treacherous footholds, and the children shrank back against the cliff.

The speed-boat roared up in a great flurry of spray. Within seconds it was alongside the headland. The engine's note changed to a deeper throb and the boat lurched slowly closer. Looking fearfully over Bill's advancing shoulder Jane could see Great-Uncle Merry standing erect, beside the blue-jerseyed figure of Mr. Penhallow crouching over the controls.

Forgetting everything in the overwhelming surge of relief, she dashed forward to the edge of the rocks, taking the boy by surprise so that he grasped at her too late and overbalanced against Mr. Hastings. The man snarled at him angrily and made a last reach for Barney as he stood pressed and staring helplessly against the cliff, his arms hanging down now limp.

But Simon, twisting up the last of his strength, snatched the grail and the long cylinder of the telescope case from his brother and slipped out of reach, dodging round him to the edge of the waves.

He shouted urgently, "Gumerry!" As his great-uncle turned, he raised his arm and flung the grail with all his might towards the speed-boat, watching agonized to see if it could cross the gap. At the controls, Mr. Penhallow wrestled to hold the boat steady. The strange bell-like cup wheeled through the air, flashing golden in the sun, and Great-Uncle Merry shot out one arm sideways like a slip fielder and caught it as it curved over towards the water.

"Look out!" Barney yelled. Mr. Hastings pivoted towards Simon as he drew back his arm to send the manuscript after the cup, darting sideways to keep out of reach. He threw: but as the case left his hand Mr. Withers, rising dripping to his feet in the dinghy, lunged out with an oar in a clumsy attempt to intercept it.

Jane screamed.

The oar struck the case in mid-flight. Withers let out a shout of triumph. But in his throat it changed to terror, as the long unwieldy case spun off the oar with the force of Simon's throw and came apart in the air. The two halves spiralled out away from the boat, scattering fragments of the familiar manuscript that they had studied so often: they saw the small lead case from the cave fall out and splash like a stone into the sea; and almost at the same moment the two halves of the telescope case, with their disintegrating parchment, hit the water and disappeared. The broken pieces of parchment did not float; they were gone at once, as if they had dissolved. Nothing was left but Jane's handkerchief, bobbing forlornly on the waves.

And then their blood stood still and cold within them, as an inhuman sound like the howl of an animal rang out over the sea. It was the second long howl that they had heard that day, but it was not the same as the first. Mr. Hastings put back his head like a dog, and gave a great shriek of pain and fear and rage. With two long bounds he leapt from the edge of the rocks, and dived with a mighty splash into the rippled water where the case had gone down.

They stared at the sunlight dancing on the water that had closed over his head, and but for the mutter of the engines and the sea there was no sound. A movement by the yacht caught their gaze, and they saw the girl being pulled aboard, with her dinghy left bobbing below.

Bill stood as immobile as the children, gazing open-mouthed at the sea turning golden now under the late sun. Then Withers shouted at him, lurching towards the outboard motor in the remaining dinghy, and as the boat moved off the boy flung himself aboard.

The children still stood watching. No one moved either aboard the speed-boat, as it swayed towards the rocks on the swell. The dinghy moved out, buzzing like an angry wasp, and then beside it they saw a dark head break the surface, and heard the rasp of desperate gulping breaths. The dinghy slowed, and the man and boy in it heaved the tall black figure aboard. It held nothing in its hand.

Mr. Hastings lay in the bottom of the boat, choking and gasping for breath, but as they watched he raised his head, the dark wet hair flattened over his forehead like a mask, and put out a hand to Withers to pull himself up. With rage and hatred twisting his face, he looked back at Great-Uncle Merry.

Great-Uncle Merry stood in the speed-boat with one hand on the wind-shield and the other holding the grail, the sun behind him blazing in his white hair. He drew himself so tall and erect that he looked for a strange moment like some great creature of the rocks and the sea. And he called across the water, in a strong voice that rang back from the cliffs, some words in a language that the children could not understand, but with a note through it that made them suddenly shiver.

And the dark figure in the other boat seemed to shrink within himself at the sound, so that the menace and power were all at once gone out of him. Suddenly he looked only ridiculous in the skin-wet black clothes, and seemed smaller than he had been before. All three in the boat cowered down, making no move or sound, as the dinghy crossed back to the yacht.

The children stirred. "Gosh!" Barney whispered. "What did he say?"

"I don't know."

"I'm glad I don't know," Jane said slowly.

They watched as the three figures swung themselves aboard the yacht, and almost at once the engine throbbed higher and the *Lady Mary*'s long white hull slipped away. The broad outboard dinghy trailed forlorn behind, but the other remained, bobbing and drifting empty on the waves.

The yacht headed out across the bay, past Trewissick harbour and down the coast, until she was only a small white shape on the sun-gilded sea. And by the time they had all climbed aboard the speed-boat, and looked again, she was gone.

• *Epilogue* •

The sound of clapping echoed through the glossy pillars of the long museum gallery, and Simon, very pink in the face, threaded his way back to Barney and Jane through the crowd of gravely smiling scholars and dons. The crowd began to move about again, and voices rose in a general chatter all round them.

A bright-eyed young man with a notebook materialised at their side. "That was a very nice speech, Simon, if I may say so. This is Jane and Barnabas, is it?"

Simon blinked at him, and nodded.

"I'm from the Press Association," said the young man briskly. "Can I just ask you how large a check the curator presented you with?"

Simon looked down at the envelope in his hand, put his finger nervously in the flap and tore it open. He took out the neatly folded check, gazed at it for several moments, and without a word passed it across to Jane.

Jane looked at it, and swallowed. "It says, one hundred pounds."

"*Gosh*!" said Barney.

"Well, that's nice," said the young man cheerfully. "Con-gratulations. Now then, what will you do with it?"

They looked at him blankly.

"I don't know," said Simon at last.

"Oh, come now," the young man persisted. "You must have some idea. What are the things you've always most wanted to buy?"

The children looked at one another helplessly.

"Young man," said Great-Uncle Merry's deep voice beside them, "if you were suddenly presented with a hundred pounds, what would you buy?"

The reporter looked taken aback. "Well—er—I—"

"Precisely," said Great-Uncle Merry. "You don't know. Neither do these children. Good afternoon."

"Just one more thing," said the young man, unabashed, writing rapid shorthand squiggles in his notebook. "What were you actually doing when you found the thing?"

"The grail, you mean," Barney said.

"Well, yes, that's what you like to call it, isn't it?" said the young man lightly.

Barney glared at him indignantly.

"We just happened to be exploring a cave," Simon said hastily. "And we found it on a ledge."

"Wasn't there talk of someone else having been after it?"

"Moonshine," said Great-Uncle Merry firmly. "Now look here, my boy, you go off and talk to the curator, just over there. He knows all about it. These three have had enough excitement for one day."

The young man opened his mouth to say something else, looked at Great-Uncle Merry, and shut it again. He grinned amiably and disappeared into the crowd, and Great-Uncle Merry steered the children into a quiet corner behind a pillar.

"Well," he said, "you'll have your pictures in all the papers tomorrow, you'll be written about in books for years to come by a lot of distinguished scholarly gentlemen, and you've been given a hundred pounds by one of the most famous museums in the world. And I must say you all deserve it."

"Gumerry," Simon said thoughtfully. "I know there'd be no point in telling people the real story behind finding the grail, but wouldn't it be a good thing at least to warn them about Mr. Hastings? I mean, he got hold of Mrs. Palk and that boy Bill and made them bad, and there's nothing to stop him going round doing it to everyone."

"He has gone," Great-Uncle Merry said. Two owl-like men in heavy spectacles, passing, bowed respectfully to him, and he nodded vaguely.

"I know, but he might come back."

Great-Uncle Merry looked down the long gallery, over the heads, and the old closed look came back into his face. "When he does come back," he said, "it will not be as Mr. Hastings."

"Wasn't his name really Hastings at all?" Simon said curiously.

"I have known him to use many different names," Great-Uncle Merry said, "at many different times."

Jane slid one foot unhappily to and fro over the smooth marble floor. "It seems so awful that a vicar should be so bad."

"He must have kidded all the bishops and things into thinking he was good," Simon said. "Same as he kidded everyone in Trewissick."

"Not at all," Great-Uncle Merry said.

Simon stared at him. "But he must have . . . I mean, they must have heard him preaching sermons on Sundays."

"No one heard him preach on Sundays. And I doubt if he has ever met a bishop in his life."

Now they were all staring at him, in such baffled amazement that the sides of his mouth twitched into a half-smile. "It's quite simple. What they call the power of suggestion. Our Mr. Hastings was not the vicar of Trewissick, nor anything to do with him. I know the real vicar slightly, he is a tall man as well, though rather thin and about seventy years old . . . his name is Smith."

"But Mr. Hastings lived in the vicarage," Barney said.

"It was the vicarage, once. Now it's let out to anyone who wants to rent it . . . the parish council decided years ago that it was much too big for Mr. Smith to live alone in it like a pea in a pod, and they found him a little cottage on the other side of the church."

"And when I went to find him," Jane said slowly, trying to remember, "I didn't ask anyone where he lived, I just said to an old man by the church, is that the vicarage, and all he said was yes . . . he was a rather bad-tempered old man, I think . . . And do you know, Gumerry, I don't think Mr. Hastings actually told me he was the vicar, I just took it for granted when he said something about his replacing Mr. Hawes-Mellor there. But he must have known I thought he was."

"Oh yes. He wasn't going to disillusion you until he'd found out what you were up to. He knew perfectly well who you were."

"Did he really?"

"From the moment he opened his front door."

"Oh," said Jane. She thought about it, and felt cold. "Oh."

"So from that moment we all went on thinking he was the vicar," Simon said, "and if ever we mentioned him to anybody like Mr. Penhallow they must have thought we meant the real vicar . . . but Gumerry, didn't you know?"

Great-Uncle Merry chuckled. "No. That's what I thought as well. For some time—well, right up to the last—I entertained the most terrible suspicions of poor harmless Mr. Smith."

Barney said unexpectedly: "But if you've been against Mr. Hastings before, surely you couldn't mistake anybody else for him?"

"He changes," Great-Uncle Merry said vaguely, deliberately looking away again. "There is no knowing what he will look like. . . ."

And there was a finality in the ring of his voice that forbade any further question; as they knew there would always be when they tried to ask more about the mysterious enemy of their days in Trewissick. This was one of the things from Great-Uncle Merry's secret world, and even though they had been so much involved, they knew he would keep his secrets as he always had.

Simon looked down at the check in his hand. "We found the grail," he said. "And everyone seems frightfully excited about it. But it isn't any use on its own, is it? The Cornishman said, if whoever found it had other words from him, on the second manuscript that we didn't even have a chance to look at, then they'd be able to understand what was written on the grail and know the secret of it all. But we shan't ever know, because the manuscripts are at the bottom of the sea."

Barney said, gloomily, "We failed, really."

Great-Uncle Merry said nothing, and when they looked up at him, hearing only the hum of voices from the crowd, he seemed to be towering over them as tall and still as the pillar at his side.

"Failed?" he said, and he was smiling. "Oh no. Is that really what you think? You haven't failed. The hunt for the grail was a battle, as important in its way as any battle that's ever been fought. And you won it, the three of you. The powers behind the man calling himself Hastings came very near to winning, and what that victory would have meant, if the secret of the grail had been given into their hands, is more than anyone dare think. But thanks to you the vital secret they needed is safe from them still, for as many centuries perhaps as it was before. Safe—not destroyed, Simon. The first manuscript, your map, will certainly have disintegrated at once in the sea. But that was no more use to anyone once it had led you to the second, and the grail. It might have made my colleagues even more excited"—he glanced round the room, and chuckled—"but that's no matter. The point is that the second manuscript, down under the sea, is sealed up in its case—which will resist seawater indefinitely if it's made of lead. So the last secret is safe, and hidden. So well hidden at the bottom of Trewissick Bay that they could never ever begin the long business of searching for it without our being able to find out, and to stop them. They have lost their chance."

"And so have we," Simon said bitterly, seeing again the picture that had never properly left his mind. He thought of the glinting brass telescope case, with both precious manuscripts sealed inside, flying from his desperate hand and then, only yards from Great-Uncle Merry's safe grasp, jerking away from the raised oar to break and plunge its contents for ever into the sea.

"No, we haven't," said Jane unexpectedly. She was thinking of the same moment, and she was out of the cool marble vastness of the museum, back on Kemare Head in the excitement and the scorching sun. "We do know where it is. I was standing by the only thing that could mark it—that deep pool in the rocks. I was just on the edge, and the lead case went down right in front of me. So we should know where to look if we ever went back."

For a moment Great-Uncle Merry looked really alarmed. "I had no idea of that. Then the others will have noticed the same thing—and they will be able to go straight to the spot, dive for the manuscript, and be away with it before anyone has time even to notice they are there."

"No, they won't," Jane said, pink and earnest. "That's the best thing of all, Gumerry. You see, we only noticed that pool in the first place because we came across it when the tide was at its lowest. By the time we were on our way back to the beach the water had covered it again. Mr. Withers fell into it, but he didn't know he had. So if there was ever a tide as low as that again, we should be able to look for the pool and find the second manuscript. But the enemy wouldn't, because they don't know about the pool at all."

"Can we go back?" Simon said eagerly. "Can we go back, Gumerry, and have someone dive for it?"

"One day, perhaps," Great-Uncle Merry said; and then before he could say any more a group of men from the murmuring crowd all round them had turned towards him: "Ah, Professor Lyon! If you have a moment, might I introduce you to Dr. Theodore Reisenstatz—"

"I am a great, great disciple of yours," an intense little man with a pointed beard said to Great-Uncle Merry as he took his hand. "Merriman Lyon is a name much honoured in my country. . . ."

"Come on," Simon said in an undertone; and the children slipped away to stand on the edge of the crowd, while the bald heads and grey beards wagged and chattered solemnly. They looked across the shimmering floor to the lone glass case where the grail stood like a golden star.

Barney was gazing into space as if he were coming out of a trance.

"Wake up," Jane said cheerfully.

Barney said slowly, "Is that his real name?"

"Whose name?"

"Great-Uncle Merry—is he really called Merriman?'"

"Well, of course—that's what Merry is short for."

"I didn't know," Barney said. "I always thought Merry was a nickname. Merriman Lyon . . ."

"Funny name, isn't it?" said Simon lightly. "Come on, let's go and have another look at the grail. I want to see what it says about us again."

He moved round the edge of the crowd with Jane; but Barney stayed where he was. "Merriman Lyon," he said softly to himself. "Merry Lyon . . . Merlion . . . *Merlin* . . ."

He looked across the room to where Great-Uncle Merry's white head towered over the rest; slightly bent as he listened to what someone else was saying. The angular brown face seemed more than ever like an old, old carving, deep eyes shadowed and mysterious above the fierce nose.

"No," Barney said aloud, and he shook himself. "It's not possible." But as he followed Simon and Jane he glanced back over his shoulder, wondering. And Great-Uncle Merry, as if he knew, turned his head and looked him full in the face for an instant, across the crowd; smiled very faintly, and looked away again.

All the way up the immense gallery, over its glistening stone floor, row upon row of identical glass cases stretched into the distance, with pots, daggers, coins, strange twisted pieces of bronze and leather and wood all shut quiet inside like butterflies caught on pins. The case which held the grail was taller than the rest; a high glass box in a place of honour in the centre of the great gallery, with nothing inside it but the one shining cup, cleaned now to brilliant gold, poised on a heavy black plinth. A neat silver square beneath was engraved with the words:

Gold chalice of unknown Celtic workmanship, believed sixth century. Found in Trewissick, South Cornwall, and presented by Simon, Jane and Barnabas Drew.

They moved round the case, looking at the grail. Its curved, engraved sides had been meticulously cleaned; and now that the beaten gold was free of the dirt left by centuries in the cave under Kemare Head, every line of the engraving was clear.

They saw that it was divided into five panels, and that four of the five were covered with pictures of men fighting: brandishing swords and spears, crouching behind shields, dressed not in armour but in strange tunics ending above their knees. They wore helmets on their heads; but the helmets, curving down over the backs of their necks, were like no shape the children had ever seen before. Between the figures, interweaving like pictures on a tapestry, words and letters were closely engraved. The last panel, the fifth, was completely covered in words, as close-written as the scrawled black lines had been on the manuscript. But all these words on the golden grail, the children knew, were in a language nobody, from Great-Uncle Merry to the museum experts, had been able to understand.

Behind them, they heard two men from the crowd come up deep in discussion, looking down into the glass case.

". . . quite unique. Of course the significance of the inscription is difficult to estimate. Clearly runic, I think—strange, in a Roman ambiance . . ."

"But my dear fellow—" The second man's voice was loud and jolly; glancing round, Barney saw that he was redfaced, enormous beside his small bespectacled companion. "Emphasising the runic element surely presupposes some Saxon connection, and the whole essence of this thing is Celtic. Romano-Celtic if you like, but consider the Arthurian evidence—"

"Arthurian?" said the first voice in nasal disbelief. "I should have to have greater proof for that than Professor Lyon's imaginative surmise. Loomis, I think, would have grave doubts . . . but indeed a remarkable find none the less, remarkable. . . ."

They moved away again into the crowd.

"What on earth did all that mean?" said Jane.

"Doesn't he believe it's about King Arthur?" Barney glared resentfully after the little man. Then they heard voices from another group passing the show-case.

"Surely all the theories will have to be revised now; it throws a new light on the entire Arthurian canon." The voice was as solemn as the rest, but younger; and then it chuckled. "Poor old Battersby—all his vapourings about Scandinavian analogues, and now here's the first evidence since Nennius of a Celtic Arthur—a real king—"

"The *Times* asked me for a piece, you know," said a deeper voice.

"Oh really, did you do that? Bit strong, wasn't it?— 'a find to shake the whole field of English scholarship—'"

"Not at all," said the deeper voice. "It's undoubtedly genuine, and it undoubtedly gives clues to the identity of Arthur. And as such it can't be overpraised. I'm only sorry about that last panel."

"Yes, the mysterious inscription. A cipher, I think. It must be. Those strange Old English characters—runic, old Battersby claims, absurd of course—personally I'm sure there was once a key to them. Lost long since, of course, so we shall never know. . . ."

The voices faded like the rest.

"Well, that sounds better," Simon said.

"They all seem to treat it as a kind of relic," Jane said sadly. "I suppose it's what Gumerry said, that the real meaning of it wouldn't have been known unless the enemy had got hold of it, and then it would have been too late."

"Well, the enemy can come and look at it as much as they like now," said Simon, "but it won't mean anything to them without the manuscript. I suppose that was the key to the ciphers in the last panel, that the man was talking about just now."

Jane sighed. "And it won't mean anything to us either. So we shan't know the real truth about King Arthur, about the—what did the manuscript call him?—the Pendragon."

"No. We shan't know exactly who he was, or what happened to him."

"We shan't know what his secret was, that Gumerry talked about and the enemy wanted."

"We shan't know about that other odd thing the manuscript said—the day when the Pendragon shall come again."

Barney, listening to them, looked again at the mysterious words engraved on the gleaming side of the grail. And he raised his head to stare across the room at Great-Uncle Merry's tall figure, with the great white head and fierce, secret face.

"I think we shall know," he said slowly, "one day."

SUSAN COOPER

SUSAN COOPER is best known for her acclaimed sequence of fantasy novels known as The Dark Is Rising which includes OVER SEA, UNDER STONE; THE DARK IS RISING (1974 Newbery Honor book); GREENWITCH; THE GREY KING (1976 Newbery Award book); and SILVER ON THE TREE. Her novels for young readers also include SEAWARD and DAWN OF FEAR. She has written three books for younger children as well: THE SILVER COW, THE SELKIE GIRL, and TAM LIN, all illustrated by Warwick Hutton. In collaboration with actor Hume Cronyn, she wrote the Broadway play *Foxfire* and—for Jane Fonda—the television film *The Dollmaker*, for which they received the Humanitas Prize in 1985. Born in Buckinghamshire, England, Susan Cooper moved to the United States in 1963 and now lives in Cambridge, Massachusetts.

A remarkable fantasy sequence by Susan Cooper, described by *The Horn Book* as being "as rich and eloquent as a Beethoven symphony."

The magic continues
with more fantasies from
Aladdin Paperbacks